"Come now, sweet torment. Tell me, if you can, that you do not want me.

"Tell me you wish to leave me. Tell me that while I take your breath away, while I make you moan. Come, make me believe it."

He pulled her into his arms, bruising her lips under his. She collapsed against him, and Morgan thought the victory won.

But suddenly she pulled back, holding him off with her palms, her eyes the ominous gray of a lowering storm. She spoke quietly at first, but her voice rose steadily with growing emotion. "You say I want you. And I do." She wiped angrily at her eyes. "You know it. And you are taking advantage of it, and..." She was shouting now, tears trailing down her face.

"I will not be your whore!"

* * *

A Dangerous Seduction
Harlequin Historical #668—August 2003

A
DANGEROUS
SEDUCTION

PATRICIA FRANCES ROWELL

HARLEQUIN®

TORONTO • NEW YORK • LONDON
AMSTERDAM • PARIS • SYDNEY • HAMBURG
STOCKHOLM • ATHENS • TOKYO • MILAN • MADRID
PRAGUE • WARSAW • BUDAPEST • AUCKLAND

ISBN 0-373-29268-6

A DANGEROUS SEDUCTION

Please address questions and book requests to:
Harlequin Reader Service
U.S.: 3010 Walden Ave., P.O. Box 1325, Buffalo, NY 14269
Canadian: P.O. Box 609, Fort Erie, Ont. L2A 5X3

In memory of my young friend Morgan Mitchell,
who left us at the age of nine

And for my grandchildren,
who are, happily, still with us—

Zachary Nathaniel, Eric Dean, Joseph Richmond,
Amber Nicole, Camille Elise, Joy Anna, Jillian Paige
and Andrew Houghton

And, of course, for Johnny

Acknowledgment

I would like to thank my friend Maria Budzenski
for her help with this story. She sent me literally
boxes of information in addition to her personal
observations of Cornwall. Thank you, Maria.

Prologue

London, England, 1808

Pain. Gripping, grinding, paralyzing pain. He lay on the grass in the pool of blood that leaked through his fingers. But how could he…?

Five, six, seven—three more steps and he would kill the bastard. But there had been no more steps. Eight… A flash of light, a blast, and he was falling. Falling forward, propelled by a blow that knocked him off his feet and onto his face.

Laughter. Shouts. Running feet. Shots. The blood stained his coat and dripped over the hand he pressed in vain against his chest.

The scurvy dog shot before the count! Shot you in the back.

And he laughed.

The laughter echoed through the darkness that was closing around him.

The bastard laughed!

Hoofbeats. The laughter trailing away.

He had thought he hated the man. Now he knew better.

In that moment was conceived a hatred as deep as his soul.

He tried to raise himself on one elbow, tried to lift the pistol still clutched in his hand. Too heavy. Too dark. Hands taking the pistol. Voices calling his name. The darkness wrapping around him in a smothering cloud. Gasping. Choking.

Breathe, damn you, breathe. A breath. Another breath. One more. Another. You can't die. Not now. The dog must pay.

He *will* pay. He will pay with everything.

Everything.

Chapter One

Cornwall, England, 1816

There it lay.

Morgan Pendaris, Earl of Carrick, drew rein at the top of the knoll, bringing the curricle to a stop. Before him over the rolling hills spread the woods, fields and meadows of his home, lush and green, neatly divided and stitched across by ancient hedges.

Nineteen years. Nineteen long years. Nineteen years dark with blood and hate. But, at last, Merdinn again belonged to him. His eyes narrowed with satisfaction, the words that had been his polestar ringing in his head, the words of Genghis Khan.

The greatest joy a man can have is to see his enemy in chains, to deprive him of his possessions, to ride his horses, to see tears on the faces of his loved ones, and to crush in your arms his wives and daughters.

He had at last deprived Cordell Hayne of every possession, including the estate that Hayne's father had stolen from his. Chains were not far behind. The cur was firmly under the hatches, his only choice debtors prison or the transport ships.

"Why are we stopping, Uncle Morgan?"

"Because we have reached the Merdinn lands, Jeremy." Morgan raked his dark curls out of his face with impatient fingers, a gesture that was the despair of Dagenham, his long-suffering valet. He smiled down at the boy seated beside him. "It has been a very long time since I have seen them."

"But you lived here when you were my age?" Without waiting for an answer he already knew, Jeremy rushed on. "When will we see the castle?"

"Soon now." Morgan flicked his reins and the curricle started down the hill. "It stands behind that bit of woods there." He pointed with his whip.

The road wound between the fields, the summer sun of Cornwall hot on their heads and necks. A sliver of silver on their left marked the sea, placid at the moment, only the tiniest waves visible. As they neared the castle, the bridge across the old ditch rang hollow beneath the hooves of the horses and they plunged into the cool shade and dank greenery of the small forest that now covered the motte. The way rose steeply as they climbed the man-made hill, flickering through the shadows cast by the twisted trunks of the trees.

Jeremy bounced in his seat. "And there are real towers and real battlements?"

"Yes, as I have told you many times, there are two towers on the seaside wall."

"But there is no drawbridge and it looks more like a big house now." The boy's voice clearly reflected his disapproval of another fact he had often been told.

"I'm sorry to disappoint you, Jeremy." Morgan chuckled. He remembered how much, as a seven-year-old boy, he himself had wished that the crumbling walls still stood, that the bridges still lifted, that he might charge across them on a fiery steed. But alas, those deeds belonged to ages past. The towers, however, remained satisfyingly intact—or at least, mostly so. They shared with the rest of the manor the deterioration of two generations of neglect, the neglect that he intended to wipe away.

And when all had again been restored to stateliness and comfort, he would bring his mother home, back to her rightful place as mistress of Merdinn.

Suddenly the trees parted and Morgan's heart swelled as his boyhood home stood before his eyes—somewhat battered perhaps, as he himself was, but still proud and strong.

Across the level ground of the bailey that had once lain inside a curtain wall, lay the gray stone of the manor itself, with the twin towers on the wall behind it standing proudly against the azure sky. Behind them, he knew, the cliff fell away over jagged rocks into the sea.

He heard beside him a small sigh of satisfaction. "There really *are* towers."

"Did you doubt my word?" Morgan lifted one eyebrow as he guided his blacks around the curving drive.

"Oh, no!" A touch of dismay sounded in the boy's voice. "I wouldn't question *your* honor, Uncle Morgan." He glanced speculatively up at his uncle. "You aren't going to call me out, are you?"

"No. Not today."

A sigh. "I thought not."

Morgan couldn't decide whether he heard relief or disappointment. "Are you so eager to engage in an affair of honor?"

"Well," Jeremy pondered, "not with you. But I think it would be famous to have a duel."

"Believe me, it is not." Morgan pulled his horses in

before the double doors of the house. "I hope you never have occasion to find that out for yourself."

As he waited for a groom to come take his horses, a surge of excitement coursed through Morgan. The success of another of his goals would be achieved within minutes. He did not expect to find Hayne at Merdinn. The bastard would be in London, trying desperately to find a way to recoup. But his wife... Ah. Hayne's mysterious, never-seen wife, the usurper of his mother's place, the cause of his sister's disgrace. She would be there.

Within minutes he would put her out of his house.

Let her go to her rotten husband. Let her go with him to whatever hole claimed him. Let her beg on the streets, for all he cared. No longer would she be a barrier to decent women, to the women he loved. Enough time had elapsed. She should already be preparing for departure.

Several minutes passed without the appearance of a groom. Hmm. Had Hayne already dismissed his staff? Was the place deserted? No. The windows were open on the second floor. "Well, then, Jeremy. It seems that we will have to take the horses to the stable ourselves."

"I can take them, Uncle Morgan, while you go inside." Jeremy looked hopefully at his uncle.

Morgan tousled his nephew's hair as he once again gave his mettlesome horses the office to start. "All in good time, ambitious one."

Another heavy sigh. Shaking his head in amusement, Morgan directed his team through the stable door and climbed down. Jeremy scrambled down after him and dashed past him to the back door of the building. Morgan sauntered after him, his critical eye appraising the lone riding mount and the sturdy cob that appeared to be the only occupants of the stalls. Hardly an impressive selection.

Perhaps Hayne had contrived to depose of his stable before Morgan could take possession of it. He scowled. Much good it would do him. Morgan now owned the paper on every debt that Hayne had incurred in a long and profligate career. Even the sale of his horses would not save him. Morgan rubbed at his chest absently. Nothing would save the cad now.

He followed Jeremy out into the sunshine behind the dark stable. At the rear of the stable and the kitchen wing of the house, a large kitchen garden tumbled down the motte. Morgan frowned thoughtfully. It looked to be a great deal larger than he remembered. And now that he thought about it, there were more flower beds in the lawn of the bailey. He wouldn't have thought that Hayne would have spent money on gardens. Perhaps it was the wife.

Two women, their hair covered with kerchiefs, worked far down the slope. They apparently did not hear him, or perhaps considered the arrival of guests none of their concern. One of them stepped with the slow movements of age, and gray hair peeped from under her scarf. The other looked young and possibly shapely under her heavy skirts. A midnight-black braid of hair as thick as her wrist dropped from beneath her head covering to her hips. It shone lustrously in the sun.

At the sound of footsteps Morgan reluctantly tore his gaze from the shining hair and the hips beneath it. Jeremy rounded the far corner of the stable, a tall, thin man in his wake. "Look, Uncle Morgan, I found someone."

"James!" Morgan hurried forward, his hand extended. "It's good to see you."

"Lord Morgan? Is it really you?" The old man

grasped his hand and pumped it vigorously. "It's a sight for sore eyes you are! What brings you here?"

"I'm home to stay, James. Merdinn is no longer in the hands of the Haynes."

"Him!" James spat on the ground. "I'll be glad to see the back of his head. He had his way he'd have turned me off long ago. Said I can't do the work no more." He patted his silvery locks. "Just because there's a little snow on the roof... But the missus keeps me on. I handle everything just fine by myself." He jerked his head toward the two resident horses. "Ain't all that much to do. But let me see to your team. Beautiful bits of bone and blood they are, too. You and the little fellow go on up to the house. I'll take care of 'em."

Murmuring his thanks, Morgan herded Jeremy out into the bailey. As they strolled toward the main door of the house he glanced at the beds of plants that dotted the lawn. To his surprise he noted that they contained as many vegetables as flowers. The effect was odd, but strangely pleasing.

Not bothering to knock, he opened the door and Jeremy darted inside. They found themselves in a vaulted hall, before them a wide set of stairs leading up. "Where do they go, Uncle Morgan?"

"To the upper levels. Hold your horses but a little longer, Jeremy, and I will take you over the whole place. For now, come into the library and let us see if anyone is about." He turned to a door on his left and led the way into a large room lined with books. He gave the bellpull an authoritative tug and sat down in the chair behind the desk. Jeremy immediately climbed the book ladder to the top and sat surveying his new domain.

While he waited, Morgan glanced at the papers on the desk. They seemed to be household books, but there were not enough of them to account for the running of the castle. He was going through the drawers when a frail young girl timidly opened the library door and poked her dull blond head into the room. When she saw him sitting at the desk and Jeremy perched like a gargoyle on the ladder, she squeaked and hastily withdrew.

"Wait!" Morgan sprang out of the chair and through the door barely in time to grasp her arm before she could disappear into the kitchen wing. Jeremy scampered down the ladder and peered around the door. "Here now. What's the matter with you? Where is everyone?" The girl cringed away from him and hung her head, giving every evidence of terror. Morgan snorted in frustration. "Is your mistress at home?"

The girl nodded. At last! A response. "Then kindly tell her that the Earl of Carrick would like a moment of her time. I'll be in the library." She scurried away and disappeared. "Am I mad or is it everyone else?" Morgan stalked back into the library and sprawled into a chair. "One pensioner in the stable and one half-wit in the house. Perhaps Mrs. Hayne is almost ready to leave."

At least she had ordered a good cleaning before going. The books looked dusted and the leather chair smelled of lemon oil. The stone floor was well polished, although the carpet was distinctly worn. It had been worn the last time Morgan had seen it. Too impatient to sit longer, he paced around the room. Where was the woman? He had been waiting for at least twenty minutes. Was she showing her disdain for him? His lip curled. If so, let her enjoy it while she may. If the curst woman would but show herself…

After another half hour his anger had grown to the point of explosion. Jeremy prudently busied himself with looking at the pictures in an old book, careful to avoid the avuncular displeasure. Morgan had almost decided to scour the castle for its soon-to-be-former mistress himself when the door opened and a woman stepped into the room. He recognized her immediately as the younger woman he had seen in the garden.

"Who the hell are you, and where the hell is Mrs. Hayne? I sent for her an hour ago. She has not yet done me the courtesy of responding." He glared at the gardener. Her gown had green stains from the plants and there was a smudge of dirt on her nose. There was also a puzzled expression in her eyes—eyes, he noted, that were the calm, transparent aquamarine of the shallows on a sunny day.

"I'm sorry you had to wait, my lord." She crossed the room to the chair opposite Morgan and sank into it gracefully. "Peggy did not tell me until a moment ago that you were here."

Morgan stared in astonishment. This woman certainly had a lot of brass for a gardener. His scowl deepened. "What's wrong with Peggy? Is she half-witted?"

"No, just fearful." She wiped at the dirt on her face, smearing it and making matters worse.

"What the devil is she so afraid of?" Morgan's eyes went to the streaked face and then to the skin beneath the dirt. It appeared to be flawless—as luminescent as a pearl. The tendrils of raven-black hair escaping from the kerchief framed softly rounded cheeks that glowed a slightly deeper rose. When she spoke he discovered that, for a moment, he had forgotten his own question. He jerked his attention back to her answer.

"Everything. Of you. Of me. Of making a mistake."

Morgan shook his head, not completely understanding. If that were the case, the young girl deserved his pity, not his scorn. In fact, it came to his attention that the woman in the chair across from him did not deserve the anger he had generated toward the elusive Mrs. Hayne. He should not have cursed in her presence, who-ever she was.

He moderated his tone. "You have still not told me who you are."

She looked startled. "Why, I am Eulalia Hayne. You asked for me?"

The sense of unreality that had been growing in Morgan reached a new height. This lovely but disheveled creature was the stylish Cordell Hayne's wife? He had pictured a cold and haughty woman, lifting herself on the backs of others as Hayne himself did. And he had pictured her living in grandeur stolen from his family. He could only stare.

"*You* are Mrs. Hayne?" She nodded and he thought he glimpsed for a moment the slightest twinkle in those remarkable eyes. "Where is the rest of your staff?"

"There is no staff except me, my grandmother, James and Peggy."

"And Hayne is content to live like this?"

For a moment the eyes darkened, as though a cloud had passed over the sun. Then a small smile curved the deep-rose lips. "My husband is very rarely here, except when he takes his sloop out. Did you wish to speak to him?"

The question of Hayne's whereabouts began to disturb Morgan. "Is he in residence now?"

"No. He rode in yesterday, but only for a short while. He left again in the *Seahawk,* saying that he had a wager on a sailing race that would bring him about." She shrugged. The movement brought the tops of two plump globes covered in pearly skin nearer to the rounded neckline of her dress. The train of the conversation again momentarily eluded Morgan. With an effort he pulled his gaze back to her face as she continued. ''I don't know what he meant, exactly, but he often races the *Seahawk*. He has been doing so a great deal of late. It's very fast, and he likes to wager on the outcome.''

''He likes to wager on everything.'' Morgan frowned. Apparently he had not succeeded in depriving Hayne of his boat. An oversight on his part. But perhaps not. Hayne would think nothing of taking out a boat that had already been foreclosed. Or of making a wager when he no longer had anything to back it.

Or of leaving Morgan to break the news to his wife that she no longer had a home.

Suddenly the shining prospect of that satisfying moment faded a trifle. He had believed that Hayne would have at least sent word to her that he had lost Merdinn, but obviously he had not. His wife sat before him with confusion in her eyes. As Morgan searched for the words that would at last avenge his mother and sister, Jeremy closed his book and edged forward to get a better look at the lady.

She turned in surprise, and the first real smile Morgan had seen bloomed in her face. ''Well, who is this?''

Morgan motioned the boy forward. ''This is my nephew, Jeremy Pendaris. He makes his home with me.''

Jeremy stepped closer and essayed a polite bow. ''How do you do, Mrs. Hayne?''

She held out a welcoming hand and clasped Jeremy's small one. ''How nice to meet you, Jeremy.''

Seeing the warm response in his nephew's face, Morgan rubbed his chin thoughtfully. Things were not going as he had expected. ''Jeremy, I need to speak with Mrs.

Hayne privately. You may explore on this floor of the building, but on *no* account are you to climb the wall or the towers. Nor are you to go down the path to our cove alone—not now or at any other time. Do I make myself clear?''

''Oh, yes, sir. I promise.'' Jeremy quickly dashed for the door before his uncle could change his mind.

When the door had banged shut behind him, Morgan turned back to Eulalia Hayne and hardened his heart. ''Mrs. Hayne, apparently it falls to me to explain your situation to you.'' Damnation! Where were the arrogant words he had rehearsed so many times in his dreams? ''Are you aware that nineteen years ago your father-in-law came into possession of Merdinn, a property that had been in the Pendaris family for generations, as the result of a dishonorable business arrangement?''

Again her eyes seemed to darken to a light gray, like the sunless winter sea. ''I know very little about the dealings of my husband's family. At that time I would have been only five years old. My family lived nearby, but I would not have remembered anything like that.''

Morgan remembered. He remembered that day in every agonizing detail. His father's impotent anger, his mother's tears, his own pain as his beloved home was ripped away from him. His own anger. It welled in him again, and a muscle jumped in his tightened jaw. At the age of fifteen he had been dispossessed of his birthright. He spoke through clenched teeth. ''Suffice to say that he did so—by defrauding my father. I have recently been able to regain what the Haynes stole from my family.''

A small pucker increased between the lady's brows. ''I am not sure I understand.''

''I now own Merdinn.''

He watched in silence as the significance of the statement sank in. She sat very still in her chair, her hands lying motionless in her lap. At last she nodded. ''I see. My husband has sold it to you?''

''No.'' The word was stark, harsh. Morgan waited a heartbeat before continuing. ''Your husband had mort-gaged everything he owned—and he was far in arrears on even the interest, let alone the principal. I have bought up all his notes—on the land, his wagers, his cattle—everything. He now owns nothing.''

''I see.'' She continued to sit like a statue, but he could see a pulse beating frantically in her throat. ''My only income derives from a small portion of the tenant rents.''

''Unfortunately, any arrangement that Hayne made is no longer worth the ink in which it was signed. All the rents are now payable to me.''

She stood and lifted her small chin. The gray of her eyes now approached the dark color of the sea in storm. ''I understand. My grandmother and I will leave as quickly as we can. Will three days be soon enough?''

''You may wait for your husband's return. You will no doubt want to go with him.''

An expression he could not read flitted over her face. ''I do not believe that it will be useful to wait.''

She left the room with a dignified tread. Morgan blew out an angry breath and slumped in his chair. He did this for his mother, and even more for his poor deceived, disgraced little sister. For Beth. Especially for her. God rest her unhappy soul.

But the triumph suddenly left a bitter taste in his mouth.

Chapter Two

Lalia carefully laid the hairbrush on the dressing table, forbidding herself to throw it, and dropped her face into her hands. Her thoughts spun 'round and 'round and back and forth like the unattended wheel of a ship in a gale. What was she to do? Where in the world could she go? And what about Daj? She was no longer young, and her bones hurt her so. She could do very little work. Lalia would have to earn their bread for both herself and her grandmother. She had almost no money to provide for them until she could find employment. She could not afford to go to London or even Bath. And what was she trained to do?

Manage a home she no longer had.

What? Where? How? When? How? Where...?

Dizziness threatened to overcome her. She jumped up from the dressing stool and began to pace. A flicker of lightning brightened the window for an instant and she paused to look out on the dark sea. The clouds had already defeated the moon. She could see nothing until the approaching storm hurled another bolt.

One thing was certain. Her husband would not rescue her.

Rain began to patter against the glass, and the wind rattled the casement, reflecting the storm that raged inside Lalia. Her feelings changed with every wave, battering her against the rocks of indecision. Fear. Anger. Grief. Her usual serenity had long since disappeared into the depths. She had become the storm.

She couldn't stand it another minute.

Snatching her wrapper from the bed, she flung it over her shoulders and raced out of the room.

Morgan threw open the wardrobe and took stock of its contents. They didn't amount to much. Apparently, as Mrs. Hayne had said, her husband spent very little time at Merdinn. But even a single cravat, a pair of stockings, an unmatched glove was too much. He began to pull shirts and coats and trousers out of the wardrobe and throw them on the floor.

Boots, small clothes... When the wardrobe was empty, he attacked the dressing room. Brushes, razors and shaving mug joined the heap on the floor. When not a solitary item belonging to Hayne remained in place in the master suite, Morgan gathered up the pile and dumped it in the hallway. Tomorrow James could take the lot to the vicar to give to the poor. He wanted no trace of the man to remain in his home.

Morgan walked to the window to watch the storm. As he stood there, a distant thump vibrated its way through the house. A door slamming. Now who would be going out into this weather? As he pondered the question, a flicker of movement on the ground below him, caught in a flash of lightning, captured his attention. Someone was abroad.

The next bolt of lightning revealed someone leaning against the parapet at the top of the east tower. As he watched, the wind blew a sail of hair back from the figure. So much hair. Eulalia Hayne.

Alarm shot through Morgan. Good God! She intended to jump! He whirled and dashed into the hallway and ran for the stairs. Taking them two at a time, he gained the lower floor and found the door behind the main staircase unfastened. Looking up, he could still see her leaning into the gale, the rain beating down on her lifted face. He ducked his own head against the rain and made for the tower.

The heavy wooden door into the tower opened easily enough, but the moment it closed, he was in total darkness. Feeling his way up the steps, Morgan had climbed only three when his foot encountered not the fourth, but open air. He caught himself on the next stair up, banging his elbow and painfully scraping his shin. Damnation!

The place had deteriorated badly since he had been here. How the devil did she get up there? Rubbing his elbow, he backed down to the floor and considered. As a boy he had known everything there was to know about Merdinn. Including the flight of unprotected steps that led from the wall around the outside of the tower to the watch platform where his quarry stood. Not a route to pursue in this kind of weather, however.

But a life was at stake. The thought gave him pause. Was it a life that he was willing to risk his own to save? Or was he willing to drive Cordell Hayne's wife to her death as Hayne had driven Beth to hers? Had it been Hayne on the parapet, he would have watched him fall without lifting a finger. But his hapless wife? Could he stand by and watch Eulalia Hayne die, even to avenge his little sister's death?

He swore under his breath and started for the wall.

* * *

Lalia closed her eyes and let the rain mingle with her tears. It poured over her, washing away her agitation and confusion. The wind swirled around her, blowing her mantle of hair first toward her and then out behind. She didn't feel the chill. She didn't want to feel. Didn't want to remember the resolve she saw in Lord Carrick's hard, glass-green eyes. Didn't want to think anymore.

Not thinking—the very thing that had kept her in this situation. Allowing herself to drift, to accept. Think she must, but she would do it tomorrow. Tomorrow. Always tomorrow.

Now Lalia only wanted the rain.

Suddenly she heard the scrape of leather on stone and before she could spin around, a large, authoritative hand grasped her upper arm and pulled her away from the parapet. Stifling a shriek, she put up her other hand to fend off whomever had taken hold of her. Her hand encountered something very warm and very hard. A flash of light revealed the something to be Lord Carrick's chest. He only tightened his hold when she tried to step away.

"My lord! What are you doing?"

"What am *I* doing? I am stopping you from leaping onto the rocks. What are *you* doing? Surely your situation cannot be that bad."

"You have no…" Before she could finish the sentence a gust blew her curtain of hair across her face, covering both her eyes and her mouth. She fumbled ineffectively with her free hand to clear it away. Before she could gain control of the errant tresses, a second large hand gathered them together and lifted them over her head, holding them firmly at the nape of her neck. The wrist rested heavily on her shoulder.

"Think, Mrs. Hayne. Is any misfortune worth your life?"

Lalia looked up into the stern face with the dark curls plastered to the broad forehead. It was too dark to see the green of his eyes, but they glittered wildly in the intermittent light. She pressed her hand against her chest where her startled heart still pounded loudly and tried to gather her composure. He seemed to expect a response.

"I… You… I'm sorry, my lord. I did not mean to alarm you. I have no intention of jumping to my death."

His lordship looked skeptical. "Then what, pray tell me, are you doing up here in the midst of a storm? Are you hoping to be stuck by lightning?"

A blinding flash and a deafening crack of thunder punctuated this question. Lord Carrick jerked her against himself as if to shield her. Lalia ducked her head, hiding her face against his shirt. After a cautious moment she decided that she was still alive and tried to draw back a step. His lordship hesitated for a second, looking deeply into her eyes, then loosened his hold slightly.

The warmth of his muscular body enveloped her. Lalia vainly willed her racing heart to slow. She could hear it banging in her ears. "I am not seeking death, my lord. I simply wanted the rain."

"You wanted… You wanted the rain?" His lordship still looked unconvinced.

"Yes. It calms me."

"I see." He did not let go of her. He lifted one eyebrow. "You are telling me that I have come out into a storm, risked my health to an inflammation of the lungs, risked my *neck* climbing a crumbling wall and an open stair slick with rain, and you tell me you simply wanted to be calmed?"

In spite of herself Lalia chuckled. "Apparently so. But thank you for your concern."

Lord Carrick did not chuckle. The next flash of light revealed an intimidating crease between his eyebrows. At last he spoke. "If you say so. Nevertheless, I am unwilling to put the matter to the test. How the devil did you come up? Surely you did not climb the outer stairs."

"I came through the old guard room, my lord. I am familiar with the broken steps in the tower."

"Very well. You can lead me back down." He paused for another frowning moment, then asked abruptly, "Have you anywhere to go?"

Lalia shook her head. "No, my lord."

"Hayne will certainly return for you."

Lalia dropped her gaze to the stone floor. She knew that would never happen. Looking once more into his face, she drew a deep breath. "I consider that very unlikely."

Lord Carrick sighed. "Then we will continue this discussion tomorrow—without the danger of being incinerated by lightning."

With every evidence of reluctance, he released her hair and ushered her toward the door of the tower room.

Having divested himself of his wet clothes, Morgan poured himself a brandy and leaned back against the headboard of the bed, pulling the quilt over his legs. He rubbed at the spot on his chest that always ached in damp weather. A fire would have been nice, but Mrs. Hayne informed him that they did not purchase wood for the bedchambers at Merdinn in the summer.

Hellfire and damnation! What had he got himself into now?

He was realizing that, if the woman truly had nowhere

to go, if her husband had abandoned her, he would have a very hard time making himself send her into the streets. After all, was his desire to avenge Beth on Hayne's woman any better than what Hayne had done to Beth? Morgan was beginning to feel a bit like a cad and a bully in his own right. Not the way he wanted to view himself. Besides—another idea had taken strong hold of his mind.

…to crush in your arms his wives and daughters.

Perhaps it was time for him to do a little crushing.

What better revenge on your enemy than to take his woman from him, to take her to your bed? No man could stand that. A cold smile lit Morgan's eyes.

He felt himself getting hard. He had been hard off and on ever since he had grasped Eulalia Hayne's arm on the tower. Her soaked nightclothes clinging to every inch of her body clearly revealed the curves whose presence he had hitherto only deduced. Lovely, plump curves covered in flawless, translucent skin. And all that hair. Black satin spread out beneath him, lying beneath those succulently rounded hips, covering those soft, generous breasts.

Morgan rolled the brandy over his tongue. He couldn't wait to get his mouth on her. He must have been mad to even consider sending away such a delicious morsel.

Lord Carrick had asked her to join him for dinner in the family dining room—one of the rooms she and her grandmother usually allowed to go uncleaned. Lalia had more than enough work, and her pride, such as it was, did not prevent her eating in the kitchen with the rest of her small household. It did, however, prevent her from serving his lordship in a dirty room. She buffed the table, her hands busy while her mind worried the problem of what she should do.

Lalia pushed her hair out of her face with a wrist that smelled of beeswax. She sensed that Lord Carrick intended to give her a reprieve, that he would tell her that she need not leave immediately. But was that the best decision for her? Certainly it was the easiest.

The question of what she would do here loomed almost as large as that of what she would do if she left. Even with her grandmother as chaperone, living here with his lordship in residence would really be not at all the thing. The memory of the heat of his body and the hardness of his chest washed over her, causing her to tremble. No, indeed. Not the thing at all!

Daj, as always, counseled patience.

"Wait and see, Lalia."

Wait and see, wait and see, always wait, wait, wait.

Apparently a small miracle had occurred. When Morgan had looked into the family dining room earlier in the day, he had resigned himself to a dinner eaten alongside the dust that had covered everything. But now the cobwebs were no more and the surface of the table reflected the fine, gleaming china and crystal his mother had not been able to take to London with her. The heirloom silver had even been polished, glinting softly in the candlelight. Another miracle that Hayne had not sold it all. Likely he never visited the pantries. Morgan leaned back in his chair with satisfaction.

Now if his dinner companion would but appear, he would enjoy a meal at his own table. And enjoy his companion. He licked his lips. Even if she appeared in the worn work clothes that seemed to be her only garments, she would outshine most of the beauties in London. He looked at his watch. Any moment now.

As Morgan slipped his watch back into the pocket of his dark evening coat, the lady stepped through the door. Or at least, he *thought* it was the same lady. Surely the third miracle of the day had come to pass.

Eulalia Hayne glided through the door in a gown of some shimmering fabric that clung to her curves like the hands of a lover. The seafoam green silk, a little lighter than her limpid eyes, caressed her breasts, swooping low across them. A rope of pearls dipped into the valley between. Her masses of shining, inky-black hair, freed from the braid, were piled in loops and swirls high on her head. The arrangement appeared to defy gravity, allowing only soft wisps to escape around her face.

For a moment Morgan could only stare. Surely if he looked hard enough he would be able to see through that gown to the luscious skin beneath it. Surely if she moved, that bodice would slide down, revealing her rosy nipples. Surely... Suddenly he bethought himself of his manners and came hastily to his feet.

"Good evening, Lord Carrick. I trust I haven't kept you waiting."

"Uh, um...not at all." Morgan pulled out her chair and leaned over her shoulder hungrily as she seated herself. That neckline was bound to move, if he just kept his eye on it. "I have just arrived." The bodice stayed stubbornly in place and he moved regretfully to the sideboard. "May I pour you some wine?" She nodded, and Morgan gave thanks to his father's ghost for hiding away his best collection of wine in the deepest, darkest cellar.

Sitting down again, he gave a thought to the wondrous dress. Perhaps Mrs. Hayne enjoyed more affluence than he had yet observed. He tried to feel anger at some possible deception on her part, but it failed to materialize. Even he could see that the garment was years from being the height of fashion. But curiosity pricked. ''Your gown is lovely. Did you purchase it in London?''

Mrs. Hayne sipped her wine and shook her head. ''I have never been to London.''

''Never?'' Everyone had been to London.

She smiled. ''I have led a rather secluded life.''

Apparently so. *Everyone* had been to London. ''Did you live in Cornwall before your marriage?''

''Yes, my father was Sir Richmond Poleven. He owned an estate not far from here. My half brother, Roger, now lives there.'' After a moment with a curious lack of expression she added, ''It was he who arranged for my marriage.''

So she was Poleven's sister. That explained some things. He knew Roger Poleven to be a crony of Hayne's. He surpassed Hayne in character by a small margin, but Morgan did not think very highly of him. ''I would think he could have done better for you than Cordell Hayne.''

Mrs. Hayne looked down into her glass, then back at him with eyes that had turned gray but steady. ''It is not easy to find a match for a dowerless, half-Gypsy sister. I believe Roger brought it about by forgiving a debt.''

Startled, Morgan exclaimed, ''Gypsy? Your mother was a Gypsy?'' It was almost unheard of for a nobleman to marry anyone not of the gentry, let alone a person considered an outcast by even the lowest peasant. Perhaps Sir Richmond had an aversion to leaving a bastard behind. But to know she had been foisted onto a scoundrel through coercion... What a blow to her pride.

If the lady felt any chagrin, he did not see it on her

face. "Yes, my father married her a long while after Roger's mother died. Mine died giving me birth."

"I'm sorry."

"Thank you. As I never knew her, I have not felt the loss, especially as her mother has taken care of me ever since."

"So your grandmother is a Gypsy."

She smiled. "Oh, yes. She has never given up her Romani ways. *Roma* is the name they call themselves," she explained. "When a woman marries a *gadjo,* a man who is not Roma, she becomes *marimé,* and no longer Gypsy. Since my father would not give me up when my mother died, my grandmother also left her tribe rather than abandon me to a strange household—but she is still Roma to the core."

The door opened and James came in with a tray bearing two plates of a savory stew with a hearty pancake-like bread useful for scooping. Morgan drew in the aroma appreciatively. "Is this a Romani dish?"

"Yes, I hope you don't mind. Romani food is all my grandmother or I know how to cook. We were never in the kitchen at my father's home." Mrs. Hayne appeared to study her dinner, speaking with a bit of hesitation. "Is your own chef coming soon?"

"In a few days. My man of business is assembling a full staff."

"I see." She kept her gaze on her plate. "We shall try to be away by then."

Morgan pushed away from the table and poured himself another glass of wine, his brows creased thoughtfully. Without asking, he refilled her half-empty glass. "You seem to be certain that Hayne will not return for you."

She took a tiny sip of the wine. "I think that it is

highly unlikely, my lord. If, as you say, he is ruined, he will not want an additional burden. And...he has never sought my company.''

Never sought her company? The man must be blind as well as a blackguard. ''Will you go to your brother?''

She appeared to consider for a moment, then shook her head. ''My *half* brother. I doubt that will be possible. I have not seen Roger in years.''

So Poleven did not want an embarrassing Gypsy relative in residence. It fit with Morgan's assessment of his nature. And with his own plans. He hesitated a moment before asking the next, potentially humiliating, question, and then decided to ask it anyway. ''Have you any money?''

''I have some, my lord.'' She did not meet his eyes and he deduced that *some* meant very little indeed. The answer also suited his purposes. She would stay because she could not leave.

If she felt ashamed, her voice did not betray it. ''I have tried to sell these pearls, but no one I know can buy them.'' Her eyes, now clear again, twinkled, and a little smile played around her lips. ''Besides—they all have their own finery.''

The light dawned on Morgan. Salvage. Goods washed ashore from shipwrecks by law belonged to the crown or the ship owner. Apparently she was not above skirting the law a bit herself. What had he expected of Hayne's wife? Roger Poleven's sister? Did she also engage in a little smuggling?

''You, uh, found the pearls?''

''A trunk appeared as if by magic in our cove several years ago.'' She assumed a very innocent expression, opening her eyes wide. ''There was no ship in sight, so how were we to know how it got there?''

In spite of himself, a bark of laughter burst out of Morgan. He knew well that where so many ships met their doom on the treacherous cliffs of Cornwall, outwitting the salvage officers had long since become a major industry. ''And the dress?''

''From the trunk, also.'' She returned serenely to her dinner. How like Cordell Hayne to leave his beautiful wife to resort to the sea for an out-of-fashion evening dress, to leave her to manage his estate on a paltry allowance.

And now he left her conveniently penniless. Morgan started to refill Mrs. Hayne's glass, but it was still full, so he poured another glass for himself. Apparently the seduction of his enemy's lady would not be accomplished by plying her with strong drink. Pity. The longer she sat across the table from him in that enticing gown, the more impatient he became.

He would have to offer her a position. But *not* as the mistress of Merdinn. Cordell Hayne's wife would never be that.

Chapter Three

What should he suggest? The position of housekeeper? Demeaning for a gentleman's daughter, but perhaps suitable for the wife of one's defeated enemy. But, no. He already had a housekeeper on the way. Besides—she might move out of the mistress's bedchamber that adjoined his and take up residence in the housekeeper's rooms.

The offer must be something temporary. Then if things did not work out as he wished, he could find a position for her with one of his acquaintances. Even if they did, he could not picture himself carrying on an affair with an employee under the same roof as his mother. No, indeed.

That thought gave him pause. An affair with an employee? Never before had he even considered such a dishonorable course of action. But she would not *really* be an employee, just a…

A woman without protection.

The notion trust itself forward unbidden. He shoved it back. Damnation! She was Cordell Hayne's wife! It was *his* responsibility to protect her. Married women had affairs all the time—after producing a few heirs, of course. It was an accepted fact of ton life.

But Mrs. Hayne must be long gone before his mother's arrival at the end of the summer. Ah! That gave him an idea. Morgan schooled his features to reveal none of his thoughts. This must be done carefully.

"Mrs. Hayne, I wonder, since you have no immediate plans, if you might be able to oblige me in the matter of Jeremy's supervision? I dismissed his governess when we left London. He is old enough now for a tutor, but I want to allow him his freedom for the rest of the summer. As I will be very busy with the renovations of Merdinn, perhaps you might agree to keep him out of trouble for me? By summer's end, you should be able to arrange a position elsewhere."

"Thank you, my lord. I appreciate your offer, but what of my grandmother?"

Apparently the grandparent came with the lady. In any event, Morgan could certainly not see himself turning out an infirm and aged woman. "She will remain as my guest, of course."

Lalia took a careful sip of her wine. The expected reprieve had become reality—and presented in a very palatable form. Not charity exactly, but a position. Not a very exalted position, true, but honorable enough. A governess of sorts. No, not quite that exalted. Rather a nursemaid. Very kind of his lordship.

Very kind.

He was up to something.

She looked steadily into his face for a moment. He looked back, politely expectant—nothing more. Yes, he was *definitely* up to something. He clearly hated her husband, so why should he feel any differently toward her? Why indeed.

Perhaps she presumed in thinking that his lordship had designs on her plump person. She was but a mere dab of a woman, too short and too well padded for fashion. No one had ever called her a beauty. But she saw…something…behind that enigmatic green gaze. Clearly the safety of her virtue lay in departing Merdinn as fast as her legs could carry her.

But when had she ever had the luxury of safety? Not since her father died certainly. And what of Daj? Her legs hardly even carried her up the stairs. Once again Lalia would have to be practical. At least the post would give her the time she needed.

All her other choices really constituted no choice at all. Once again she must accept the inevitable. The very thing she had always done. Accept and make the best of it. Accept the position of an ostracized half-Gypsy daughter sheltered on her father's estate. Accept the guardianship of a half brother who married her to a ne'er-do-well at the age of sixteen, because he didn't want to be bothered with her well-being. Accept a husband who took no thought for her well-being at all.

Now, if she stayed, what might she be asked to accept?

"Very well, my lord. Until the end of the summer then."

If she could avoid her husband, she certainly could avoid Lord Carrick.

The next morning Lalia had her first inkling that Lord Carrick might prove a little harder to avoid than her usually absent husband. Just as she and Jeremy were climbing into the gig outside the stable, his lordship came running toward them up the lane. Good heavens! What could be the matter? She tossed the reins to James and, hastily jumping down, hurried toward Lord Carrick. He ran easily up to the carriage, his long legs pumping, the muscles flexing inside the skintight britches. He came to a stop beside her, his breathing only slightly deep.

"My lord! What is it?"

He bowed carelessly and tossed sweaty curls off his forehead. "What is what?"

"Why are you running? Is there some emergency?"

"Oh, that. No, I often run."

He smiled down at her, his eyes warming, and suddenly Lalia's own breath caught in her throat. He had pushed his rolled sleeves above his elbows, revealing sculptured forearms, and his open collar showed the cords of his strong neck. A sense of power flowed off of him along with his scent and the heat from his body, embracing her in a mesmerizing cloud.

Lalia took a step back. "Oh…uh…" She drew a sustaining breath. "You alarmed me. I have never known a gentleman to…"

"To run? Most gentlemen do not have my motivation. I suffered an injury to my lung. Running has helped me to regain my stamina." The smile dimmed a bit and the seductive light in his eyes went out. Somehow the expression changed to something just a little menacing.

Lalia stepped back again. "I—I see. That must have been very difficult for you."

"Yes, at first." He move a pace nearer, and Lalia retreated again, bumping against the gig. The horse sidled and his lordship steadied it with a hand on the bridle. "Where are you two going?" He casually put his hands on her waist as though to help her into the carriage.

And he took his time about it. Drat the man! Lalia

braced herself and prepared to be lifted. "To see Widow Tregellen. I am taking her some of our fresh vegetables."

The hands that had tightened around her were abruptly removed and she almost stumbled in surprise as she found herself still on the ground. Lord Carrick stepped back. "I see. As you have been doing as lady of the estate."

"Well, yes. I guess you might say that. The tenants have no one else on whom they may depend."

"*Had* no one else. The situation has changed. That is no longer your responsibility, Mrs. Hayne."

Lalia's cheeks grew warm. "I—I had not thought of that. I did not mean to… It is just that she can no longer manage her own garden, and I thought she would especially enjoy the green onions."

"No doubt." His lordship crossed his arms over his chest, his expression unyielding.

"Very well. If you don't wish her to have them… James, you may unhitch the gig. Come, Jeremy."

"Aw, Uncle Morgan." Jeremy made to climb down. "We were going to see the lighthouse."

Damn the woman! Morgan perceived that he had been cast neatly in the role of villain—an uncaring lord denying an aging dependent a few fresh vegetables and his nephew an outing. Now what was he to do? He held up a restraining hand. James stopped his preparations to lead the carriage away, a carefully neutral expression on his lined face.

"I did not say I did not want her to have them." Morgan grimaced. Damnation! Now he sounded defensive.

"You could come with us, Uncle Morgan," Jeremy put in hopefully.

Not a bad idea, three of them crowded onto the seat. Morgan glanced down at his sweat-stained clothes. But not at this particular moment. He turned to the lady who waited quietly. "Are you a competent driver?"

James chortled. "At least, *she* never put the gig in no ditch, as I seem to recall a certain young gentleman doing."

Morgan scowled, then grinned ruefully. "That was a long time ago, James. I have since learned caution. Very well, Mrs. Hayne. Please deliver the produce with my compliments and greet Old Tom for me. Tell him I will stop in at the lighthouse at my earliest opportunity."

"If you wish it, my lord." She turned back to the gig and Morgan again seized her waist and tossed her up. As she took the reins, he waited until he could capture her gaze. When she looked at him in inquiry, he smiled slowly and allowed his gaze to travel briefly to the bosom concealed beneath the shabby pelisse. When he saw the blush climb from her neck to her cheeks, Morgan turned and withdrew, checked, but in good order.

Now what had *that* look been all about? As if she didn't know! Lalia guided the cob down the road toward the widow's house, considering. In the first place he had been determined to put her out of countenance, retaliation for her presumption—in short, to show her her place. Well, he could just put his mind at rest. She would certainly never act in her former role again. A spark of anger crept through the calm facade she showed the world.

Then, of course, there was the second place. Did he think she would so easily fall into his bed? She did, after all, have marriage vows to remember—not that her husband had ever given them a moment's consideration.

Again the wind of wrath ruffled her still waters. Why must she be chained to such a scoundrel—drunken, abusive, neglectful of everything but his pleasures and his schemes?

Oh, yes. She had heard the schemes. On the rare occasions when he graced his home with his presence, always deep in his cups, he pounded her ears with his talk. He even had the goodness to regale her with his amatory adventures. As if she cared. Apparently he hoped that jealousy would open her door to him, but she long ago had learned better than to do that.

She knew just when, before he had quite finished the third bottle, to make good her escape and turn the key. If she left him too soon, before he grew helplessly drunk, he would come after her and drag her back. If she waited too late, he would begin to paw her where she sat. Let him batter her door. That was better than his battering her body.

And now the Earl of Carrick appeared, smiling temptation thinly covering his anger. But for all that, he represented a very tempting temptation, indeed. How she would love to… No. No, she would not think of that. She, at least, would keep the vows she had made before God.

She drove silently for a few moments, recovering her tranquility. Repining did no good. It merely cut up her peace. She looked around her and drew a deep breath. She had a lovely day to enjoy, and Jeremy was chattering happily beside her. Time to once more put away what could not be remedied.

"Forgive me, Jeremy. I wasn't attending. What did you say?"

"I asked you if I must call you Mrs. Hayne."

Lalia pondered the question. "I don't know. Do you not wish to call me that?"

"No-oo." The boy lowered his gaze. "I don't like the way it sounds when Uncle Morgan says it. He sounds as though he doesn't like it, either."

That made three of them. Lalia didn't like it very much herself. "I suspect that is because he is angry with my husband. What would you like to call me?"

Jeremy brightened. "I don't know. I know I shouldn't call you by your given name." He paused, squinting up at her in the bright sunlight. "You do have a given name, don't you?"

Lalia chuckled. "Of course. It's Eulalia."

"Yoo…lol…ya. That's a very long name."

"My family calls me Lalia."

"I could call you *Miss* Lalia." He looked at her hopefully.

She smiled and ruffled his hair. "I think that would be nice."

That must have been very difficult for you.
Yes, at first.

If only the woman knew. *Difficult* had hardly been the word at first. That came later. At first the word had been *agonizing,* lying propped on a stack of pillows, blood frothing on his lips, every breath an excruciating effort. Everyone knew Morgan would die. But they didn't understand. He couldn't die—wouldn't. He survived to bring the bastard low.

Although, Morgan had to admit, at the moment he had not yet brought the scum quite as low as he had thought. The man was still at liberty, entirely without chains, and still on English soil. But Morgan would soon change that state of affairs. He strolled into the stable and surveyed the meager array of livestock.

...to ride his enemy's horses...

That portion of his revenge was not going well, either. Aside from his own team of blacks, he saw only one horse—the cob, of course, being busy elsewhere. Even counting that functional if unglamorous animal, a stable of two horses did not provide much scope for revenge. Even the lone mount on which Hayne had ridden lacked quality.

Oh, well. Perhaps he should place Hayne's sloop in the horse-riding category. He had no doubt that the small yacht would be better kept than the stable. It represented the only passion, greater than gambling and seducing women, that Hayne had. In place of the horse riding, sailing Hayne's boat should pain his enemy even more. If he could find it. But Morgan, after all, owned numerous shipping vessels.

He would find it.

Horses and boats were a minor matter, in any case. His larger problem lay in deciding just how to bring about the desired crushing in his arms of Hayne's wife. She would not hold him off for long. He could see that in her eyes, in the way she stepped away from him when he crowded her, in the way her breath quickened. She felt the tug of desire, just as he did. Hayne had obviously neglected her, leaving her hungry for the touch of a man. Yes, Morgan judged that he would soon prevail.

But he must not let her think that she would ever again be the mistress of his home. *His* mistress perhaps, but not the lady of the manor. Yet, upon reflection, he felt a grudging appreciation for her desire to see to the welfare of his people. At least they had had someone to turn to in his absence. The lady appeared to have a caring heart behind those delectable breasts. But as soon as Merdinn was again livable, he would bring his mother home to assume those tasks. Mrs. Hayne must learn her new place.

She would soon have other duties.

"Uncle Morgan, Uncle Morgan!" Jeremy slammed through the main door and raced into the library. "There's a shipwreck! There are pieces of ship and dead people lying all over the cove!"

"Dead people?" Morgan scowled at his nephew's caretaker as she followed her charge through the door at a more sedate pace.

His nephew glanced at him uncertainly. "Well, I think they were dead, because Miss Lalia would not let me go down to see."

Morgan looked inquiringly at the lady. She nodded as she removed her frayed bonnet and smoothed her hair. "I fear so, my lord. The wreck occurred in Sad Day Cove, just this side of the lighthouse, some distance from our cove. The currents there are very strong and the rocks are vicious. I spoke with Old Tom where we met him on the road. He said that no one seems to have survived. I brought Jeremy straight away."

"We did not get to see the lighthouse," Jeremy rushed on, still excited, "because Mr. Tom was going to look at the wreck. But just think…I saw a real shipwreck!"

"No doubt a high treat, but I'm sure you'll forgive me if, as a ship owner, I don't share your enthusiasm," Morgan responded dryly. He turned back to Mrs. Hayne. "Is there any indication as to who owned the vessel?"

"Tom thought it was a French ship—perhaps carrying

passengers only. There seems to have been little cargo washed up.''

Morgan lifted an eyebrow. "Stranded goods rarely stay in evidence for long.''

"True, but from what I heard, there was not much to be seen when fishermen first noticed the debris just after dawn. Everyone was very disappointed.''

Morgan's mouth quirked at this matter-of-fact assessment, but it bothered him that there had been so much loss of life. Unfortunately, when the booty looked rich, more than one struggling survivor had been known to die after reaching the safety of the beach. He got to his feet. "I'll ride over and have a look.''

From the top of the cliff the rocks looked to be covered with ants. Two-legged ants. Both men and women swarmed over the rocks below him, searching in every cranny for anything valuable, or even useful. Breakers, crashing over the boulders as the tide advanced, wet everyone and threatened the bravest who teetered on the outlying stones. Several men climbed a rocky cleft, straining to keep hold of a rope attached to a grim burden. As they neared the top of the cliff, Morgan stepped forward and grasped the rope, adding his strength to pull the body onto level ground. While the other men caught their breath, he knelt and lifted away the covering sheet and studied the bruised face.

It had belonged to a young woman. About Beth's age. The age Beth had been. Morgan winced at the thought of the tender body being pounded against the cruel rocks. What fear had gripped her as she fought the clutching breakers in the black darkness? He could only hope she had drowned before encountering the jagged stone teeth. He rose and stood looking thoughtfully at her, the questions in his mind still unanswered.

"It's a sad day, me lord."

Morgan started at the familiar voice. "Well, hello, James. I didn't see you."

James nodded at a second body, wiping his face. "I been doing my possible to help bring 'em up, but that ain't as much as I'd like anymore. Good thing that's the last one."

"I'll lend a hand. I'd have come sooner if I had known." Morgan clapped his henchman on the shoulder. "You bring my horse."

Morgan took James's place and, encouraged by fresh help, the bearers resumed their burdens and carried them away from the edge of the precipice. They arrived shortly at a small, level spot where several bodies were laid out. A fair-haired young man in the uniform of the preventive services stood looking glumly at the corpses, casting an occasional glance toward the ocean.

Morgan approached him. "Good afternoon. I'm Carrick. Nothing to salvage, Mr....?"

The officer touched his hat respectfully. "Hastings. Nay, my lord. Not worth the battle with that lot." He nodded toward the cliff. "Even most of them will go home empty-handed—unless the tide brings something in."

"Do you know what happened to her?"

"No, my lord. The wind wasn't all that high last night. I can't see why..." The man shrugged. "You invest in shipping?"

Morgan nodded. "I have shipping interests, yes."

"I see. Well, if I learn something I'll send you word. Good day, sir." The officer bowed and walked off toward the cliff.

Morgan strolled to where the village doctor knelt examining the dead, his white hair and side whiskers shining in the sun. Morgan extended his hand. "Dr. Lanreath."

The doctor turned in surprise. "Lord Morgan! Or I guess I should say 'Lord Carrick' now. I heard you were back. It's good to see you."

"Thank you. Have you found anything of interest to a sailor here?"

The doctor narrowed his eyes shrewdly. "Do you mean, have I found evidence of foul play?" He shook his head. "Not that I can see. Looks like the sea did the work, but it's impossible to tell for sure. I'll tell you this, though. None of them have anything valuable on them."

Morgan looked around at the men still hovering near the cliff top. None of them returned his gaze. Well, that didn't surprise him. Lanreath straightened from his work, coming stiffly to his feet. "Nothing more I can do here. They may as well bury them. Join me for a tankard at the Pilchard?"

"With pleasure." Morgan retrieved his horse and followed the older man's gig to the village. The tavern, identified by a worn sign featuring a sad-looking fish peering from a stargazey pie, looked much as it had nineteen years before. They found a place at a table in the tap room, the cool shade welcome after the warm day.

Morgan surveyed the assortment of patrons collected there, most of them talking about the wreck. Some of them he vaguely recognized, but the bull-necked man with the completely bald head serving the drinks was a stranger to him.

He returned his gaze to his companion. "Has Wendrom given up the Pilchard?"

"In a manner of speaking." The doctor took a long draught of his ale. "He died of a fever last year, and his wife sold the tavern to Killigrew there. Don't know why he came here—speaks as though he hails from London. Don't like him above half myself. Mean customer. Doubtless into smuggling."

Morgan raised an eyebrow, watching as the man, his massive muscles bulging, easily hoisted a keg and lifted it into the rack. "Aren't all innkeepers?"

"Oh, aye, but this one..." Dr. Lanreath shrugged. "I'm only thinking out loud, and not very loud at that. Some sorts of thinking can prove to be very bad for one's health. Don't want to become my own patient."

Morgan nodded thoughtfully, but didn't pursue the subject. "I don't recognize many of these fellows. I guess they were just lads when I went away."

"Aye, that they were, and many of them have been abroad fighting Napoleon. A large number of fishermen were impressed into the navy, as I'm sure you know. Now they're home, and with damn little work for them to do, unless they want to work for the preventives—which they don't. Put that with a man like Killigrew... Well, I'm talking out of turn again."

"Just so. Best you be careful on that subject." Morgan swallowed down the last of his ale and shook hands with the doctor. "I better get back to Merdinn and see what my scamp of a nephew is up to. Stop in to see us when you're passing."

Morgan emerged into the sunlight and started for home. Everyone in the district seemed to have driven out to have a look at the scene of the disaster. By the time Morgan had spoken with half a dozen old acquaintances met along the road, he barely had time to wash and change his clothes for dinner.

He tied a fresh cravat with a bit more than his usual care, wondering if Eulalia Hayne would wear the same mouthwatering dress, or whether the magically discovered trunk had yielded more than one. He was humming as he made his way downstairs to the dining room.

The humming came to an abrupt stop as he approached the table. Only one cover had been laid, resting in solitary splendor at the head of the table.

Hmm. The suspicion blossomed in Morgan that he had just been shown *his* place.

Chapter Four

The hell with this!

Halfway through a plate of some kind of spicy meat rolled in cabbage leaves, Morgan threw down his napkin and picked up his plate. Eating alone was *not* what he had in mind, even if he was the master of the house. Apparently Mrs. Hayne was giving him the opportunity to regret his reminding her of her new status. On inquiry, James had assured him that she was presently dining in the kitchen as she always did, so possibly she was simply following her usual custom. But she was bound to know that he intended his invitation the previous night to be of a standing nature. Wasn't she?

In any case, he did not relish lordly solitude.

He grabbed the wine bottle and made his way down the steps to the kitchen. How to handle this? His first thought had been to let the lady sulk. But that would deprive him of her voluptuous company. He might have little time to spend with her in coming days, and he required proximity for his intentions to become reality. This situation must be nipped in the bud.

And it must be done subtly. If he confronted her directly, he would merely confirm the fact that her withdrawal had nettled him. That would not do. No, he would do better to sound magnanimous—the gracious lord politely delivering a command disguised as an invitation. The gracious lord not too high in the instep to join his overworked staff in the kitchen until help arrived. Yes, that should set the tone nicely. Never mind the gracious lord who wanted to keep his prey in his eye.

Pleased with this strategy, Morgan strolled into the kitchen nonchalantly. Mrs. Hayne came immediately to her feet, delicate eyebrows drawn together. "Lord Carrick! Is something wrong with your dinner?"

"Oh, no. On the contrary." He set the plate and bottle on the table and slid onto the bench opposite her. "I find that good food requires good company to be properly appreciated." He let his gaze rest on her face for a long moment. "And I don't wish to add to your work unnecessarily. The rest of the kitchen staff will be here day after tomorrow. I'm content to eat here until then."

She did not speak until Morgan asked, "Where is my nephew?"

"In his room, my lord. He was hungry earlier, so I gave him his dinner and suggested he play quietly until I come to tuck him in."

Morgan nodded approval.

He lifted the wine bottle, offering for them to join him. Mrs. Hayne shook her head and sat down again. James jumped up with alacrity and brought two cups to the table. Peggy stared at her plate. Morgan glanced at the elderly woman sitting at the foot of the table. This must be the grandmother. She calmly finished the last of her food and, without a word, handed her plate to Peggy and left the room. Peggy scurried into the scullery.

Feeling a bit like the skeleton at the feast, Morgan

nevertheless took his time finishing his dinner. He and James talked a bit about the wreck, speculating as to the cause until the bottle of wine had been emptied. Mrs. Hayne contributed nothing to the conversation, but listened attentively.

He was on the point of asking about her grandmother when that lady reappeared. Still without speaking, she began to spread thick slices of bread with jam and clotted cream. She brought a plate of this delicacy to Morgan's place. He turned to face her at her approach.

She quickly stepped back and said something Morgan did not understand. He looked inquiringly at her granddaughter.

"She said, *'Bolde kut, kako.'* With the Roma the men are always served from the back. A woman must not pass in front of a man or between two men," Mrs. Hayne explained. "Therefore she asks you to turn away." Morgan obediently faced forward and the plate was set before him.

Apparently only he merited this service. The old woman placed the bread and containers on the table, and the rest of the group served themselves. When all had finished the plain dessert, Morgan rose and thanked the ladies for an excellent repast, refusing to acknowledge the awkwardness around him. He smiled.

Let Mrs. Hayne reap what she sowed.

"I'd best go up and see to Jeremy." Lalia rose from her bench and started out of the room.

"I'll come with you and tell him good-night." Lord Carrick hastily stepped ahead of her to open the door, but he did not provide quite enough clearance for her to exit without brushing against him.

So… His lordship was still up to his tricks. Lalia would ignore it. He offered her his arm. Refusing to smile her thanks, she laid her hand on his sleeve. That was considerably harder to ignore. Lalia felt the hard muscle through his coat and could smell an almost smoky scent that surrounded him. She schooled herself not to react.

"I hope," he said, smiling down at her, "that when more help arrives, you and your grandmother will do me the honor of joining me for dinner each evening. Eating alone is very dreary."

Was that a gentle reproof? Lalia couldn't be sure. She resisted the temptation to point out that she was no longer mistress of the house but a lower servant. But that kind of spite was certainly beneath her dignity. Nor would she give him the satisfaction. Besides, there must be peace, at least, between them for the rest of the summer.

And she could never hold a grudge, anyway.

"Why, thank you, my lord. I should be delighted." Well, perhaps something a little less than *delighted*. His lordship's masculine presence tended to put a severe strain on her self-possession. "I cannot speak for my grandmother. It is very difficult for her to climb stairs. That is why she moved to a room in the service wing."

Now what accounted for that look of satisfaction on the man's face?

Before Lalia could decide, they arrived at Jeremy's room just in time to witness the annihilation of a troop of cavalry by a hail of artillery fire. Jeremy lay on his stomach shooting crockery marbles into the ranks of the wooden soldiers, making too much noise to hear them enter. "Boom! Boom! Boom!"

Lalia put her hands to her ears. "Jeremy! I said play quietly."

The barrage ceased as the boy leapt to his feet and bowed politely. "Oh, hello, Miss Lalia. Uncle Morgan. Have you come to tuck me in?"

They both assured him on this point, and Lalia sent him behind the screen to wash his face and change to his nightshirt. She watched in some surprise at the tenderness with which Lord Carrick tucked the covers under his nephew's chin. Apparently his lordship's harshness and conniving were reserved for her and her husband.

Afterward, he insisted on walking her to her bedchamber in spite of protests that she could walk the few yards alone quite safely. At the door he somehow succeeded in capturing her hand before she could escape into her room. With his gaze never leaving her eyes, he carried her hand to his lips. In spite of Lalia's determination, her fingers trembled.

That look of satisfaction again in his hard green eyes, he reached past her to open the door. Lalia slipped hastily through the narrow space he allowed, her breasts brushing his chest slightly before she could get the door closed, sighing with relief.

That encounter had been a near run thing.

Morgan resisted the impulse to pace. He hated not being able to sleep. The level of brandy in his glass had sunk almost to the bottom. Perhaps he would have another. But, no. He had drunk too much already. His wits would soon be wandering. Besides, rather than dampening the feelings that persisted in tormenting his lower body, the wine seemed to increase them. He was ready and more than ready to crush his enemy's wife in his embrace. And the lady was nothing loathe, he was sure.

He could hear her quick intake of breath when he touched her, could see the warmth kindle in her eyes.

Ah, those eyes. So changeable. So expressive. What color would they become in the throes of passion? He would soon know. He could sense her weakening.

The thought of her lying in the next room in the big bed wanting him, needing him, made his mouth water and his groin ache unbearably. No, this state of affairs could not go on much longer.

Lalia had not been asleep. How could she sleep with the foundations of her life crumbling? Lalia had been staring at the faded canopy of her bed, wondering for the hundredth time—no, the millionth time—what sort of work she might do. And how to resist his disturbingly seductive lordship. The noise in the corridor had been so muffled that it almost failed to pierce her consciousness—a light thump, as though someone had collided with the chair outside her door. She sat up listening.

The sound did not repeat itself, but the furtive quality of it disturbed Lalia. Lord Carrick had come up to bed an hour ago and she had not heard the door of the adjoining room open since then. Perhaps Jeremy needed her and had lost himself in the dark.

Lalia swung her feet over the side of the bed and lit the candle. Pulling her wrapper over her cotton nightgown, she eased the door open and put her head out. Seeing no one, she slipped into the hall and held the candle high. Still no one. In her bare feet she padded silently to Jeremy's room and peeked in. The boy lay lost in the slumber reserved for the just and the very young.

Puzzled, Lalia retreated to her own door, then glanced at his lordship's. Should she alert him? She took two more steps, but hesitated as she reached the portal. Did she really want to wake him? An encounter in a darkened passage might be… Well, it would be too… But… If someone were prowling… Lalia lifted her hand to knock, but stood frozen by indecision. Was he awake or asleep? Cautiously she laid her ear against the panels.

Suddenly the door swept open, knocking her back against the wall. The candle fell to the floor and went out.

Hearing a startled squeak issue from behind the door, Morgan stepped into the hall and peered behind it. He beheld the object of his recent plotting leaning against the wall with her hands held up to ward off the collision. So she *had* come to his bedchamber!

"Good evening, Mrs. Hayne." Smiling with satisfaction, Morgan leaned his hands against the wall, one on either side of her head. "Have you come to keep me company in my lonely room?"

"Uh…" Her voice sounded strangled and she cleared her throat. "N-no, my lord. I heard something in the corridor." She still held her hands before her and now she pushed against his chest tentatively, as if to move him away.

Morgan didn't budge. She heard something? Ha! "So why were you listening at my keyhole?"

"I—I didn't know if you were sleeping… I didn't want to…"

He shifted one hand to gather a handful of silky black hair, pinning it to the wall. She pushed again, harder. Morgan leaned into the pressure, bringing his face nearer to hers so that she could feel his breath on her lips. "You didn't want to what?"

"I didn't…" She stopped in midsentence and looked into his face. "My lord, why are you doing this?"

The question took Morgan by surprise. He moved

back a bit. "Why? Because you are lovely, and I want you. And you want me."

She shook her head. "That is not the real reason." Her voice was now calm and certain. She did not push again, but seemed still and waiting. "You hate my husband. Why would you want me?"

Shrewd as well as beautiful. Well, then...she asked. "Because you are his. I want everything that is his— especially you. No man can stand the thought of another man taking his woman, holding her, touching all the places that are his alone." He moved his lips nearer, brushing them against her face between words. "The way I want to hold you...touch you."

Her laugh almost startled him into releasing her. "For all your hate, you don't know my husband very well, do you, my lord?"

This was not going well. Morgan increased the distance between them slightly. "What do you mean?"

"Let me tell you a story, my lord." She made no further attempt to escape. "You must understand that my husband seldom came here. He could be very... unpleasant when he did appear, and I learned to avoid him. It angered him, but...well, he soon left again." Her quiet manner had captured Morgan's full attention. "One day he came bringing two other men with him. By evening they were all very drunk. I was on the way up to my room when I overheard their talk. He owed them gambling debts. I heard him propose that in place of the money he owed, they might...might... share me throughout the night."

Morgan dropped his hands to his sides and stepped back. Good God! What was he doing? "What happened? Did they...?"

"No." She stepped away from the wall. "I ran to my

room to lock my doors, but when I looked for the keys, they had been removed.'' She no longer looked at Morgan, but seemed lost in remembering. ''I suppose he took them earlier. I could hear them coming up the stairs… They were laughing.'' She glanced at his face. ''Do you know about the hidden stair in my room?''

''Yes, a priest's hole. It has been there for centuries—comes out above the path to the cove.''

She nodded. ''I knew they would catch me if I used it. They were too close. So I opened it and hid in the wardrobe. I heard them make for the stair, laughing and shouting and hallooing as though they were hunting… Which I guess they were.''

Morgan winced at the image.

She continued calmly. ''The panel can only be opened from inside my room, so I closed it and ran back the other way and hid in the tower guard room. You saw the condition of the steps there. I thought that, as drunk as they were…''

''That they would break their necks climbing them.''

''Well, I did not think they could come up, and they didn't. They all went away the next day.'' She smiled a sad little half-smile. ''But you see, you will not harm my husband in this way.''

Morgan moved away from her a few more steps. ''Mrs. Hayne, I find myself taken at fault. I beg you will forgive my boorish behavior.'' He heard the coldness embarrassment injected into his voice and made an attempt to ameliorate it. ''I assure you, however, that my actions were based more upon feelings engendered by you than on those I hold toward your husband. Nonetheless… I apologize.'' He walked around her, picking up her candle as he passed. ''I'll have a look around for what you heard before I go back to bed.''

Opening her door, Morgan cursed himself for a cad and stood well back, giving her plenty of room to enter.

He should have known that he would not force himself on an hesitant woman, the crushing precept to the contrary notwithstanding. Convincing himself that she shared his desire was blatant wishful thinking. True, as the veteran of a number of affairs, Morgan knew encouraging signs when he saw them, and he felt sure he had seen them in Eulalia Hayne. That, however, brought him around to what should have been obvious to him by the second day of their acquaintance.

In spite of the fact that polite society condoned discreet affairs in married women, this lady did not. This lady would keep her vows, even when they trapped her in a hideous marriage. This lady, for all her soft, gentle manner, had courage, resilience and character. She made Morgan examine his own.

On reflection, he did not regret one moment of ruining Hayne. The man was a predator from which society needed protection. Had Morgan been able to kill him in a fair fight, he would gladly have done it. But subjecting Hayne's wife to further abuse...

Unforgivable.

It put him firmly in the category with Hayne himself. That thought made Morgan want to take a bath. The devil was in it, though, in that he wanted the woman as much as—no, more than—ever. He couldn't quite give up his determination to have her in his arms, to taste her sweetness.

But he could not do it as an act of revenge.

The pile of vegetables in the basket beside her grew steadily as Lalia's sure hands picked them and plucked dead blossoms from their neighbors. A few feet away

Jeremy, not so sure, attempted to master the mysteries of what constituted a weed. She smiled. The bed would be short a few flowers by the end of the day, but he seemed to enjoy the challenge if not the work.

Usually working with the plants lifted Lalia's spirits, but today even the cheerful sun and soft ocean breeze did not help. Despite her optimistic nature, the future looked bleak. She had not realized how much her home meant to her. Now that she had only a few more weeks to spend in it, even the relentless drudgery and loneliness seemed dear. And she would greatly miss visiting the tenants. They accepted her—most of them, at least.

What would she do with herself, aside from caring for Jeremy, for the next three months? Already Lord Carrick had taken away most of her duties. He himself had greeted the crew of workers who had appeared earlier in the morning, explaining to the overseer what he wanted done first. He had made it very clear to her that he did not want her help.

Another in a long line of people who did not want her. She didn't know whether to welcome his apology of the night before or to regret it. At least he seemed for a moment to want *her*. But Lalia knew from bleak experience that Carrick's approaches did not count as wanting her. The future looked lonely indeed.

Lost in these melancholy thoughts, she jumped when the subject of her thoughts spoke right behind her.

''You two are busy to a purpose this morning.''

''Oh! Good morning, your lordship. You startled me. Have you… No, Jeremy, not that one. That's a delphinium.'' Lalia turned back to smile up at Lord Carrick from her spot seated beside the flower bed.

He knelt on one knee and examined the bed, pulling

out what was obviously a dandelion. "Do you always plant vegetables in your flower beds?"

Lalia nodded. "We need them. I considered putting the whole bed to them, but I can't bear to give up all the flowers."

"Can't you just buy some of the local produce?"

"We could, of course, but..." She paused and turned her head back to her work. "But the tenants need what they grow for their families, and it...it is more economical to grow them myself."

"Well, soon you will not have that necessity. The new gardeners start next week, and I have hired enough help to reopen the home farm."

Lalia swallowed around a lump that had suddenly appeared in her throat. So... Soon she would not even be allowed to garden. Unless... A ray of light appeared. Perhaps she could hire herself out as a gardener. To work all day at what she loved—at last, a heartening thought.

Lord Carrick stood and brushed the dirt from his knee. "Jeremy has been plaguing me to take him down to the cove. The cleaning in the great hall seems to be well under way, and the tide is out. I thought this would be a good time."

"Hooray!" Jeremy bounced to his feet. "Come on, Miss Lalia. I'm tired of being a farmer."

Lalia smiled, shaking her head. "I must take these to the kitchen and help Daj. I will see you when you return."

"Unnecessary." Carrick bent and scooped up the basket. "Another local woman has been hired to help in the kitchen. We will take these in before we explore the cove."

Lalia sighed. Another role removed.

* * *

Morgan extended his hand to help Lalia down a rough portion of the path. He knew she didn't really need the help, but it gave him an excuse to touch her. Exulting in the crackle of awareness between them, he clasped her fingers and rested his hand lightly on the small of her back as she passed him. No, the lady was by no means as cool as she would have him think. Perhaps there was hope for him. She kept her gaze carefully on the path, avoiding puddles left by the tide, while Morgan enjoyed his view of the dainty curve of her neck.

Jeremy scrambled down the rocky track easily. A small stream had cut a narrow defile through the cliff. The old trail ran beside it, switching back and forth across the width of the cleft in the steeper spots and around a few twisted trees, dipping and rising with the broken ledges. Above them loomed the precipice, crowned by the towers of Merdinn. The cove boasted very little in the way of sand, but Morgan knew that the spaces between the guarding boulders allowed a medium-size vessel to come through and shelter there. Jeremy immediately made a dash for the water, quickly wetting himself to the knees.

"Don't step out very far," Lalia called, hurrying toward him. "The currents are not safe."

"Yes, ma'am. I want to see what's up there, anyway." The boy pointed at a small dam of stones holding a tidal pool. He sprinted away.

"He will be well enough. I'll keep my eye on him." Morgan strolled along the waterline examining and discarding shells. It had been nineteen years since he had lived by the ocean. He looked forward to having a personal sailing craft close by again—when he found

Hayne's. If he didn't find it soon, he would have his own sloop brought in. He turned to Hayne's lady.

She was investigating another tidal pool, waving at his nephew. "Look, Jeremy. There are crabs."

Morgan moved closer to observe the crabs—and the lady. Careless of her threadbare gown, she knelt beside the puddle, turning stones on the bottom with a piece of driftwood. He hunkered down beside her, and she smiled, her usual wariness dissolved in her enjoyment of her discovery. Her face glowed with pleasure.

Breathing in the scent of sunshine and woman, he resisted the desire to touch her again. Her caution would certainly return, and he liked the way she looked now, happy and carefree, her petite figure almost childlike. Far be it from him to spoil her mood. Besides, the sea and the sun made him feel young and carefree himself. And perhaps a little foolish. He reached into the pool and drew out a small but indignant crab.

Turning suddenly he thrust waving pinchers toward Lalia's face. She shrieked very satisfactorily and jerked away. Overbalancing, she tumbled backward onto sand, skirts flying. Morgan caught a glimpse of beautifully shaped leg before she sat up, laughing, and subdued the unruly garment.

"My lord! What a wicked prank! You will be teaching Jeremy bad tricks."

Tossing the crab back into the puddle, he held out his hand and grinned. "No one needs to teach boys that sort of mischief. They come by it quite naturally." He pulled her to her feet. "Forgive me. I forgot the dignity of my years."

"Humph." She straightened her clothes and brushed at the sand clinging to them, twinkling eyes denying her stern tone.. "I do not see one particle of penitence in your countenance, my lord."

"I'm hopelessly corrupt." He favored her with his most winning smile. "Here, let me help you." He limited his assistance to whisking the dirt off her shoulders, regretfully restraining himself from more interesting areas. Bethinking himself of his nephew, Morgan looked around for the whereabouts of that fearless young man. He was discovered to be tugging vigorously at something jammed between two rocks a few yards away.

Morgan sauntered in his direction. "What do you have there, lad?"

"I think it's part of a boat. Maybe the one that got wrecked." A final wrench freed the object and Jeremy sprawled backward, following Lalia's undignified example. "Ow!" He got up sucking his finger.

"Oh, dear. Let me see." Lalia took his hand in hers. "Yes. It's a splinter." She grasped the sliver and pulled before Jeremy could object and withdraw his hand.

"Ouch! Don't!" He stuck his finger back in his mouth, mumbling, "Did you get it out?"

"I think so. Let me see. Stay still a minute. How can I…?"

Ignoring the tussle with the splinter, Morgan stood, brow furrowed, studying the battered lettering on the length of wood Jeremy had retrieved. He turned to Lalia. "What did you call Hayne's vessel?"

"The *Seahawk*. Why?" She glanced at what he held, then froze. "Oh, my."

Chapter Five

Morgan knew that the wreck of the day before had not been the *Seahawk*. That had been a much bigger vessel than Hayne's private yacht. A ride along the cliff tops revealed several more pieces of flotsam the color of Hayne's boat lodged against the rocks, but no sign of Hayne. Inquiries in the village brought no further enlightenment. All declared that no one had seen him since he sailed away several days before. Nor did anyone seem very interested in searching for him.

Possibly because they already knew where he was. A man of Hayne's caliber must surely have friends among the rogues who plied the smuggling trade in the district. It defied belief that the *Seahawk* had never carried a cargo of run brandy. Hayne always needed money. But if his yacht had come to grief, and no body was to be found, where was Hayne? He returned home with the question unanswered to find his library occupied.

He studied the man sitting across from the desk with a carefully neutral expression. Morgan did not like Roger Poleven. He surveyed his guest with as much courtesy as he could muster. The family resemblance between Lalia Hayne and her half brother did not extend beyond the blue-green eyes. His did not even show the brilliant clarity of hers, but looked bloodshot and murky. Neither did the dark brown hair shine as her black braid did. He certainly did not demonstrate any of her gentle nature.

Poleven lounged carelessly in the chair, brandy in hand. "I found it expedient to rusticate for a time, so I thought I would call and greet my sister. How long have you been in Cornwall?"

Morgan took his time in pouring his own brandy and seating himself behind the desk. From what Lalia said, the man had not troubled himself to greet her in years. What, then, was this show of brotherly affection? "I'm afraid you have missed Mrs. Hayne. She has driven out with my nephew. I don't expect them back for another hour."

"Ah, well. Another time." Poleven waved a disinterested hand. "Your nephew, eh?" A knowing smirk appeared on his face, but he quickly removed it as Morgan directed a cold look at him. Poleven hastily changed the subject. "The talk is that you have bought up Hayne's mortgages?"

Morgan nodded silently.

"And my sister is still in residence? I would have thought you would have remedied that by now."

Morgan's continued silence slowed Poleven a bit, but didn't daunt him.

The man's face took on a sly expression. "Well, I can't blame you. She's a pretty enough chit. In any case, that's Hayne's problem, not mine. Can you imagine? My father left not one shilling for her maintenance."

Morgan raised one eyebrow. "No doubt he expected that you would provide a home for her."

"Me? Keep a thieving Gypsy in my house? No thank

you. He was touched in his upper works. At least I found a suitable match for her. Cost me a pretty penny and so I'll tell you.''

Good God! The man was every bit as despicable as Hayne. ''Perhaps you know where your sister's husband is to be found?''

''Not I. No one's seen him this age. Probably with someone else's wife somewhere.'' Poleven tossed off the rest of his brandy and looked hopefully toward the decanter.

Morgan stood. ''I'll tell your sister you called.''

''Oh. Yes, of course.'' Poleven got reluctantly to his feet, one eye still on the decanter. ''I say, Carrick, I was just wondering as I rode up…I'm a bit embarrassed at the moment. Perhaps you might help me out with a few pounds until I come about?''

So that was it. The rascal wanted money. Obviously he already knew he would find Morgan at Merdinn. Perhaps he fancied that he had some leverage. Morgan gave him a flint-hard look. ''I'm afraid it will not be possible for me to oblige you.''

Poleven shrugged. ''No matter. I'll stop in again sometime.'' He collected his hat and gloves and ambled out the door.

When Watford arrived, Morgan's first instruction to his butler would be that Roger Poleven should never again set foot within the walls of Merdinn. The man's attitude toward his sister was vile—unpardonable. One did not abandon one's relatives because of some irregularity of birth. If he ever heard Roger Poleven call Eulalia Hayne a ''thieving Gypsy'' again, he would probably plant him a facer.

''Beg pardon, ma'am.'' Gwennap, the foreman of the renovation crew, stuck his head through the door.

"Where might I find his lordship?"

Lalia looked up from trying to find a place for more vegetables in the cool of the cellar. His lordship's chef had arrived the day after their discovery in the cove, along with the rest of the staff, but while she had become unwelcome in the kitchen, no one had yet driven her out of the garden. "He is not here. He took his nephew down to the village. May I help you?"

Gwennap looked perplexed. "Well, I can't rightly say. We've finished cleaning the great hall, and I don't know what he wants done next."

"Have you asked Mrs. Carthew?"

"The new housekeeper? She's gone to the market, ma'am."

"Very well, I'll go with you to look. I'm sure the large dining room needs a great deal of work." She led the workman up the stairs to the ground floor.

At the door of the room formerly used for large dinners, she paused and waved a hand. She had long wanted to turn it out for a good cleaning. "Everything needs work—the floor stones need scrubbing, the paneling must be cleaned and polished... And the furniture...well, it is probably still usable if scrubbed and the chairs recovered, but... You will have to ask Lord Carrick if he wants the draperies cleaned or discarded. In any case, they must be taken down. Here..."

Within a few minutes the work force had invaded the room, and Lalia dived into supervising, lending a hand here and there. She was happily engaged in bundling up the old draperies when his lordship sauntered through the door. Lalia sneezed.

"Oh, excuse me, my lord. These are very dusty." A quick glance suddenly informed her that he did not look best pleased. She dabbed at her nose with her handkerchief. "Is something wrong?" She sneezed again.

"What are you doing in here?"

"They have finished in the…" Another sneeze interrupted her response. "Oh dear, I'm sorry." She fished for her handkerchief again. "They finished cleaning the hall and did not know what to do next. I thought they could spend their time…"

Carrick scowled. "I thought we had agreed that you need not concern yourself any further with their work."

"But I don't mind. I hadn't anything else…" Yet another sneeze burst forth. Her small handkerchief had become too damp to be useful, so Lalia sniffed behind her finger as quietly as she could.

Morgan took her firmly by the arm and led her out of the dust into the corridor. How the devil could he express his displeasure to a woman who kept sneezing? And sniffling. He handed her his handkerchief. "Now…why are you involving yourself in this? You now have other duties."

"Very few, my lord." She blew discreetly. "Thank you." She put his handkerchief in her pocket. He wondered if he would ever see it again. "You and Mrs. Carthew were both away, and Gwennap came and asked me what to do. But I don't know what to tell him about the draperies. Will you replace them?"

Morgan tried another frown. Somehow he was not getting through. These decisions were no longer her responsibility. "That will be for my mother to decide. When the work is complete, this will again be her home."

At last she looked at him with something approaching comprehension. The smooth skin of her brow wrinkled.

"I see." Her eyes clouded over. "Then you will write to her about them?"

"Yes, I will ask her."

"Very well. Perhaps she can select new fabric in London. I really wouldn't recommend…" She sneezed and reached in her pocket. "These are just too dirty."

"I will convey your opinion to her."

I will convey your opinion to her. And what would his lordship convey to his mother about Lalia's continued presence? The lady must not like her being here any more than Lord Carrick liked it. Somehow Lalia must stop thinking of Merdinn as her home. She had no home. She would be leaving in a few months.

Again the frightening specter of where she would go in the fall arose. Other than her tenants, she knew so few people. She had no idea where to start looking for a position. Would his lordship know of something? She hated the thought of having to ask him, but the unpalatable fact was that she needed his help. If she didn't have Daj to think of it might be much easier. But she did, and she would contrive somehow. Just as always.

She had just washed her face and hands and looked in on Jeremy's activities when Watford found her. "The Reverend Nascawan wishes to know if you are in?"

It had been so long since Lalia had the assistance of servants that for a moment she couldn't think how to respond. "I… I…" Everything was so disrupted by the cleaning… "Yes, of course. I'll talk to him in the library if his lordship is not using it."

She made her way down to the book room to find the good parson sipping a glass of brandy to which he had helped himself. Lalia had tried hard to like the man. She truly had. Somehow she never quite succeeded. Tall and gaunt, his emaciated face and wispy hair made her think of a graying cadaver. He always wore a resigned expression, as if he had given her up for lost but felt duty-bound to keep trying. At least he no longer exhorted her to brave the snubs of his congregation by attending services. He bowed.

"Good afternoon, Mrs. Hayne." He held out a small, damp bundle. "I have brought you something you might find useful."

It would be a collection of worn-out clothes. He often brought them. These smelled of seawater and mildew. She reached for them politely, and his bony hand, chill and clammy, lingered against hers as he released them. Why must he *always* do that? Lalia repressed a shudder. "Why, thank you, Reverend Nascawan. How thoughtful of you."

"And I must ask you—when did his lordship bring his household here?"

Oh, dear. A lecture loomed. "A few days ago."

The clergyman drew his eyebrows together and folded his hands before him. Yes, definitely a lecture. "I must say, ma'am, that I am very surprised to see that you are still here. Certainly you must know that for a lady to reside with a gentleman not her husband..." He turned toward the door. "Ah. Lord Carrick?"

Carrick stood in the doorway, his face expressionless. "You have the advantage of me, sir. You are...?"

Lalia, still holding the smelly bundle, hastened to make introductions. Carrick stepped out of the doorway but remained standing. "I see. It was kind of you to call on Mrs. Hayne."

Nascawan hesitated. Even he could not completely disregard the dismissal, but apparently he felt obliged to make one more sally. "My lord, I must point out to you that your living in the same house with…"

His lordship raised one eyebrow. "Must you?"

Lalia listened in astonishment, all admiration for Lord Carrick. Obviously he did not suffer busybodies gladly. At last she was about to see the redoubtable cleric routed foot and horse.

The pastor, however, was still game. He put on a stern expression. "Sir, under these circumstances Mrs. Hayne's reputation must be called into question."

"Not in *my* house."

The chilling response stopped Nascawan in his tracks. He blinked and drew himself up. Handing Lalia his glass, he mumbled a haughty goodbye and abruptly took himself off, his dignity trailing behind him.

Morgan moved into the room and took the clothes out of her hands, his nose wrinkling. "What the devil is that?"

"Reverend Nascawan very kindly brought me some used garments." She grimaced. "He often does so."

"Clothes? Do you use them?" No wonder her wardrobe looked so shabby.

She shrugged. "Sometimes, if Daj or Peggy or I can wear them. Otherwise, I give them away or use them for cleaning rags."

Her answer gave Morgan pause. Was her poverty such that she had actually been reduced to accepting that sort of charity? The lady had endured a great deal indeed. He tossed the bundle through the door into the hall. "Surely you won't use those?"

She smiled. "No, I fear they are past praying for. They did not fare well in their encounter with the sea."

Morgan settled himself behind the desk and invited

her to sit with a wave of his hand. "Do you think they came from the recent wreck?"

"I would think so. The things he brings often do." She seated herself in the chair opposite him.

"So the good pastor is not above a little scavenging?"

She smiled. "No, nor a little smuggling, I feel sure. He does like a good glass of brandy."

"In common with many Cornish clergymen. Did you offer it to him?"

"Oh, no." She looked shocked. "I would not make free with your wine. He must have helped himself." She giggled. "No doubt a privilege of the cloth. He means well, I'm sure."

"I'm not." Another thought occurred to Morgan. The man had been noticeably preoccupied with where Eulalia Hayne was sleeping. "He seemed very interested in our living arrangements. Has he ever accosted you?"

"Mmm...no." Morgan did not miss the slight hesitation in her voice. "No, not exactly. He just... I don't know. He is married, after all. Very likely I imagine it."

"No, you do not." He recognized that with the certainty of a man who senses a rival for the woman he wanted. "He doesn't seem very highly principled, and you are very..." He let the sentence go. No need to rekindle her wariness of himself. Of course, the old rascal wanted her—her appetizing curves, her luscious skin. What man wouldn't?

"Well, I do appreciate your sending him on his way. I am very tired of lectures on one subject or another."

He brought himself back to the conversation with an effort. "You are too kind and polite. You do not have to receive him, you know."

"I guess not." She seemed startled. "Now that there is a butler in residence..."

"I suggest you make use of him."

* * *

Climbing the stairs to her room, Lalia pondered his lordship's advice. Too kind and polite? Perhaps so. Perhaps the reverend mistook that for encouragement. Surely not? She had not been *that* kind and polite. And he knew her to be married. Would a man of the cloth really…? Hmm. Yes, she would take Carrick's suggestion. She would instruct the butler to deny her to Reverend Nascawan in the future.

How luxurious to have a butler! And how luxurious to have someone to defend her good name. His lordship had surprised her. Having him protect her from Nascawan's innuendos had been… Well, a luxury she had not had since her father's death. She had expected never to have it again. If only… Never mind. It was not likely that she would enjoy that protection for long.

The stonework in the great hall, one of the oldest parts of the house, had sustained quite a bit of damage over the centuries. Not since Morgan's grandfather's day had the family fortune been sufficient to keep the place up as it should have been. The graceful arches showed cracks and chunks of limestone had even fallen out in places. Morgan had spent the entire morning working with the stone mason, determining the needs.

He was closeted with the architect, arguing as to whether to keep the original fireplace, when his housekeeper appeared at the door. Morgan looked up in annoyance. He didn't have time for interruptions today. "Yes, Mrs. Carthew?"

"I'm sorry to bother you, my lord." She curtsied. "We seem to have an usually large number of summer vegetables in storage. Many of them cannot be preserved and will spoil before we can use them, and there is no more room in the cellar. James tells me that Mrs. Hayne is accustomed to giving them to those in need. I thought perhaps, if you don't mind…''

Morgan waved a hand at her, turning back to the architect. "Of course, of course. Feel free to take them to someone.''

The housekeeper curtsied again. "I would, my lord, but I'm needed in the large dining room at the moment, and I see that you are occupied. I thought that if Mrs. Hayne is not busy today, perhaps…''

Morgan turned slowly to look at her, eyes narrowed. She looked perfectly innocent, if a little startled by his scrutiny. Apparently Mrs. Hayne had obeyed his previous order, but… "Did Mrs. Hayne suggest that?''

"No, my lord, but it would be a big help to me. I believe it will require more than one trip.''

"James?''

"James has gone to the smithy.''

Damn the woman! Must she grow enough vegetables to feed the entire district? He did not want her acting in the role of lady of the estate. He had made that clear. Several times. She had never exactly defied him, but somehow she… Well, it would be petty of him to refuse. Better to be the gracious lord again.

Morgan's mouth quirked wryly. "Very well. Please ask Mrs. Hayne if she will do me the service of delivering the bounty to the deserving.''

Chapter Six

Lalia sat stiffly upright in the gig, her face carefully controlled, watching the sun slip slowly toward the horizon. She had readily relinquished the reins to James. She couldn't concentrate on driving now, much less on the breathtaking colors painted on the sea.

The men had come to the house shortly after she and Jeremy had returned from distributing the vegetables. In a way she had been expecting them, yet it did not seem possible that the brute to which she had been tied for eight years might actually be dead. They had found his body, the men told her, washed into a cave in the cliffs. All of them had been careful not to specify why they had gone to the cave.

And everyone else had been careful not to ask. Very likely her husband had fallen out with his smuggling confederates. He'd probably cheated them, just as he did everyone. They *thought* it was her husband. Would she please come to see if she could verify the fact? Small need. They knew good and well whose body lay in that cave. But nonetheless, she now must go through the motions of viewing a body too decayed to be easily recognized.

The man couldn't even have the decency to be shot by a jealous husband before witnesses!

As James pulled off the road, Lord Carrick, who had ridden ahead, separated himself from a small crowd of men who stood with their attention focused on something that lay on the ground in their midst. He handed her down from the gig and offered her his arm. "Are you sure you are willing to do this? It will be very unpleasant. The sea had the body for some time."

Lalia paused for the space of three heartbeats and considered, staring at her toes. Why was she doing this? The answer came to her in an instant. She wanted to know—to know for sure and certain that she was free of him, to see him lying dead on the stony earth. She glanced into Lord Carrick's face.

"I will look."

"Very well." He guided her to the group and the gawkers parted to make way for her.

In spite of herself Lalia cringed from the ghastly mound of flesh that lay rotting before her. She covered her mouth and nose with her handkerchief and made herself look again. The hair was certainly as blond as her husband's had been, and as thin at the temples, but the face was only a pulpy mass. The eyes no longer existed, but the receding lips bared the familiar missing tooth. The coat he wore the day she last saw him covered the bloated body, and the signet ring on the pale, swollen hand…

His hands, his hard, clutching hands…groping…hot…

The hand now had only three fingers.

Lalia whirled. The blood drained from her face, leaving her cold to the core. She had to get away! She took one blind, running step and fetched up against a solid barrier. Lord Carrick grasped her shoulders to steady her. She looked into his frowning face and gasped, "It is he."

The next moment the world turned black and disappeared.

It had been a difficult day. Still weak from her faint, Lalia had sat in the gig feeling dazed as she listened to his lordship give orders for a hasty and unceremonious burial of the noisome pile of flesh that had once been Cordell Hayne. She thought, perhaps, he had asked her preferences, but when she did not respond, he made the decisions without her. It was not until she had returned to the house that her head began to clear. She must remember to thank him.

Her thoughts far away, Lalia jumped and almost dropped her brush when a light tap sounded at her bedchamber door. At her murmured, "Yes?" the door opened and one of the new maids put her head in the door.

The girl dropped a quick curtsy. "Good evening, ma'am. I'm Sarah. His lordship sent me to ask if you would like your dinner brought to your room?"

Good heavens. How comfortable her life was becoming. Lalia pondered the offer. Eating in her room would be quiet and undemanding, but…lonely. She did not want to be alone tonight. "No, thank you, Sarah. I'll come down."

"Then let me help you dress." Without waiting for agreement, the maid went to the wardrobe and opened it. Of course, it held but one gown acceptable for dinner with a lord—one that she had already worn several times. Sarah removed it without comment and placed it on the bed. "I do love to dress hair, and yours is so pretty…here, let me.'' She picked up the comb from the table.

Before she knew it, Lalia was suitably, if repetitiously, arrayed and on her way down to dinner. Lord Carrick met her at the door of the small dining room and, with the greatest formality, held out his hand. Hmm. Proper manners tonight. Lalia offered her own hand in an almost forgotten response, and he brought it to his lips. The warmth of his fingers tingled up her arm and his distinctive fragrance took her breath. The tingle somehow ended up in her lower body.

How had that happened?

Reluctantly she brought her gaze to his face and found the green eyes looking into hers. Tonight, rather than seeming cold, a slow fire flickered in their depths. Something in Lalia warmed in answer. Just before the extended silence required a comment, his lordship smoothly tucked her hand into the crook of his arm and led her to the table.

''I didn't know if you would feel up to having dinner. Have you recovered from your faint?'' He pulled out her chair, hovering over her shoulder but for a few heartbeats. His lordship was being very thoughtful. He must be on his good behavior.

''Thank you.'' She nodded as he offered the sherry bottle. ''A little wine would be welcome. I have never fainted before. Thank you so much for dealing with the burial. I…I just couldn't seem to think.''

''No great wonder in that.'' He filled first her glass and then his own. ''I thought, considering the condition of the body and the heat, it was best done quickly. But tell me how you are feeling now.''

''I feel well enough now…just… I don't know… shaken. It seemed that he would always be there, lurking somewhere out of sight, always my husband, and yet…not my husband. I can't quite take in that he is gone.''

"I'm sure. But he *is* gone.'' Lord Carrick spoke gently. "Tell me…I have noticed… I've never heard you call him by name.''

"Have I not?'' Lalia turned the matter over in her mind. "No, I don't. He has never really seemed like a *person* to me, more a…''

"A problem?''

"You might say that.'' The word she had been thinking of was *beast*. "Nor have I ever thought of myself as really his wife, just…''

His prisoner.

"Do you object to being called Mrs. Hayne?''

"I don't object. I just don't think of myself that way.''

Carrick leaned back in his chair and looked thoughtful, waiting until the footman had brought in the first course and departed. When they were again alone he said, "I wonder, then, if I may ask a favor of you?''

"Of course.'' *I think. Probably.*

"I notice that Jeremy addresses you as *Miss Lalia*. May I have the same privilege?''

"Why…yes. If you prefer it.'' Oh, dear. The comfortable barrier of formality between them had just crumbled a bit, leaving a sense of increased vulnerability. She did not ask him what she should call him.

"And I would like for you to call me Morgan.''

He had been thinking of her as *Lalia* for several days. He no longer wanted to think of her in connection with Cordell Hayne. Morgan poured himself his bedtime glass of brandy and leaned against the head of the bed. Cordell Hayne. His unworthy foe. Dead.

Morgan didn't know what to feel. Death, of course, must be the ultimate revenge. Beth was dead. Hayne was dead. It was fitting. But it seemed unsatisfying that the scoundrel would never know poverty or prison or that Morgan had taken his woman for himself.

Assuming, of course, that he succeeded in doing the latter. That issue had yet to be resolved, but Morgan remained optimistic. She was attracted to him. He could tell that. And Hayne's death at least removed the obstacle of the lady's wedding vows. Widows had a great deal more freedom than either spinsters or married women. Yet, he must school himself to patience. She was in shock. This was no time to pounce on her.

Patience? Damnation! He was rapidly running out of that commodity. He actually held her this afternoon—scooped her up into his arms when she fainted. As he had carried her to the gig, he had ached with the awareness of how tiny and soft she felt against his chest. Of her scent. Of her mantle of hair tumbling out of her bonnet as he laid her on the seat of the gig.

And of her complete vulnerability when she opened confused eyes and looked helplessly into his.

Hands. Two hands. Reaching out of the darkness. Pale, bloodless, seeking. She lay paralyzed, watching the hands approach. One of them brushed her cheek. She could see the bones where pieces of flesh had dropped away. They pinched her breast viciously, squeezed her throat, hovered over her eyes.

And, one by one, the fingers began to drop off.

One struck her chest, her shoulder, her face…

The scream ripped through her, searing her throat. She fought her way up, tearing aside the bedclothes, knocking over the candle. She couldn't see. Her eyes would not open. She screamed again.

Pounding. Shouting. "Lalia, unlock this door!" Running footsteps. More pounding. More shouting. "Open, damn it!" Loud thumps. He was trying to get in. She mustn't let him...a crash. Footsteps. Hands reaching for her. She screamed again—

"Lalia, Lalia! Wake up." The hands gripped her shoulders and shook her gently. Lord Carrick's voice. His hands. But she couldn't see. She fought to a sitting position and felt herself gathered into a pair of strong arms, held against a muscular chest. A hand stroked her hair.

"You are all right now. Wake up, Lalia. You had a nightmare."

Consciousness gradually returned and Lalia started to cry. "It was his hands. They were all rotted, and they hurt me, and the fingers... Oh, my God." She moaned softly against his chest. "The fingers fell off."

Morgan held her close and let her cry, smoothing her hair and murmuring comforting words. She had dreamt about the body. No wonder in that. It had been a gruesome sight. He was just grateful that he hadn't dreamt about it himself. Her fragrance and softness teased his awareness, but this was no time to take advantage. She did not trust him overmuch as matters stood. A wrong move now and he would never get near her again.

Suddenly a light appeared in the doorway. He looked up to find Lalia's grandmother standing there, Jeremy peeping around her skirts. He would not have thought that the old woman could have heard the commotion from her quarters near the kitchen, much less climbed the stairs so rapidly, but there she stood fixing him with a steely eye. What the hell was the lady's name? He couldn't call her Daj. And what was she thinking? He wore only hastily donned britches. This did look rather...

But he couldn't let Lalia go. She clung to him, her tears dampening his bare chest. Morgan cleared his throat awkwardly. "She...she had a nightmare."

Lalia sobbed. "It was his hands..."

Her grandmother crossed the room and motioned for Morgan to move. *"Muló,"* she stated firmly.

Morgan edged aside and she took his place, gathering her granddaughter into her arms and crooning what sounded like Romani endearments. Morgan beckoned to Jeremy and picked him up. The boy's eyes were huge in his pale face.

"Did someone hurt Miss Lalia?"

"No, not at all." Morgan wished he could be more sure of that. She had been terribly frightened. What would have made her so afraid of her husband's hands? Was it just the decay, or...? Morgan didn't want to think too much about that. "She just had a bad dream." He turned to her grandmother. "You'll stay with her?" The old woman nodded.

"Then I'll put Jeremy to bed."

He must remember to have someone repair the broken lock tomorrow. She would not feel safe without it.

The next morning Morgan found Lalia harvesting, with Jeremy's energetic if not enthusiastic help, yet more peas. He covered his eyes for a moment and sighed. Apparently the job of feeding the hungry of the estate would continue to be the purview of Merdinn's most recent former mistress for some time to come. Very well. Enough argumentation. His mother could resume her former duties when she came to stay. At the moment he was more concerned with whether Lalia had recovered from her fright of the night before.

She straightened as he approached and picked up her basket, her smile a bit wan. He took the basket from her and held it out for Jeremy to add his last contribution. Having done so, the boy dashed across the lawn after a butterfly, and Morgan, smiling down at her, strolled with Lalia in the direction of the kitchen. "You seem to be determined to feed every tenant on the estate."

She returned the smile. "Not all of them. We will dry these for use this winter."

"Very provident of you. But I'll warrant that the tenants will still see a fair number of them. How are you this morning?"

"Feeling rather stupid." Lalia grimaced. "To have been so completely undone by a dream…" She shuddered. "But it was horribly real. I—I hadn't realized how I felt about his… I thought…" She gave up the explanation and shrugged. "Daj says it was his *muló*— his ghost. The Roma view all the dead as malicious, even people who were good in life. They believe the goodness passes on and the mean parts remain. She says my seeing his corpse attracted him to me." She bent to pluck a withered blossom from the bed they were passing, hiding her face.

"She…she says he is jealous of you."

Morgan laughed. So far, much to his chagrin, jealousy, human or spirit, hardly seemed appropriate. His Khanian revenge was definitely not living up to his expectations—no chains, no deprivation, no horses, not even a boat, and so far absolutely no crushing. "His envy is a bit premature."

He allowed himself the luxury of tucking in a lock of glossy hair that had escaped from her braid. She suddenly stumbled and Morgan caught her arm. Yes, she was as aware of him as he was of her. Perhaps his future held a little crushing after all. He diplomatically released her arm. *Don't push.* "Do you agree with your grandmother's beliefs?"

"Well, no, not really." Lalia dealt with several more dead flowers. "My father discouraged most of her customs, so I don't really believe in all of them. Still, he did not forbid them, and I have been influenced a great deal by her. I know there are no such things as ghosts, and yet…I find it hard to discount them, especially when…" She stopped speaking and looked out toward the sea.

"When one visits your dreams?"

She nodded, but made no further answer.

Morgan took her elbow and steered her toward the house. "Understandable. I realized last night that I do not even know your grandmother's name. I gather that *Daj* has a Romani meaning?"

"Yes, it simply means *mother*. Her name is Carolina Veshengo."

"Ah. Does she speak English?"

Lalia gave him a startled glance. "Of course. Why?"

Morgan shrugged. "I don't remember her ever saying anything directly to me. I thought perhaps…" He grinned. "Now I suspect that she just doesn't like me much."

Lalia flushed a little, but didn't contradict him. "She feels unsettled—as do I. I have been meaning to ask you… Do you know of anyone who might be in need of a gardener? That is something both of us can do, and often an estate has a cottage for the gardener. She and I could then…"

He raised an eyebrow. "Hardly a position for a lady."

"I know." She sighed. "Perhaps that is wishful thinking, but I don't how, otherwise, to…"

"I will give it some thought." Morgan opened the door for her and called to Jeremy.

Actually, he would give it a lot of thought. It might be a long time before he could find a suitable place for Eulalia Hayne and Carolina Veshengo. At least until the end of summer.

It didn't look right. No matter from which angle he looked, it just didn't produce the effect he had hoped to achieve. Morgan had instructed his captain to personally select the rug from the bazaar in Turkey. The colors were exactly as he had specified, the design magnificently complex. The silk glowed with a warmth all its own.

And it did not look right in his library.

Morgan shoved his hair off his forehead impatiently. Damnation! What was wrong with it? He stood, arms folded across his chest, glowering at the offending carpet, nudging the fringe with a booted toe. The effect did not improve. A quiet step sounded behind him. He turned and directed his glower at the intruder.

"My lord, Jeremy wants…" Lalia paused hesitantly in the doorway. "Oh, excuse me. Did I interrupt?"

"What? No. I am merely viewing my latest acquisition." Morgan motioned her into the room irritably. "Well, don't just stand there. Come in."

"I see." Eyeing him cautiously, she stepped into the room and glanced about for the source of his annoyance. "What a nice rug," she offered carefully.

Distinctly lukewarm praise. Morgan's glare deepened. "It is a very fine carpet."

''Oh, yes,'' she added hastily. ''It really is. Quite beautiful.''

She didn't sound convinced. He rounded on her. ''Please do not be so dashed polite. What's wrong with it?''

''Nothing, my lord. Nothing at all. It is a lovely piece.'' She edged toward the door. ''I'll return later, when…''

''Oh, no, you don't.'' Morgan stepped quickly into the doorway, blocking it with his arm. ''You don't like it, either. Why not?''

She stopped abruptly, almost colliding with him, then backed away a step. ''I think, my lord, that you should ask your mother's opinion about that. Now if you'll excuse me, Jeremy…''

So that was it. He was being reminded of his earlier edict. Confound it! Couldn't the woman understand when to mind her own business and when to… Morgan checked himself. When to what? He *had* told her to stay out of the redecorating. And she had done so since then. But now he wanted… Why couldn't she just do what he wanted her to do when he wanted her to do it? Was that too much to ask?

Suddenly the absurdity of that notion hit Morgan full-force. He was being ridiculous. His ill humor lightened and he chuckled. He would have to give ground, but he did not intend to do it without extracting at least a small reward for being forced to be reasonable.

He lounged against the door facing, arms folded, a wry grimace on his lips. ''Must you insist on throwing my words in my teeth?''

''No, my lord. I just think it better that you ask your mother. You are completely in the right about that. It is her home and I no long—'' Lalia raised a protesting hand, and he captured it, planting a kiss on her fingers.

''Yes, I know what I said, but now I am asking for your opinion.'' He touched his lips to her wrist.

Lalia tugged discreetly. His lordship grinned at her, but did not relinquish his grip. He drew her toward him. Both his large hands now enveloped her small one. Strong hands. Long and lean, well-muscled. Warm. So different…

She forced her gaze to his face and saw, in the green eyes fixed so intently on hers, laughter and a growing heat. He cupped her cheek and stroked her chin with his thumb. Lalia shivered. Apparently time had expired on the good behavior.

She essayed a stern expression. ''Come, my lord, give over.''

''Not until you give me either your opinion or a kiss.''

The rascal was teasing her. The last week had done much to relax the strain between them. She gave him another reproving glance and his grasp loosened. Lalia turned to consider the carpet. ''It truly is handsome, my lord.'' She stepped back into the room, and this time he let her go. ''I don't think the carpet is the problem.''

''Then what is?'' He followed to the center of the room where she stood surveying the furnishings.

''The chairs and the drapes. They have faded badly, and that russet would have never complimented the carpet.''

Morgan squinted at the chair. ''I think you are right. I need to have them redone. But in what fabric?''

Lalia shook her head. ''That decision…''

Morgan shook his finger at her, laughing. ''Remember the forfeit. Your opinion or a kiss.''

Lalia looked at him out of the corner of her eye and,

in spite of herself, giggled. She had always liked that room. How she would love to redo it. She really shouldn't, but... "A deep Turkey red, I believe, like that in the carpet. Perhaps have the drapes the same with a royal blue stripe..." She could see it in her mind's eye. The glowing jewel colors of the rug setting off the rich, dark paneling and bookshelves. "Or, if you would prefer..."

Morgan held up a hand. "I'll write to my mother to ask her opinion and to ask her to send an upholsterer with a selection of covers. Then we will choose."

"Very well. That will be best. But now I must take Jeremy out for the drive I promised him. We will see you at dinner."

Morgan watched the alluring sway of her hips as her figure retreated down the hall, considering the unfathomable ways of women.

Somehow, he had just badgered her into doing the very thing he had emphatically forbidden her to do only a few days before.

Lalia lay in the darkness, trying to determine what had wakened her. Something nagged at her senses. What was it? Something familiar, something disturbing. She sat up and gazed around the room. Moonlight spilling through the open window revealed nothing unusual. She slipped from the bed and made her way to the casement.

Then she smelled it.

Cigar smoke. Drifting in from outside. *His* cigar smoke. Lalia jerked back from the window, momentarily confused. When had her husband come? No... No, it couldn't be. Her husband was dead. He could not... Lalia shuddered as a cool breeze wafted another whiff of burning tobacco into the room.

It must be someone else. Perhaps Lord Carrick… But he never smoked cigars. Someone should go and see who was prowling about. But *not* his lordship. Lalia had no intention whatsoever of wakening him at this time of night. Their previous late-night hallway encounter had clearly demonstrated the unwisdom of that course of action. She would go look herself.

She pulled on her wrapper and glided silently down the stairs. Creeping to the door that gave onto the lawn between the house and the seaside wall, Lalia unlocked it, eased it open and put her head out. No one in sight. She searched the darkness with straining eyes. Not so much as a flicker of movement. The odor had faded. She could not detect a trace of it now. It must have been her imagination.

She stepped fully onto the lawn, letting the door swing to behind her with a light thump. Lalia strolled around the lawn for a few minutes, enjoying the quiet rushing sound of the sea and the soft light of the waxing moon. She considered going to her room in the tower, but decided she was too sleepy, so she let herself back in through the door. She stepped quietly into the corridor.

And someone seized her and flung her up against the wall.

Chapter Seven

"What the devil!" Morgan registered the size of the body a heartbeat after he grasped it, but not in time to prevent the bone-jarring collision with the stone wall. He heard a distinctly feminine gasp for air. "Lalia?" Confound the woman! Couldn't she stay in her bed at night? He lowered the pistol in his other hand and reached out to support her. "Are you all right? I·heard the door close. What were you doing out there?"

"I—I smelled something."

"You *smelled* something? I see." Morgan sighed, leaned one arm on the wall beside her, and asked resignedly, "And just what did you smell?"

"Cigar smoke. You don't use them do you?"

He shook his head. "No, I don't care for tobacco." Her eyes, luminous in the moonlight filtering in through the door, gazed up at him, wide with…something. Fear? If she was afraid, why was she down here? "If you thought someone was lurking about, why did you come down alone? Why didn't you wake me?"

Lalia opened her mouth to reply, but Morgan stopped her with a gesture and a grimace. "Never mind. I know the answer to that. But if I promise to behave myself, will you promise to stop making these midnight forays by yourself? You have but to tap on the connecting door. What if there *had* been an intruder?''

''I didn't think…'' Lalia shrugged and studied her bare toes. ''It was the sort *he* always smoked.''

''Ah. Another visitation. Hayne?''

''Don't say it!'' She put her hand to her mouth. ''Don't say his name.''

''Why mustn't I say it?''

''To speak the name of the dead calls the attention of their *muló* to you.''

''Lalia.'' Morgan made his voice stern. ''What is this nonsense? Surely you don't believe that.''

A hint of a smile played around her lips. ''Not in the daylight.''

''There is nothing to be afraid of. There is no one here.'' He brushed her flowing hair out of her face. ''Except me.'' Woefully in danger of breaking the promise he had just made, he let his hand linger against her cheek, looking intently into her face. He was saved from this perfidy by a sound at the end of the hallway.

He spun around, pistol once more ready. Lalia's grandmother stood at the end of the hall, watching silently. Morgan hastily lowered his weapon and stepped away from Lalia. She touched a finger to her lips quickly, but briefly, and there was no mistaking her message.

''Good evening, Mrs. Veshengo. I'm sorry to have disturbed you. I thought I heard something sinister, but it was only Mrs. Hayne.''

''Daj, you should not be up. The air is too cool.'' Lalia hurried toward the older woman. ''Let me help you back to bed.''

Morgan realized that Mrs. Veshengo was leaning

heavily on a stout walking stick. Lalia took her arm and guided her labored steps back toward the housekeeper's suite. He could hear the murmur of conversation between them, but the old woman still had not spoken a word to him. How had she heard them from her room? Her hearing could hardly be that acute at her age.

But she could probably still wield that cane to good effect.

No, it was a good thing for him he had moved away from Lalia when he did. He might have had some very embarrassing bruises to show for his trouble.

It was a glorious day. Birds wheeled in a blindingly blue sky, and Lalia could hear their cheerful calls as they tended their nests in the adjacent trees. In the sunshine her fears of the night before seemed distant and foolish. Probably she had been dreaming again, or possibly the cigar smoke had been carried by the wind from a passing ship. Unlikely, but…

Lalia sat with Jeremy on the path above the cove, watching the breakers of the high tide pound the lower trail and the beach. He had wanted to go down to play, but the water was much too high. The boy never seemed to get enough of the ocean. They settled for watching the action of the waves, a pastime she enjoyed as much as searching for shells. Jeremy, however, was finding the entertainment a bit slow.

As Lalia was wondering what to do with him for the rest of the morning, she heard a step above her and turned to find Lord Carrick on the path behind her. He was dressed for driving in buckskins, top boots and a fashionable black coat, his dark curls carefully arranged in a dashing style. Lalia was suddenly very aware of her faded dress and kerchief. And her braided hair.

"Did you pass the rest of the night undisturbed?" He looked down at her and smiled.

"Yes, although it took me a long time to fall asleep again."

"What did your grandmother have to say?"

"Nothing to the purpose. I didn't tell her about the smoke." Lalia shrugged. "I knew all too well what she would say."

"And you do not want to hear it." He watched her solemnly for a moment. "It frightens you."

Lalia rubbed at arms that had suddenly developed gooseflesh, avoiding his gaze. "But she knows, nonetheless." She stared off at the sea. "She always knows."

His lordship settled on a rock outcropping beside her, and Jeremy immediately jumped up and ran to him. "Where are you going, Uncle Morgan?"

Morgan put his arm around the boy. "I came to see if you and Miss Lalia would care to go for a drive to the village."

"In your curricle? Hooray!" At his uncle's nod, Jeremy bounced up and down. "Come on, Miss Lalia."

"That's a fine idea." Lalia heaved a sigh of relief. That should keep young Jeremy nicely occupied until afternoon. She stood and brushed off her skirts. "You'll enjoy that, but I think I better go back to the house." What she would do with herself once there was another question. There was always mending, of course. She sighed.

"Oh, no. You must come with us. Mustn't she, Uncle Morgan?"

"Of course." Lord Carrick took her elbow and helped her over a rough spot. "She is definitely to accompany us."

"Thank you, my lord, but I think not. I am not dressed

for going out." *Nor do I have anything in which to dress to go out.* She left the thought unspoken and smiled at the two gentlemen. They looked very much alike, she reflected, although Jeremy's coloring was a bit lighter, his hair more auburn. A very handsome pair. She certainly could not equal their smart appearance. "I best remain here."

"I won't hear of it." His lordship firmly guided her in the direction of the waiting curricle. "I have already told my cook that we will not require a luncheon. You might starve."

Lalia laughed. "I imagine I might avoid that fate. He is always cooking something." She pulled back against his tug. "I surely can't appear in the tavern looking like this."

"We'll take the private parlor." He took her by the waist and lifted.

Obliged to brace herself on his shoulders, Lalia found herself sitting on the carriage seat. Jeremy scrambled up on the far side, and Carrick climbed in behind her, sandwiching her between them. He signaled his groom to step away from the horses' heads, and soon they were tooling down the road toward the village, Lalia their not altogether reluctant captive. A ride in a sporting carriage with a stylish gentleman was infinitely more appealing than mending her second-best bonnet.

"It's kind of you to treat us, as busy as you are." She smiled up at him. "I fear Jeremy is often bored. He needs a playmate, and I have never known much about playing."

"Something we must remedy." He returned her smile. "All work and no play makes Jill a dull girl."

Lalia laughed. "Alas, I'm afraid that is true. I have become a very dull girl."

"I don't find you so at all." There was something else in his glance now. "And I've heard no complaints from Jeremy."

"He is a very good-natured child. Fortunately, he seems to enjoy helping me in the garden, although he is very firm that he does not want to be a farmer. But with the new staff, we…"

An oath suddenly escaped his lordship as they rounded a curve only to be required to scrape the hedge to avoid another open carriage being driven in the opposite direction at a gallop. Lalia flung an arm around Jeremy, clutching Carrick's coat with her other hand.

He brought the curricle back to the road without mishap and glanced over his shoulder in annoyance. "If I am not mistaken, that was a relative of yours."

"Roger?" Lalia released her grip and looked back in the direction of the disappearing vehicle.

"I told you he called on me."

"Yes, and I find it very strange that he came to the house. He never does so. Nor does he usually stay in Cornwall this long."

"I'd like to know why he is doing it now. He asked to borrow money that day, but… I had the impression that was not his real purpose."

Lalia wrinkled her nose. Her half brother was as much an embarrassment to her as she was to him.

The men in the smoky taproom turned to stare as the three of them came through the door. Lalia resisted the temptation to smooth her skirts and hair. These people were nothing to her, she told herself. She turned her back to them and smiled serenely at the burly landlord. He rewarded her with a surly scowl.

Lord Carrick fixed the man with a cold look. "We require your private parlor, if you please, immediately."

Killigrew nodded brusquely and turned to lead the way. At that moment one of the younger men behind her guffawed and said something to his companion that Lalia was just as glad she did not understand. The only words she could discern were "...his bed now." Hot blood flooded her cheeks.

His lordship turned slowly and stared. The man grinned insolently for the space of three heartbeats, but the grin began to fade when Lord Carrick took a step toward him. Carrick continued to regard the offender silently, one eyebrow raised. The man squirmed a bit but did not turn away until his lordship spoke softly, his voice silky. "I beg your pardon. I am sure I did not understand what you just said. Would you care to repeat it?"

The man shook his head sheepishly. "Nay, m'lord. It was nothing."

"Then I may assume that you will not repeat it again?"

"Nay, m'lord."

The man turned back to his companion awkwardly, and Carrick followed Lalia and Jeremy into the parlor. He held her chair and squeezed her shoulder. "Pay no attention to the likes of him."

"Thank you. I appreciate your gallantry, Lord Carrick, but I should not have come."

"Morgan."

"I beg your pardon?"

"Please call me Morgan, and why should you not have come?" He pulled out a chair and sat.

"I avoid public places." Lalia studied the hands clasped tightly together in her lap. "My husband was not well thought of in this area, nor is Roger. And of course, they all know that my grandmother is…'' She jumped as his open hand cracked down against the table.

''Enough. You are the daughter of a gentleman and an honorable woman who has done far better than most could have done in such difficult circumstances. You have no reason to hang your head, nor to avoid the public—except to protect yourself from boors of that sort.'' He leaned back in his chair and frowned. ''But forgive me for not realizing what you have been putting up with. And believe me—I will personally see to it that you will not have to put up with it in the future.''

Lalia's heart began to warm, the glow spreading out to her very toes and fingers.

''Thank you, Morgan.''

Ordinarily, Morgan was no more given to introspection than the next man. However, it seemed that for the last several days he had spent a great deal of time occupied with that exercise. His desires and his principles were becoming more and more at odds, and he could no longer justify his actions as a part of his revenge. Hayne was dead. Morgan could no longer hurt him.

But Lalia was wrong about one thing. She believed that her husband had not cared that she might be taken by another man. He had even offered her to his cronies. But Morgan knew that Hayne would have cared, and cared a great deal if that man was Morgan Pendaris. Hayne's enmity had been as strong as his own. Perhaps his ghost *was* jealous of Morgan's intentions toward his widow.

Morgan heartily hoped so.

But now he had just vowed that he would put a stop to the slurs that Lalia had been forced to endure. How could he stop them if, in fact, the slur that they had overheard in the tavern described exactly that which he was attempting to achieve? All would be well until his mother and Jeremy's tutor arrived in the fall. Lalia had a legitimate reason to remain at Merdinn. At that point, however, he would have to consider impeccably discreet arrangements for Lalia Hayne.

And some arrangement for her suspicious grandmother.

Lost in his contemplation, Morgan stepped through the door of the drawing room and almost fell on his face. Something small and gray tangled itself in his feet, and only by grabbing the door frame did he keep himself from sprawling headlong. Searching the shadowy room for the cause of his trouble, he at last discovered a very small tabby kitten peering at him from under the dust covers that shrouded the sofa.

"So. What the devil are you doing in here?" Morgan knelt and reached for the tiny cat. It scrunched backward out of range. Morgan leaned his shoulder against the seat, groping with one arm into the space underneath.

"Ow!" Sharp little teeth sank into his hand, and he jerked back, banging his shoulder against the frame of the sofa.

"Damnation!"

"My lord! What happened?" Morgan stood, rubbing his shoulder as Lalia dashed in, casting furtive glances around the room.

"I suspect that what you are looking for is under the sofa." He shoved a booted toe into the space and sucked the spot on his hand where the kitten had bitten him. "It retreated there after almost causing me to break my neck. That was before it bit me, of course."

"Oh, dear." Lalia put fingertips to her lips. He

couldn't tell if she was hiding chagrin or a laugh. "I'm so sorry, my lord. I didn't think you were using this room."

"I'm not using it, but I wish to use it, and I intend to have the workmen up here next. It is time we had a presentable drawing room. I suggest you take the livestock to the stable."

"I can't. You see her mother is lost and…"

"And no doubt she will starve without your aid. Another hungry mouth." Morgan held up a hand to halt explanations. "Very well. Take her to the kitchen."

"Oh, my. You don't understand. If Daj saw her she would be going about the house purifying everything. The Roma do not approve of pets in the house."

"One matter in which Mrs. Veshengo and I are in complete agreement."

"Did you find her?" Morgan's nephew barreled into the room, coming to a screeching halt when he saw his uncle. "Oh, good morning, Uncle Morgan." Jeremy sidled up to Lalia and spoke out of the side of his mouth. "I told you, you mustn't let him see…"

"You are too late. I have already seen. The object of your concern is under the sofa."

"Oh. Well, then…" Jeremy lowered himself to his stomach and slithered under the divan, emerging after a few moments with the kitten cradled in his arms. "I know you don't like animals in the house, but you see, Uncle Morgan, she is too little to live in the barn and…"

"So I understand. But now that the two of you have the matter in hand, will you please find a location for the orphan that is out of both my and Mrs. Veshengo's sight?"

"Her name is Smoke." Jeremy carefully rubbed the top of the small head with one finger.

Morgan sighed. Something told him that once a pet had a name, it would be very difficult to eject. "Just keep her out of the way of the workers, and, Jeremy..."

"Sir?"

"Keep her out of *my* way."

Lalia had hoped that Morgan's eviction of the Reverend Nascawan might be permanent. Unhappily, that did not prove to be the case. Two days later he not only appeared in the entry hall as she had the ill fortune to be passing that way, he had obviously let himself in the front door. Apparently, Watford had recently been effective in excluding him when he knocked. He bore the inevitable cloth bundle, this time all black.

"Ah, Mrs. Hayne. I am indeed fortunate today." Lalia backed away from him a bit. He favored her with a mournful look, taking immediate steps to prevent her escape by deftly maneuvering her into the angle of the corridor formed by the wall of the great hall. His expression became distinctly reproving. "I have been attempting to bring these to you for several days. I know that you will wish to be appropriately attired after the death of your husband."

Lalia took the clothes from him, willing herself not to wince at the chill of his fingers against hers. At least this parcel wasn't wet, even if it smelled no better than the last lot. "That was very thoughtful of you, Reverend Nascawan."

He was standing much too close. She edged away from him along the wall. He took a furtive step to block her path and she slid back the other way. Predictably, he moved with her. She stepped back. So did he. She was about to try the other direction again when it struck her. This was ridiculous! The two of them dodging back and forth like prizefighters.

Lalia stopped in her tracks. She was finished with being kind and polite. "Reverend Nascawan." She pushed at him with her palm against his chest. "I must ask you to step back."

Instead of complying, the preacher grasped her hand and pulled her closer. "Now, Mrs. Hayne, do not say that you do not return my regard. I'm sure I have observed in you a partiality for me. I cannot have been mistaken." He got an arm around her waist. "Your reticence is, of course, very becoming. I have tried in vain to restrain my feelings, but now that there is no obstacle in our way..."

No obstacle in their way? And just what did he consider his wife? Let alone Lalia's own reluctance. He bent his head toward her lips and her voice rose in panic. "Sir! You mistake the matt...please don't..."

She shoved with all her might, but he drew her inexorably closer. His mouth, damp and hard and cold, came down on hers. She was kissing a corpse! Nausea rose in her throat and she began to struggle frantically, a scream trying to force its way out.

Suddenly she was free, the clergyman jerked back and flung away from her. He stumbled across the corridor and fetched up against the sideboard that stood against the opposite entry wall. Vases went crashing to the floor, flowers scattering in all directions. Lalia's knees failed her and she began to slide toward the floor. Morgan advanced on Nascawan, murder in his face. Twisting his left hand in the preacher's shirt, he lifted him onto his toes and drew back his right fist. A tense moment ensued.

"Damnation! I can't strike a man so much my senior,

but hear this, Nascawan. You had better never set foot in this house again. And if I ever find you further molesting Mrs. Hayne, your cloth and your years are not going to save you.''

''She is a lewd woman. She caught me in her toils just as she has you.'' The preacher's whine grew louder. ''The devil is in both of you.''

Morgan's lip curled in disgust. He dragged the man to the door and thrust him through it. The black clothes lay on the floor where they had fallen. Morgan gathered them up and heaved them out after Nascawan. The door crashed shut and Morgan strode across to where Lalia sat on the floor, her hands covering her face. He gently pulled them away and she stared into his face.

''His mouth was so cold and wet, and he…'' She shuddered.

Morgan lifted her to her feet. ''He is gone now.'' He smoothed her hair. ''I doubt very much that he'll be back.''

''Did he really think I wanted him?'' Lalia pressed a fist to her lips. ''I can't imagine that I…''

''The man is an idiot. Even *I* know when to back off.'' Morgan drew her hands into his and gazed down at her. ''Do not take the blame for him. Your comportment is never anything but modest.'' He smiled, and his voice lightened. ''At least your grandmother cannot attribute this disturbance to your husband's ghost.''

Lalia returned his smile, comforted by his reassurance. ''Don't be too sure of it, my lord. She will say that a *muló* can inhabit another body.''

''Ha!'' He snorted. ''The only thing inhabiting that slimy rascal is his precious devil and unmitigated lust.''

And in just what way did he, himself, differ from the slimy parson? Morgan sealed the last letter and franked it. Pouring himself a brandy, he propped his feet on his desk to consider that uncomfortable question in the silence of the sleeping house. Had his outrage stemmed from his disgust of the liberties the man had been taking with Lalia, or from the fact that Morgan preferred to have those liberties reserved to himself?

They did not differ in the matter of lust, certainly, but he did not trap women in a corner in order to kiss them. At least, not unwilling women, he modified conscientiously. When Morgan had realized that, even though Lalia might be attracted to him, she did not intend to fall into his arms, he had had the grace to quit pushing her. Most of the time. He had even very righteously given her up as an element of his revenge.

Not that he had given up wooing her. That was different. Or at least he kept telling himself it was. He had come to truly like the woman, apart from the way her gorgeous alabaster skin molded to her high round breasts. He liked her generosity—working herself to exhaustion to grow not only enough produce for her own tiny household but half her—his—older tenants, as well. He liked the kindness she showed Jeremy and the slow, sweet way she smiled. He even liked her willingness to protect a helpless kitten and to provide the boy with a pet.

A circumspect affair based on mutual liking between two unmarried adults—nothing wrong with that. Her outward serenity made her a comfortable companion, even though he now realized how much pain it concealed. Morgan would like to wipe away some of that pain. The lady had done nothing to deserve it. When he thought how little protection she had against a cruel world, he wanted to hit someone. Several people, in fact.

Well, he could protect her against some things, and he would. If she could be persuaded to move into a more intimate relationship, he would be able to offer her more. The question, of course, was whether she might be so persuaded. The time for flirtatious touches and heated gazes had passed. Lalia did not play the game of dalliance, in any case. He must look for an opportune time for some plain speaking.

That decided, Morgan tossed off the rest of his brandy and picked up his night candle. He made his way silently up the stairs, cautious of waking Jeremy or Lalia. She had had enough midnight alarms. At the top of the staircase he turned to snuff the candles in the wall sconce. Having dealt with that chore, he stepped back.

His foot encountered something soft. Damnation! Morgan tried in vain to arrest the step, but his momentum carried him backward. He lost his balance and went sprawling, narrowly avoiding the stone staircase. Jarred to the teeth, he found himself lying on his back on the stone floor, staring up at the ceiling. Somewhere in the darkness he heard a faint sound.

"Meow."

Chapter Eight

The first light tap on her door filtered dimly through Lalia's dream. The second one broke it, the fragments dissipating into the dark. She sat up, pushing her hair out of her eyes. "Yes? Is someone there?"

"It is I."

"Morgan?"

"The same. May I come in for a minute?"

What now? Lalia slid off the bed and struggled into her robe. Having lit the bed candle, she opened the door a crack. She did, indeed, behold his lordship. She widened the opening slightly. "Has something else happened?"

"You might say that." He lounged against the door frame, holding something in one hand toward her. Oh, no! Smoke. She took the kitten and glanced cautiously into his face.

A sardonic smile played across his lips. "Nothing important, of course." He straightened and stepped into the room. "Unless you place value on my neck, which oddly enough, I tend to do. This time I narrowly missed tumbling down the stairs."

"I'm so sorry, my lord." Lalia cuddled the little cat

against her breast. "I thought she was in the morning room. How she got up here…"

Morgan pushed the door closed, aiming a questioning look in her direction. "Do you mind? I have an uncanny feeling that your grandmother will suddenly mysteriously appear."

"Perhaps…" She moved back from him uncertainly.

He stopped a few feet away from her. "I have given you my promise to behave." He grinned. "At least up to point."

"Very well." Somehow Lalia was not as comforted by this assurance as she might have been. Not that she doubted his word exactly. No, not that. It was more a matter of how she felt with him in her bedchamber with his coat off and his neckcloth untied. He seemed suddenly very big and very… She drew in a quick breath as his scent reached her.

He extended a finger and stroked the kitten under the chin. The finger did not quite touch her breast. Smoke emitted a tiny purr. "What are we to do with this troublesome beast? I suspect she escaped captivity from Jeremy's room."

Lalia lifted the cat and rubbed her cheek against its fur. "That isn't where I left her, but you may be right. He needs someone to play with. Children who are only with adults can become very lonely."

"As you were, I think." Morgan petted the cat and then touched her cheek. She lowered the kitten, but his hand stayed against her face. "Are you terribly lonely, Lalia?"

She should move away from him. His proximity disturbed her too much. But the warmth of his hand and the warmth in his voice comforted her, assuaged a bit of that very loneliness he had discerned in her. "Not always."

His hand now rested on her shoulder. He gazed intently into her eyes. "You know that I find you very beautiful, don't you?" She shook her head, but he continued. "I do—both beautiful and good. You must know that I want you."

Both his hands now caressed her shoulders. Lalia studied the bundle of fur in her arms. "I *don't* know, my lord. I know you sought to punish my husband."

"Not now. I did not know you then." He tipped her chin upward with the edge of one hand. "Look into my eyes, Lalia. Do you see hatred or passion?"

Lalia declined this invitation, staring, rather, at his throat. That also proved to be a mistake. Something about the muscular column ignited feelings she did *not* want at the moment. She swallowed, finding nothing to say.

His lordship refused to relent. "Do you feel no desire for me? Can you honestly tell me that?"

"No, my lord, I will not try to tell you that." She turned away from him and carried the kitten across the room to a chair. With a gesture she invited him to sit opposite her, and he did so, his gaze never leaving her face. How could she explain to him? It was all so complicated. She pulled her attention back to what he was saying.

"I appreciate your determination to respect your marriage vows. I think much the better of you for it, but you are no longer tied to Cordell Hayne. You are free now to do as *you* wish."

"It is not that simple, my lord." Lalia finally found enough calm to look into his face. "My word is important to me. I could not break any vow easily. But that is not all. You must also remember my grandmother's influence on me. The Roma put great emphasis on behavior that is *vujo*—pure. To them a woman's lower body is *marimé*—unclean—to any man save her husband.''

Morgan scowled. "Unclean? I hope you don't adhere to that belief?''

"No, but I see the value of it. It protects the woman from unwanted attention, and of course, it also keeps her faithful. Who would wish to endanger her lover?''

"I hope that doesn't apply to widows!" His lordship looked distinctly alarmed.

Lalia chuckled. "I really don't know. Should I ask Daj?''

"Perish the thought!" Morgan grinned at her. "I still have not given up hope. Kindly do not set up another barrier.''

"There are so many barriers, my lord." She sighed. How could she make him understand? "All my life I have been under the domination of some man. My father's was kind and protective, but very isolating. Roger's…'' She waved a hand. "Mercifully brief. And my husband's—'' She broke off and stared out the window.

Morgan's tone grew serious. "Have the likes of your husband and Reverend Nascawan given you a disgust of physical intimacy?''

She had to think about that. Had they? Certainly they were no recommendation for it, but… "No, only for them, I think.''

"I am relieved." Morgan leaned back in his chair. "So what then?''

"I have never had any choices. I simply had to accept my situation and make the best of it. It is far more profitable to concentrate on the good and try to avoid the bad.'' She stroked the kitten. ''And far easier. I have simply drifted with the wind.'' She looked into his face. ''It would be very easy to drift into an affair with you— to accept your protection—for as long as that lasts. But then what? I must find a place for myself.''

''I see.'' He stroked his chin thoughtfully. ''Be assured that I would never abandon you—however long our time together. Nonetheless, I see that you must consider your decision further, and I will respect your right to do so. Now...'' He stood and lifted her to her feet. ''May I at least kiss you? Only a kiss, on my honor.''

Lalia had no idea how she wished to answer that question. It proved not to be necessary. He pulled her braid over her shoulder and wound it around his hand. ''Your hair is wonderful.''

His lips brushed her forehead, touched her eyelids, her ear. Then he gently covered her mouth with his. Its warmth seeped through her, comforting her, inviting her to lean into him—to lean *on* him. After a few moments he drew in a shuddering breath and dropped a kiss into her hair.

He looped the braid lightly around her neck and took the kitten out of her hands. ''I'll put her back into Jeremy's room.''

The next minute the door closed and he was gone.

Morgan was tired of looking at that dress. As deliciously titillating and tantalizing as he found it, no lady should own but one dinner gown. But he had sufficient experience with the opposite sex to know where an excellent modiste might be found. And he had sufficient money to ensure both discretion and speed. A very few days had passed since he posted his letter to this tactful entrepreneur, but already he had a reply that his order had been dispatched by carrier.

With so much work being done on the house, carriers arrived almost every day with boxes of supplies. To accommodate the influx, Morgan had established a ware room in the stable where the merchandise could be sorted and inventoried. Recognizing that guile was called for, he made it his business for the next several days to appear at the stable late in the day to hunt for the particular shipment in which he was interested. At last it appeared, and without even trying to suppress a smug smile, he went in search of James.

He found him in the tack room, mending a harness. The old man glanced up as Morgan came through the door and started to rise, but at Morgan's signal for him to keep his seat, he went back to his task. "Evening, me lord."

"Good evening to you. You're working late today."

"Aye, a bit. Can't depend on these young'uns to do nothing right. All this new help is well and good, but about all they're good *for* is hauling hay and currying hides. What brings you out at this hour?"

"I have a little job I need for someone to help me with—quietly."

"Aye?" James's expression took on more interest.

"Yes. I have something that needs to be found in the cove."

"Now, Lord Morgan, you don't need to tell me you're up to no good. I knowed you too long." The groom laid the bridle aside. "What's the lay?"

Morgan grinned. "Old retainers are supposed to forget boyhood indiscretions."

"Humph. I ain't forgot nothing, nor remembered too much, neither." James picked up the harness again.

"You're not going to get me picked up by the preventives, are you? I'm getting too old to run."

"Not this time." Morgan shook his head. "This is more of a diplomatic mission."

The old man squinted at him speculatively. "Sounds like a woman in it somewhere."

Morgan smiled. "How well you know me—but I merely wish to give Miss Lalia a gift."

"Ah." Frowning, James stood and hung the repaired tack on its peg, then glared at his employer. "What sort of gift?"

"What's this scowl about? It's just a gift."

"Miss Lalia is a right decent woman—a real lady."

"I am well aware of that." Morgan glowered in turn. "And she doesn't need you for a guardian. She already has her grandmother. Besides, I assure you, my intentions at the moment are of the most honorable. I know she won't accept a gift if she knows it comes from me. The lady needs some new clothes."

"That she does. Pity—a pretty lady like her, wearing castoffs from the parson. What have you got?"

"A big traveling trunk—too big for me to carry down the path and lodge in the rocks at the high tide mark by myself. You up to it?"

"Ain't I always?" James stood and, pulling a handkerchief out of his pocket, mopped his forehead. "Hot tonight."

Something glittering tied in the corner of the kerchief caught Morgan's eyes. Before the old man could stuff it back into his pocket, Morgan reached out and fingered the delicate gold chain that had escaped the knot. Uneasiness gripped him.

"What's this?" There was no real reason the groom

shouldn't have a bauble, but fine gold on his income...
Morgan held his retainer's gaze for several moments.

James shrugged. "Just a trinket, me lord." He untied
the handkerchief and held out a small gold locket for
Morgan's inspection. "Found it on the beach at the last
shipwreck, lying under one of the bodies."

Morgan continued to observe him with one eyebrow
raised. The old man looked back at him, puzzled at first
and then indignant. "Here now, you don't think I've
took to robbing the dead, do you? I ain't sunk that low—
even if there are plenty who have."

"No." Morgan shook his head thoughtfully. "No, I'm
sorry, James. I didn't mean to accuse you of anything.
Everyone helps themselves at a wreck." Morgan patted
him on the shoulder and James tied the locket back into
his kerchief. "It's just that there is something about that
last one that bothers me. There should have been more
goods washed up."

James stuffed the handkerchief back in his pocket.
"Aye. Strange, that. A big disappointment. You ready
to move that trunk?"

The next morning careful timing placed Morgan near
the door just as Lalia and Jeremy came down the stairs,
dressed for the seaside. He held the door for them and
strolled along in their wake as they headed for the path.
His nephew ran ahead gleefully, charging down the trail.

"Wait until I get there, Jeremy." Lalia took the hand
Morgan offered to help her make her way over a washout. "I told him he may wade today, if he remembers
to take off his shoes. The weather is warm enough."

"Yes, indeed. I may wade myself." Morgan kept a
wary eye on his nephew and an ear open for the expected
shout. Jeremy disappeared around the next switchback.

No shout arose. Damnation! Had someone beat them to the trunk?

A moment passed…then…

"Uncle Morgan! Miss Lalia! Come look. Look what I found."

Ah. They hurried down the track and around the next bend. No trunk appeared where he and James had left it. Surely… As they turned the next corner, he heaved a sigh of relief. The tide must have been higher than he expected. It had washed the trunk downhill a few yards. He fervently hoped nothing had gotten soaked.

Jeremy bounced in excitement as they came into view. "Look! It's a trunk. I found it myself. May I keep it? Maybe it has treasure in it."

Hmm. Another unforeseen complication. However, considering the contents, Morgan didn't think Jeremy would be that eager to lay claim to them. "Well, you certainly have salvage rights, but perhaps we should open it."

"Yes, how does it work?" Jeremy tugged at the catches.

"Wait a minute." Morgan knelt on one knee by the trunk. It had been turned upside-down by the waves. "Let me right it."

He reached for one handle, and Lalia, leaning forward, reached for the other. This action brought her magnificent bosom disconcertingly close to his face, the scooped neckline right at his eye level. Frozen in place, Morgan stared. He couldn't help himself. Egad!

"Come on, Uncle Morgan, hurry."

Morgan gulped and tore his gaze away from Lalia's breasts. Damnation! He was going to have to do something about this situation and soon. He didn't want to think what might be revealed by his britches when he stood. Thank God he wore buckskin rather than knit.

To Jeremy's excited encouragement, he and Lalia tugged on the trunk until they managed to set it upright across two boulders. Then Morgan went to work on the straps and buckles, at last flinging the lid up with a flourish.

"Aw-w."

"O-oh!"

Morgan grinned. As expected, two distinctly different responses. Jeremy put his hands on his hips and looked disgusted. Lalia knelt by the chest, her face shining. "How beautiful!" She lifted a deep aqua gown of glowing silk a few inches, running her thumbs over the fabric. "So soft and smooth."

No more so than her skin. Morgan's mind flashed to an image of Lalia wearing the dress. Of him removing the dress. Of the dress in a puddle on the floor of his bedchamber. Of soft, smooth...

"Is there anything else in there?" Jeremy leaned into the trunk, rummaging. "Oh, look!" He emerged holding a roughly carved wooden sailboat with a tiny canvas sail.

Now how the devil had that gotten in there? Morgan scratched his head. James must have come back and done it later.

Jeremy dived back into the chest. "Is there more?"

"I don't know. Here let me..." Lalia took over the search of the trunk before Jeremy could spill its contents on the wet ground. "I don't see anything else except clothes, Jeremy, and...and these..." With an appreciative sigh she held up a necklace of silver and aquamarine, extending her hands to the boy. "Here...here is your treasure."

With a fine disregard for a small fortune in jewelry

and ladies' wear, Jeremy turned toward the beach. "You may have them, Miss Lalia, and all the girl stuff. I want to sail the boat."

Lalia laughed. "Thank you, Jeremy. That is very generous of you." She turned her smile on Morgan, holding out the necklace. "Properly, these belong to you—it's your cove."

He took them from her, turning them in his hands, as if seeing them for the first time—which, in fact, he was. They—and the dress—were exactly the color of her eyes, just as he had ordered. Morgan held them up to his chin. "I don't think they suit me." Grinning, he stepped behind her and fastened them around her neck. "You may as well have them. They match your eyes."

"Oh. Oh, my lord. I couldn't! They are much too dear to give away." She reached to unfasten the clasp.

Morgan, still standing behind her, quickly caught both her hands in his. Ignoring her gentle tug, he bent over her head, drawing in the scent of sun on her hair. He let his outward breath ruffle her hair. From this vantage point the aquamarines were perfect against her skin. When he spoke, his voice sounded husky. "They need you…"

The words hung in his throat. She stilled, and he could sense a warming flowing from her, a melting. Then she stiffened and tried to step away. Reluctantly, he let her go, clearing his throat and lightening his tone. "Besides, they are not mine. They are yours. Jeremy gave them to you, and they were his by right of discovery." He grinned. "In Cornwall, finders are keepers."

She gave him a long, searching look. He decided not to give her time to reply—or to think. "You stay with Jeremy. I'll go get help to retrieve the booty."

Lalia watched him for a moment as his long, strong

legs carried him effortlessly up the path, listening to the scrunch of his boots on the stones. Then she turned and followed Jeremy down to the sand. Perhaps she was unduly suspicious where his lordship was concerned, but she again had the distinct impression that he was up to something. She smiled to herself. The same something as always. The rascal knew that she would not let him give her clothing—certainly not jewelry. But would he contrive so elaborate a scheme when he could not claim credit for the gifts?

Yes.

Yes, he might, counting on her to deduce the truth. She smiled again as she worked her way down to the beach. At least, it was a tribute to her intelligence. And to his generosity. Even if he had no interest in her, he might have arranged for a few dresses for a dependent in need. But not jewelry. No, he wouldn't go that far out of charity. Out of desire...?

A moment ago, with his breath in her hair and the heat of his body wrapping around her, she had been all but unable to breathe. Her breasts had tingled under his gaze and her legs threatened to drop her to the ground. How long could she continue to resist him, living in the same house, sleeping in adjoining rooms? Wearing his silk gowns? What would it be like to simply give in, to lie with a man she wanted, who wanted her—*her*, Lalia, not just a convenient female to rut?

And was that man Morgan Pendaris?

She feared she might never be sure.

A feral smile on his face, he stood over the girl and slowly fastened his britches. She lay as he had left her, her skirts rucked up around her waist, her breasts already showing bruises through the ripped bodice. Blood stained her thighs. She turned her face away, refusing to look at him, whimpering softly deep in her throat. Very satisfying. Thrilling in fact. But the greater thrill was yet to come. He lifted the belaying pin and struck. And struck again. And again. The whimpering stopped.

Chapter Nine

The look on his lordship's face as Lalia swept into the dining room that evening brought a hot blush to hers. She wore the aquamarine gown with the jewels, and Lalia felt—for the moment—like a very grand lady. The alacrity with which he hastened to hold her chair gave her a rush of a feeling—a heady combination of power and desire that almost caused her knees to buckle.

Lucky the chair was behind her.

Without asking, he poured two glasses of sherry and handed one of them to her. His gaze never left her eyes as he raised his glass toward hers. "To you, beautiful lady. You quite take my breath away."

Flustered, Lalia looked down at her lap. She murmured her thanks and quickly took a sip. She could still feel Morgan looking at her, could feel the hunger on his face. She cast about in vain for a way to change the subject as he seated himself. Then he spoke, removing the necessity. "The gown seems to fit you well."

Lalia sighed in relief. "Yes, it was a bit too long, but Sarah and I shortened it. I hope you don't mind my taking advantage of her offer to help. She arranged my hair, too."

"Not at all. I would like for you to consider her your personal maid."

"That is very generous of you, but I really don't need a…"

He waved a dismissive hand. "All ladies need a maid, and I like looking at her handiwork."

"Well, thank you, anyway." She might as well enjoy the luxury while she had it. "My lord, I do appreciate your generosity, and I love wearing these fine things, but can't feel right about accepting them. Especially the jewelry."

Morgan's eyebrows drew together. "I told you, they are not mine. The sea washed them up. I have no use for them, in any event."

"But couldn't your mother…"

"I have given my mother more jewelry than she wants."

"What about your brother's wife? Is she still living?"

His expression darkened. "I have no brother."

"You don't?" Lalia looked up from her dinner, startled. "But I thought Jeremy was your brother's son. His name is Pendaris…" She stumbled to a halt, realizing that she had blundered into dangerous territory. A glance at his expression confirmed her fears.

"Jeremy is my sister's child." He tossed down a swallow of wine.

"I—I'm sorry, my lord. I seem to have been less than tactful."

He sat silently for an awkward moment, twirling his glass in his fingers. At last, he sighed and looked up at her. "No, it is not your fault. Everyone in London knows the story. I might as well tell you."

Lalia waited quietly. Morgan poured himself another glass of claret. Finally, drawing a long breath, he spoke.

"Beth was only eighteen—in her first Season. A lovely girl—as fair as I am dark. She was so young—only twelve—when my father died. I tried to take his place. She was…" Another long pause ensued. "She became my child…the apple of my eye."

"My lord, this is painful for you. You don't have to tell me…"

"No, but I want to. There is no reason to keep you from knowing what everyone else does. Even less." Morgan waited for the footman to set a fresh plate before them and leave the room. "Beth went with my mother to a ball, and while my mother was in the retiring room, Beth's dance partner coaxed her into a walk in the garden. It was foolish of her to go so deeply into the grounds, but he was older and polished and capable of great charm." He fortified himself with another sip of wine. "To make a long story short, he flattered her into allowing him to kiss her, and then raped her, telling her the while that she invited him with her kiss—that it was her own doing, that she was a slut. She believed him." His hand clenched on the table, his fist beating a soundless tattoo on the wood.

Lalia waited, spellbound by his grief and anger. He seemed to thrust them away with an effort and took up the tale again. "When he finished with her, he left her there in the garden, bleeding and sobbing. My mother found her after a prolonged search and brought her home. I confronted him, of course, beat him with my fists until his friends interfered. Then he laughed and said vile things about her." His eyes sought hers again. "Jeered that he could not marry her because he was already married."

Understanding crashed down on Lalia. She covered her face with her hands. "My husband."

"Yes."

Lalia could only stare at him dumbly. No wonder he had been so hostile to her when he first arrived. She listened with rapt attention as he continued.

"I challenged him, but I did not succeed in killing him. He shot before the count." His hand moved to his chest, rubbing it absentmindedly. "I understood then the depth of his hatred. Why he did that to Beth. It was his hatred and envy of me."

"But why did he hate *you* so? He had possession of your land."

"I think that was why. He knew Merdinn was not rightfully his. He would never be the earl of Carrick, only a ne'er-do-well and a usurper, hanging on the fringes of society." Morgan leaned back and sipped his wine, apparently lost for the moment in the past.

"Had he always hated you so?"

Morgan took a deep breath. "Not at first. I can see now that his hatred had been growing for years. But during those years I could not spare a thought for him. My father had just died. I became the head of my family, responsible for the support of my mother and little sister—and with almost no money left in the family coffer. My whole attention was taken with providing for them. I worked unceasingly for six years. I did everything my father had neglected to do, to bring our shipping interests back to profitability. I captained ships, kept the books— I even loaded and unloaded cargo myself—anything that needed doing. I had no time to think about Cordell Hayne."

"But he was thinking about you."

Morgan nodded. "When he could still squander the income from my land while I toiled, he could feel superior, could scoff at me—a gentleman working with my hands. But he was piling up debt faster than the rents were paid. When at last I became successful enough to enjoy the fruits of my labor a bit, he envied me my affluence. He called me the spoiled son of an earl. He blamed his own situation on bad luck, of course. His hatred grew until he at last punished me through Beth.''

''What happened to her?''

''She was with child, of course. After Jeremy was born, she took ill. The doctors said that she might have lived had she wanted to.''

''Oh, God. I'm so sorry, Morgan. What can I say? The man was a monster—I know that myself. But this means that Jeremy is…might be thought of as my stepson.''

''No!''

Lalia gasped as his fist made the dishes jump on the table.

''I will *not* have him thought of as Cordell Hayne's get. He is all I have left of Beth. I have spent the last seven years trying to make the world think of him as my heir, to regain his inheritance. I would like for him to be the next earl of Carrick, of course, but my legal advisers tell me that is not possible, considering his illegitimate birth. The land is not entailed nor attached to the title by patent, so I can leave it to him through a settlement, although right now he is more interested in the shipping. I expect that to change in time.''

''You will probably have a son of your own one day. Wouldn't you want him to have the estate?''

He gazed at her thoughtfully for several heartbeats. ''That's possible, I suppose. But I am not expecting it.''

Lalia found herself pondering the significance of that statement until she finally blew out her candle for sleep later that night.

* * *

Lalia lay in her bed in the dark and shook. No matter how much she willed herself not to be foolish, she was afraid. Someone—or something—had scratched at her door. Perhaps a thump had waked her, but then—very clearly—she heard the scratching, the rasp of fingernails on wood.

"Morgan?...Jeremy?" No reply. "Is someone there?" No answer. She would have to get up. She would have to go to the door and listen. She would have to look.

She couldn't. Everything in Lalia's being rebelled. Perhaps she could brave an ordinary ghost—a wavering shadow in the hall, a chill breeze. Perhaps even a mournful moan. But the *muló* of her dead husband—the rotting vestiges of his flesh, his bared teeth. His hands. His dead, decaying hands. Oh, God! She yanked the covers up to her face. She just couldn't.

And then she began to hear another sound.

Dripping. Water dripping just outside her door.

Lalia's breath almost stopped. Water... Oh, heaven. Water. She tried to call out. "M-m...?" Her throat almost choked off the sound of her whisper. She would have to get up, knock on his door. Panic welled up in her. She couldn't move. "My lord?" A little louder this time. Again. "Morgan?"

The handle of her door rattled. Lalia stifled a shriek.

"Lalia, are you calling me? Open up." Morgan's voice. He was shaking the handle of the connecting door.

"C-coming." She flung back the sheet and raced for the door. Her shaking fingers fumbled with the key. At last, she flung the door open and fell into his startled arms.

"What?" He steadied her with hands on her arms and looked down into her face. "What's the matter, Lalia?"

She pointed to the door to the corridor. "Out there. Something is out there."

"Something… Wait a minute." He went back into his room and returned with the night candle.

The sight of his strong arms and shoulders heartened Lalia. She took a deep breath. "Can't you hear it? Water dripping? Someone scratched at my door, and then I heard the water."

Morgan strode across the room and opened the door to the hall. Holding the candle high, he scanned the darkness for signs of life. Against the wall to his right stood a table with a vase of flowers. The vase had been knocked over, the water running onto the floor. "Aha! Here is your dripping water, and unless I miss my guess, that was the scratching culprit that just disappeared into Jeremy's bedchamber."

Lalia edged into the hall. "Smoke?"

"I would think so. But wait…what is this?"

He held up a cloak that had been flung across the table. It smelled of seawater and decay, and trailed a shower of drops across his feet. He held it out toward Lalia, a question in his face.

The hall spun around Lalia as blackness closed in.

The next moment she fainted at his feet.

Morgan hastily dropped the cloak and knelt beside Lalia, calling her name. Then he heard a thumping and turned to see her grandmother struggling up the stairs with her heavy stick. Not again. This time with Lalia wearing nothing but a filmy nightdress.

But the old woman didn't give him a glance. She stood staring at the wet cape where it lay on the floor, poking at it with her cane. Morgan lifted it and held it out.

"Do you know what this—" As the cloak swung back toward him, the hem came within inches of Lalia.

"No!" Her grandmother snatched the garment out of his hands. "It must not touch her. It is *his*." She bundled it and her stick into her arms and started back down the stairs, dragging the tail of the cape and clutching the handrail for support.

"Mrs. Veshengo! Wait." Afraid she would fall, Morgan hurried toward her, stopped, looked at Lalia lying motionless on the floor, hesitated, then reached for the old woman, clasping her arm. "I'll help you down. But I must see about Lalia first. Just sit down a moment."

She paused, looking at him with fathomless black eyes. Then she nodded toward her granddaughter, and he went back to Lalia, scooping her up off the floor and carrying her to her bed. She felt cold to the touch, so he tucked the quilt around her tightly and glanced about for some brandy. There was none in her bedchamber, so he dashed into his own room and returned with the decanter and a glass. Lifting her head on one arm, Morgan dribbled a bit of the liquor onto her lips. At first he thought she would not respond, but then she moaned and turned her head away from the glass. He laid her against the pillows.

"Lalia. Lalia, can you hear me?" Her head moved and she opened her eyes. Morgan rubbed her hand with both of his. "Say something. Are you all right?"

She shook her head, but didn't answer. He lifted her again and held the glass to her mouth. "Come, now. Drink a little. It will do the trick."

Her lips parted and he eased a little brandy between them. She choked and gasped at the fiery liquid, but accepted a second sip. Tears began to leak from her eyes and run into her hair. Morgan set the glass aside and gathered her to him. Stroking her head, he murmured comforting nonsense. She shivered in his arms, sniffling quietly.

"Don't cry. I'm here. Nothing can hurt you."

"But how did it get there? It was his, and it was soaked with seawater, as if…"

"How it got here is a very good question—one for which I hope to soon have an answer. I do not believe in ghosts—nor in *mulós*. That cloak arrived here by none other than human agency." He scowled. Someone was playing nasty tricks, tricks he would soon put a stop to. But right now Lalia still quivered in fear, her arms still held him with panicky strength.

"Were you so terrified of him when he was alive?"

"I suppose I must have been. I would not let myself feel it—I couldn't. I had to deal with him, had to think, had to escape to my little room in the tower. Thank God he came here infrequently, and when he did he usually left shortly thereafter in the *Seahawk*. I don't know what I would have done else."

Morgan tightened his arms around her. "And he hurt you?"

"Usually, if I could not get away. And he treated me much as he treated your sister, except that he wasted no charm on me. I was his. He had a right to me. But he cursed me and reviled me, calling me clumsy and blaming me when he was too drunk to…to do as he wished."

A growl rumbled in Morgan's chest. "The bloody mongrel! I hope his soul is burning in hell."

"I—I just hope it is not *here*—in this house."

At last Morgan had been able to return to his room, firmly putting aside his desire to hold her throughout the night. He could not trust himself for that. In her need she would probably come to him, but he no longer wanted her that way. He wanted her when she was ready, wanted her to come joyfully to his arms. So he gritted his teeth and left her with her candle lit and the connecting door standing open.

He had never in his life achieved a greater victory.

When he had finally bethought himself of Mrs. Veshengo and went to look for her, she was, of course, gone. She had probably waited only for him to go into Lalia's room before disappearing with the dripping cape. Only a few damp spots on the stone steps testified to her uncanny presence. How had the old lady known of the disturbance? There had been no noise this time, but as Lalia had said, she knew. Morgan shook off an uneasy shiver and headed to the breakfast parlor.

Lalia was there ahead of him, looking wan and subdued. Morgan stopped behind her chair and placed a hand on her shoulder. "How do you feel this morning?"

She shrugged. "Better than Daj, I suppose. I collect that she came upstairs last night, though I don't remember that, and this morning she is in too much pain to rise from her bed. I don't know how she even managed to get there. She is getting much worse."

"I'm sorry to hear that. *I* don't know how she knew anything was amiss." He ladled scrambled eggs from the buffet onto a plate and added a generous slice of ham.

"She always knows things." Lalia toyed with a scone, crumbling it onto her plate.

"You, however, are the lady I am concerned about." Morgan scowled at the scone. "You need to eat that, not play with it."

A faint hint of mischief rekindled in her eyes. "Yes, Papa."

"Humph." A grin worked its way through Morgan's scowl. "Just eat. Every bite. You need your strength." He poured coffee for himself and refilled her cup. "We need to discover who is behind this prank. That garment did not walk itself in, nor did it rise from the sea in the hands of a ghost. You're sure it belonged to Hayne?"

Lalia nodded. "It was such a strange color. I've seen it many times, lying wherever he left it." She glanced down at her plate. "He often wore it sailing in the winter."

"Where did you last see it?"

She pondered a moment. "I believe I put it back in his wardrobe."

"Then it must have been in the lot that James took to the parson. That man does have a penchant for old clothes." Morgan rubbed his chin. So, Nascawan had possession of the cape. Interesting. He wouldn't be the first Cornish cleric with unsavory associations.

Lalia felt a glimmer of hope pushing through her fear. Morgan was so matter-of-fact, so calm. In the daylight, listening to his steady voice, last night's fright seemed distant and out of proportion. She smiled at her next thought. "I don't think either of us is in a position to ask him."

Morgan laughed. "No, but James can. I'll have him do so. Then I'll decide how to proceed." He finished his coffee and stood, nodding at her soft green, muslin gown. "I haven't seen that dress before. Very becoming. Is it from the trunk?"

"Thank you. Yes, there quite a few gowns there, as well as...well, other things." She blushed at the thought of the sheer batiste shifts and silk nightdresses. What a pleasure to have something different to wear. Most of the garments seemed to be quite new. Perhaps it had been a bride's trousseau. That thought made her sad, wondering what had happened to the bride. But of course, the whole thing was probably a scheme of his lordship's. She dismissed the sadness and gathered her thoughts.

At that moment Watford appeared in the doorway. "My lord, a young person who appears to be a preventive officer is asking for you."

"Oh? Very well. Is he in the library?"

"Yes, my lord."

Morgan excused himself to Lalia and headed toward the library. A new feeling of dread gripped her. She knew in the depths of herself that another terrible thing had occurred. She followed him and slipped into the book room behind him. He looked startled, but motioned her to a chair and turned to the officer.

"Good morning. How may I be of service to you, Mr. Hastings?"

The man bowed. "My lord. Ma'am." He added a bow in Lalia's direction. "I thought you would want to know that there has been another wreck—just a short distance this side of the last one."

Morgan's brow furrowed. "Do you know what ship?"

"Yes, sir. It's pretty broken up, but this time the name was on a piece of the flotsam. It's the *Swallow*."

Morgan's tension flowed across the room and into Lalia. She held her breath.

"The *Swallow*." His jaw tightened. "Yes, that's mine. Are there any survivors?"

"We haven't found any. I'm sorry, my lord."

"I'll come at once. Thank you for informing me."

"I'll be there, sir." Hastings bowed again and hastily took his leave.

Lalia reached a comforting hand toward Morgan, but he had already cleared the door. Her hand dropped helplessly to her side.

Again Morgan looked down from the cliff at the scene of chaos in the cove. As before, he could see bodies sprawled on the shale and wedged between the rocks. And as before, he saw very little in the way of cargo. Dismounting, he led his black stallion nearer the row of bodies lying in the grass. He tied the horse to a bush and knelt by the first corpse. A stranger—perhaps a passenger. He moved on to the next. At the sight of this one his heart began to beat harder and his stomach clenched.

His first mate, a promising young sailor whom Morgan had hoped to develop into a captain. Gripped with sorrow, Morgan covered his face with one hand. What a waste. What a damnable waste!

He began to make his way down the cliff. A few of the swarm of people nodded to him, but continued the business of scavenging for anything of value. He ignored them and started examining the bodies. Some of them could hardly be recognized, the faces bruised and battered. Another fair-haired girl. Several sailors that he recognized. Good men—or, perhaps, some of them not so good, but all of them his people.

Surely someone had survived. He searched on in vain, his heart growing heavier at each new identification. All dead. The cargo or the cost of the ship never entered his mind. It was the people—people who had depended on him and on whom he had depended—lying dead and tattered on the strand, that brought tears to his eyes and a lump to his throat.

A hail from behind a pile of boulders claimed his attention. He looked up to see Hastings beckoning to him. "My lord, come have a look at this."

Morgan crossed the strand and climbed into the rocks. Hastings and a pair of his men were tugging at the husky body of a man that had lodged between two boulders. Even from a little distance Morgan recognized the captain of his ship. Stainton, a sturdy seaman from Northumberland, had been with Morgan since he'd taken over the shipping. Had been his confidant for fifteen years. Kneeling, Morgan gripped the flaccid arm and gazed into the face of his friend.

"Angus." The word escaped with something very like a sob. Morgan cleared his throat and drew a sustaining breath. He felt the hand of the preventive officer against his shoulder.

"I'm sorry, my lord, but I'm afraid there is worse." Hastings rolled the body onto its face.

The hands were bound behind its back.

Morgan stared for an uncomprehending moment. Then the significance of that unbelievable fact struck him with the force of a fist in his gut.

"Bloody hell!" He sprang to his feet, rage flooding his being, washing away the grief. "Someone did this! Some godforsaken, scurvy bilge rat killed him. Wrecked my ship. Killed all of them!"

The preventive crew stepped back from him warily. He knew what they saw in his face. He must look like a madman. Angus. They had killed Angus.

And they had done it deliberately.

He hadn't felt so much hatred since Hayne had shot him in the back. He clenched his fists and ground his teeth. Closing his eyes, he forced himself to breathe, to calm down. When he felt less dangerous, he turned to Hastings. "You know what this means?"

The officer nodded grimly.

"Piracy."

Chapter Ten

It was a somber dinner. Lalia had donned a gown of some soft gray material that reflected her troubled eyes and Morgan's mood. The pearls hung between her breasts, drawing his eyes but not his thoughts. Startled, he glanced up at her face when she spoke.

"I'm so sorry, my lord. I wish I could say something to ease your pain. It is very difficult when one friend dies, let alone a shipload of them."

"Thank you. It *is* hard, but this evening my grief is so laced with anger I can hardly speak. Angus Stainton. They killed Angus Stainton. A better man has never lived, and they let him drown—nay, *caused* him to drown." He rubbed a hand over his face. "When he saw the clubs falling on the others, he alone had the courage to leap into the sea with his hands bound and thus let the world know what had happened."

"It has been many years since we've had pirates in this area. Now we know why so few goods washed ashore in the last wreck. They must have unloaded them first before guiding the ship onto the rocks." Lalia toyed with a bit of fish, finally putting it into her mouth. "What is being said in the village?"

Morgan broke off a piece of his own fish, but left it on his plate. Neither of them had any appetite. His chef would be insulted. "I think most of the people are shocked—and more than a little frightened. Salvaging from shipwrecks is a time-honored practice here, and above half the men engage in a little smuggling, but piracy is different. One never knows where pirates will strike."

"I know. My father told some terrible tales of the predations of pirates during his youth."

"As did mine. At one time they even took children from homesteads and villages to sell as slaves in Africa. This is not the first time I have been their victim, but if I have my way, it will be the last. They have struck too close to my heart." Morgan slammed his fork down and reached for his wine. "I will find them, Lalia."

"Do you believe it is someone in the area?" She gave up the pretense of eating and also sipped her wine.

Morgan narrowed his eyes in thought. "Yes, I'm inclined to think so. Hastings and I discussed that, and whoever it is, they are familiar with this coast. They know where the worst barriers are and how the currents move. It takes skill to send a ship into a cove like that and make sure it breaks up—and to arrange for the bodies to end up on the beach—a diabolical touch." His lips hardened into a line. "Clubbing my people into insensibility and giving them to the sea with no chance at all. Someone will pay for that. I am well practiced in revenge."

"Yes." Lalia gazed at her hands for a moment without speaking before returning her attention to him. "Do you suspect anyone?"

Morgan considered. "I suspect everyone at the moment. I went into the Pilchard after I finished with Hastings, to hear what I might. Of course, everyone was talking about the wreck and the possibility of pirates, but I heard nothing to the purpose." He shrugged. "No great wonder. I have been away too long for people to be open with me. I was, however, surprised to see your brother drinking with the Reverend Nascawan and Old Tom. That seems an unlikely trio."

"My *half* brother," Lalia corrected. "Yes, that's odd. I certainly have never known Roger to cast his shadow on the door of a church. The only interest I know of that they share is brandy, and of course, Old Tom is well-known to be foxed more often than sober."

Morgan smiled wryly, giving up on his dinner and leaning back in his chair. "Typical lighthouse keeper. In any event, they share that interest with most of Cornwall. Most likely they were chance met. The new taverner— what is his name, Killigrew?—had his head together with theirs. Perhaps they are good customers."

"I would not have thought that Roger was in residence enough to be that good a customer. Like my husband, he preferred the excitement of London. I cannot fathom why he has remained in Cornwall for several weeks." Lalia pushed her plate away.

"Hmm. Perhaps I should make some inquiries into his activities. Now, who do we have on staff that knows the area?" Morgan paused in chagrin. "And whom I can trust not to be in league with the villains?"

"A harder question." Lalia smiled ruefully. "But surely some of the new stable hands, or perhaps one of the footmen, are trustworthy. Several were hired locally."

"I'll give it some thought. There is bound to be someone." Morgan would like to set James to the task, but the image of the gold locket forced itself, unbidden, into

his mind. Surely the old man would not involve himself
with pirates. Morgan had known him for all of his thirty-
four years, and he had never known him to be cruel. Nor
had he had any reason to suspect him of anything worse
than receiving smuggled goods—a practice common
throughout the duchy. Still... He must think about it.

He thrust the subject away and let himself take a long
look at Lalia and her pearls. With such a beautiful dinner
companion, it was a pity to waste the opportunity on
painful and vengeful thoughts. He didn't want to let himself become completely distracted from his wooing.

Lalia was tired. Even though no preternatural occurrences had marred the last several nights, she found herself too tense to sleep soundly. In the past when she felt
restless, she would seek out her retreat in the tower,
leaning against the parapet outside the former guard
room with the wind or rain in her face. When she felt
relaxed, she would fall asleep in the bed in the room
itself. She had always felt sheltered there.

But while decaying stairs and a sturdy bar might stop
a drunken husband, it would prove no deterrent to his
muló. What did the dead care for a bad fall? If they
might rise from the grave, what barrier was a mere door?

During each day, Lalia scolded herself for being silly
and resolved to visit her sanctuary that evening. But
when the slow, warm darkness of summer fell, she could
not make herself go up alone. What would happen if
Morgan could not hear her? Could not come to drive the
specter away? Would it drag her down the stairs or, perhaps, fling her into the sea below?

Or—oh, God help her—might it clutch her with rotted
hands, the bones cutting into her flesh, the yellow teeth
sinking into her breast as he once...

The image itself choked her, caused her to start up in panic. Lalia wanted to call out to Morgan, even to go to his room and let him comfort her. She wanted to be harbored by his clean, muscular body, to feel the crisp hair of his chest against her breasts—for him to kiss her with firm, gentle lips, driving away the horror that stalked her.

But she knew, if she did that, what must follow. She weakened more every day, her need and desire for him eroding her good intentions and her will. But she had not yet made up her mind to succumb to his lordship. An affair between them could be only of short duration, and her poor, foolish heart already yearned for what it could not have. She could not lean on him forever, though the need was as seductive as the man himself. She must protect herself—as best she could.

So she lay with the night candle lit and tossed until morning.

Much to his surprise, Morgan got the opportunity to talk to Lalia's half brother without any plotting on his part at all. He had climbed to the top of the wall to better use a small telescope to see what vessels he might spy on the horizon. Sir Roger Poleven came sailing into the cove aboard a small sloop at high tide, skillfully avoiding the menacing rocks.

Morgan took his time climbing down, giving the newcomer a chance to secure his dinghy and climb to the top of the cliff. Sauntering in that direction, Morgan waited until the man cleared the defile leading to the cove and strolled across the lawn toward him. Roger bowed, and Morgan nodded, not wishing to extend any more hospitality than absolutely required. "Good afternoon, Poleven. To what do we owe this pleasure?"

"Oh, just out for a sail. Thought I'd stop in. I'm told the ship that wrecked most recently was one of yours?" He cast a speculative glance at Morgan. "A great loss to you, I'd think."

"Bad enough. I lost a number of good men."

"Oh, aye. Your men." Apparently Poleven's sympathy waned rapidly. "She carrying much cargo?"

"I haven't had an accounting yet." Morgan began to suspect that his guest's purpose was to fish for information from *him*. He began to doubt that he would learn anything of use from Poleven and started considering the quickest method of ridding himself of him.

Roger suddenly looked past Morgan's shoulder. "Well... I believe I see my little sister approaching. She's grown into an attractive lady."

As Lalia and Jeremy came within earshot, Morgan bit back an acid comment as to how long it had been since the man had laid eyes on his sister.

"Why...! Roger?" Lalia stopped, looking startled, and gave her half brother a long inspection. "I didn't even recognize you."

He stepped forward and planted an unenthusiastic kiss on her cheek. "Lalia. How do you go on?"

"Very well, thank you." She backed away a step, and Morgan, from the expression on her face, fancied that she restrained herself from wiping the kiss away with the back of her hand. Turning to Jeremy, she nodded at her brother. "Roger, may I present Jeremy Pendaris. This is Sir Roger Poleven, Jeremy."

"How do you do, Sir Roger?" Jeremy made a credible bow, his little boat tucked under one arm.

Roger grinned slyly, but nodded at the boy without looking at Morgan. "Good afternoon, Jeremy. Are you planning to sail that?"

"Well, I *want* to, but Miss Lalia says the tide is too high."

Lalia shook her head smiling. "Nothing would do but that he come and look for himself."

"Best listen to her, lad." Roger jerked his head at the waves pounding the path to the cove. "When it's like this, it's no place for landlubbers."

"I am *not* a landlubber!" Jeremy propped indignant fists on his hips. "When I grow up, I am going to be a sailor. I am going to be a captain on Uncle Morgan's ships, and I am going to have my own castle on an island and sail my ship there."

"That's a fine ambition, but best wait until next week to pursue it. Well, I must get back to my craft. Your servant, Carrick." He bowed in Morgan's direction, then turned to Lalia. "What do you say, little sister, to my coming to visit for a few days? We can get re-acquainted."

Morgan took a quick step forward. Best to scuttle that notion without further loss of time. "I'm sorry, Poleven. We are renovating Merdinn and cannot entertain guests at present."

"Oh, well. Perhaps later. I may be in Cornwall for a while. Servant, Carrick. Lalia." With this fond farewell, he climbed back down the trail to his boat.

Morgan watched him with narrowed eyes. "What do you make of that?"

Lalia frowned. "I don't know. Perhaps he wants to live off your bounty. He must be in really serious financial straits. I can't think of any other reason he would want to come here."

What other reason, indeed? Morgan would have to give that question some serious thought.

* * *

"Jeremy? Jeremy, where are you? It's time for your bath." Lalia strolled toward the stable, an eye open for her charge. He had been so cross for the past two days because the high tide in the afternoon had prevented him from sailing his boat that James had offered to take him to the smithy. Lalia had sent him on his way with relief and spent the time with Sarah altering the gowns from the providential trunk. She had seen the two return from their mission an hour ago, but Jeremy had been happily following James at his chores—the old man good-naturedly giving him small tasks—so Lalia had not disturbed them.

A quick look into the stable showed her no sign of them. She hailed one of the undergrooms. "Where are James and Mr. Jeremy?"

"I dunno, ma'am." The young man paused in his work and gave her a quick bow. "The last I saw they was pushing a barrow load of straw to the cove path. His lordship's got some of the lads shoring up a washout near the top, and they need the straw to hold the dirt."

"Oh, I see. Thank you." Lalia headed for the cove, only to encounter James, the empty wheelbarrow and several stablehands on their way back to the stable.

James paused and wiped his brow. "Evening, ma'am. We're calling it done for today."

Discomfort stirred in Lalia. "Where is Jeremy? I thought he was with you."

"Yes, ma'am, he was, but he went back to the house just a few minutes ago. Didn't you see him?"

"No." Lalia didn't feel the relief she expected from this statement. Why hadn't Jeremy passed her? James and his crew continued their retreat to the stable, and she hurried in through a side door, encountering a workman in the hall. "Did his lordship's nephew come in this way?"

"I haven't seen him, ma'am, and I've been here this good half hour polishing the flags. He ain't been this way."

Serious alarm rose in Lalia. Surely he was too obedient a child to defy his uncle and return to the cove alone. Wasn't he? Was any seven-year-old boy? The temptation was great. And if not there, where was he? She dashed back out the door and headed for the cove. "Jeremy! Jeremy, answer me."

Was that a faint response above the sound of the surf? Lalia lifted her skirts and ran. The tide was rapidly reaching its zenith, flooding most of the rocky path. She hurried down the zigzags until she reached the spot where the waves lapped the track. "Jeremy?"

Again she heard a indistinct call off to her right. Casting about, she saw the boy at last in a small cul-de-sac on a switchback a level below her. He stood on a boulder that yet lifted him out of the water, but the surf beat at the path on either side of him. He still clutched his boat. Lalia raced down the trail until she was directly above him and, kneeling, leaned over the ledge and tried to reach his outstretched arms. She couldn't do it. Oh, God.

"Here, Miss Lalia, I'll stand on my toes." He elevated himself a scant four inches, wobbling on his perch. "There's water in my shoes."

Sparing a glance for his feet, Lalia saw that, indeed, the waves were surging upward, now wetting his legs. She turned so that she could sprawl stomach down, lying lengthways on the narrow trail. Thank heavens! She could just grasp his hand. He lifted both arms to her.

And dropped the boat.

"My boat!" He turned and started to lunge after his toy.

"No!" Lalia's shriek was whipped away by the wind. She all but threw herself over the edge of her precarious perch, grabbing for his hands.

She got one of them. A larger wave thrust him back toward her, and she was able to catch the other. "Jeremy! Let the boat go. We will make you another." She strained downward and finally reached his wrist. "Help me. Hold on to my wrists, as I have yours."

He did as instructed, and Lalia sighed. Now she could secure him against the waves, but she couldn't lift him. Her position, face downward on the stony path, was too awkward.

"The w-water is up to my waist, Miss Lalia." The quaver in his voice betrayed a small crack in his courage. "It's getting higher."

"I see that, Jeremy, but don't worry. The water will help us. It will lift you until I can pull you up to me." She prayed that it were so, and that the uneven path above them would remain clear. Even now she could see that the dips were filling. Was this a spring tide or a neap tide? She couldn't remember. If it was a full tide, they might yet be cut off. If the tide was too low, it might not lift him enough. Well, she would just stay here all night if she had to.

But he was already shivering. Could such a small body stand that much exposure? Could she? "It will be all right, Jeremy. Hold on to me and don't let go."

"I—I'm trying to be brave, Miss Lalia."

"You are being very brave. Just a little longer now." *I hope.*

Suddenly, over the pounding of the sea, she heard the rattle of falling stones behind her. She couldn't turn to look, but a highly polished boot appeared on the path a few inches from her face. Morgan! Thank God.

"Good girl." He knelt before her. "I can't reach him this way. Hold him. I'm going to have to get into position with you."

Lalia felt him cautiously step over her, placing a foot between her legs on the shallow shelf of rock. Then his weight gradually came down as he stretched out full-length on top of her. A sob of relief burst from her as two long arms moved past her face and two large hands clamped around Jeremy's arms.

"H-hullo, U-Uncle Morgan."

"Hullo, yourself. You sound cold." Morgan shifted his weight. Lalia winced. "Damnation! I can lift him now, but have nowhere to put him. Am I hurting you?"

The sharp stones of the track were cutting into her in a dozen places. She gasped. "N-no. I'm fine. Just get him up."

"Very well. Can you hold him around the waist when I lift him a bit?"

"I think so." Morgan pulled and Jeremy's body moved past her face. His added weight crushed Lalia farther into the rough ground, but she clamped her teeth over her lip, refusing to make a sound.

"Now." Morgan waited while Lalia locked her arms around the boy. "Don't let go and don't move. I'm going to stand behind you." He pushed away from the edge with one hand, still holding one of his nephew's arms with the other.

Lalia clung to the small form with all her might. At least she could breathe as Morgan's bulk shifted off her.

"I have him now."

As she felt the upward tug, Lalia forced herself to

release her grip on the boy. She collapsed limply against the earth.

"There you go, Jeremy." His lordship's voice had never been more reassuring. "Climb up while I push. That's my lad. Now—sit down and *do not move so much as a finger* until I tell you to do so."

As Lalia pushed herself to all fours, strong hands gripped her around the waist and pulled her to her feet. A welcome pair of arms wrapped around her, holding her upright as she ordered her bruised knees to work. She covered her face with her hands and forced herself to breathe.

"Can you climb? We best go straight up. The track ahead of us is going under." She nodded, and he cupped his hands. Lalia stepped into them, letting him toss her up. She got a hand on a rock and, while his lordship pushed from below, pulled herself safely, if not very elegantly, onto the ledge above them. She moved aside while Morgan, with a leap and a scramble, drew himself up beside her.

"We can make it from here." He took a firm grip on Jeremy with one hand and Lalia with the other, and marched the two of them up to the house.

Lalia knew she would never be able to look him in the face again. Her negligence had all but cost their precious Jeremy his life. Why, oh, why, had she relinquished him to James even for a moment? His lordship would hate her forevermore. And surely he would send her away immediately and hire a more responsible guardian for his beloved nephew. The months in which she had hoped to find a position dwindled into hours.

Chapter Eleven

While Lalia bathed, Sarah clucked and fussed over her ruined dress and the bruises and cuts that covered Lalia's arms and body. Lalia brushed away her concern. What were a few scratches compared to a child's life? It was time to dress for dinner, but she declined the dinner gown Sarah produced from the wardrobe and chose instead a simple morning dress. Lord Carrick would hardly want her company for dinner tonight.

She had Sarah braid her hair while it was still wet, ignoring the girl's protests that it would dry all crinkled. This was no time for vanity. Lalia was reaching for her kerchief when the knock she had been dreading fell on her bedchamber door.

Sarah held the door while the footman delivered his message.

"Mrs. Hayne, Lord Carrick requests that you join him in the library, if you are quite recovered from your experience."

"Yes, of course. I will be right down." Lalia tied her scarf over her hair and marched slowly toward her fate, fighting for composure. She found his lordship seated behind his desk, sipping brandy. She sat in the chair across from him and tried to meet his eyes.

He took one look at her and poured another glass. Walking around the desk, he pressed it into her hand. "You are white as a sheet." He ran an appraising eye over her. "What? Have you put on sackcloth and ashes? That's a little premature. Jeremy is not dead, and only a little the worse for his adventure."

Lalia covered her mouth with one hand to hold back a sob. She had hoped to address him with dignity, but that capability was rapidly slipping away from her. "I—I don't know what to say to you, my lord, except that I am w-wretched with shame that I very nearly allowed Jeremy to come to grief. How I c-could have…"

Morgan knelt on one knee before her and lifted her hand away from her lips, enclosing it with both of his. "Come now. Had I never been a seven-year-old boy, perhaps I might blame you, but I remember all too well the ploys I used to escape my various governors. Nay, Lalia. Don't cry."

But she could not obey that injunction. The boy had almost drowned. One sob after another burst through her control, until, taking the brandy from her and placing it on the floor, Morgan drew her head onto his shoulder and patted her back comfortingly.

"I engaged you to supervise Jeremy's care, not to be his constant gaoler. There is no reason you should have not allowed him to go to the smithy with James or to accompany him later. I loved doing so myself as a lad. James is very good with children. Jeremy simply took advantage of the situation to give you both the slip."

After several rather damp moments, Lalia was finally able to bring her tears to an end. Morgan pulled his handkerchief from his pocket and dried her face, then handed it to her.

She blew her nose and put his handkerchief in her pocket. "I'm so sorry, my lord. He is such a dear child, and I have become so fond of him. I would never forgive myself had he come to harm, and I am overcome with gratitude that you…"

"Nonsense. The boot is on the other leg." He restored her glass to her and stood. "Here, drink that. It is I who am grateful for your quick action. Without it, he very likely would not have survived this escapade, and had I not come looking for the two of you, you might have perished with him. I know you never would have let him go. The debt is mine. Now—let us have the real culprit down here to face us."

A few minutes later a very subdued Jeremy appeared under escort of a footman. The man left them, Morgan again sat behind the desk, and Jeremy was arraigned before the bench.

"Well, young sir, what do you have to say for yourself?"

Jeremy studied his shoes.

His uncle went on relentlessly. "I believe that you have completely understood that you are not to go into the cove unless either I or Miss Lalia is with you. Is that correct?"

"Yes, sir." A barely intelligible murmur.

"So why did you go there alone?"

Another inaudible mumble.

"Speak up, and look at me, if you please."

Jeremy reluctantly raised his head, expression sullen. "Someone called me."

His uncle raised an eyebrow and regarded the boy warningly. "Jeremy."

"Well. I *thought* someone did."

"And who did you think it was? A man? A woman?"
The miscreant hung his head again. "I dunno."

His judge considered him sternly. "Jeremy, not only
did you disobey, I suspect that now you are telling me
an untruth. I am very disappointed." The boy bit his lip,
and Morgan continued. "You are to go to your room
now and go to bed without your supper."

A spark of life blossomed in the condemned. "But
we're having blackberry tart!"

"Perhaps missing that will remind you to be more
obedient."

Lalia ventured a small intervention. "My lord, do you
think that wise? He was so very cold. He needs something…"

Morgan held up a hand. "Do not intercede for him.
He deserves a sound thrashing. But perhaps a long and
hungry night will be sufficient to remind him of his duty.
Let him take his punishment like a man."

Jeremy squared his shoulder resolutely. "Yes, Uncle
Morgan." He turned and marched bravely out of the
room, only pausing at the door long enough for a whisper to drift back to them before he disappeared into the
hall. "I *did* hear someone."

Morgan hated to admit how much the incident had
frightened him. He sat alone in his library after dinner,
Lalia having gone to her room early, and tried to read.
Jeremy should count himself lucky that he was still able
to sit. Morgan had been so scared and angry, he didn't
trust himself to administer the rod. The memory of the
moment he had first seen them struggling against gravity
and the surf chilled him to the bone. Egad! If he had not
finished his work and wanted a few minutes of their

company to round off the day, he would very likely have lost them.

Both of them.

The thought stopped him in his tracks. When had Eulalia Hayne become so important to him? Not a question he wanted to answer. Certainly not something he was ready to admit. Still, there it was. She had assumed a significant role in his life. And he hadn't even had the pleasure of her company in his bed.

He thrust the thought away and considered instead his nephew's misconduct. Much more pleasant, he reflected wryly, than considering his own. Why had Jeremy disobeyed him to that extent? He had never done so before. Nor had he ever lied to escape retribution. The boy's claim that someone had called to him bothered Morgan. Too many strange things had been happening at Merdinn. Perhaps he had been too hasty in accusing the lad of lying.

And perhaps Lalia was right. After a chill dunking, a child needed food. Morgan didn't want Jeremy becoming ill. And, too, perhaps his love for his sister's son made him a bit foolish. Well, if he were, then so be it. Better safe than sorry. He put down his book and headed for the kitchen.

A short while later, a saucer covered with a napkin in his hands, he nudged the door of Jeremy's bedchamber open with his boot. "Jeremy?" Morgan looked around the door, gratified to find his nephew in bed where he was supposed to be. At least the lecture seemed to have had the desired effect. "Not asleep?"

"No, sir. Not yet." The boy sat up, looking suitably attentive.

Morgan crossed the room and sat on the corner of the bed. "Not feeling ill?"

"No, sir."

"Good. I want to speak with you further. Tell me…" He paused as his gaze fell on an empty plate and glass on the bedside table. He scowled. "What is that?"

"Oh, that." Jeremy followed his gaze. "Daj sent it. She said that disobedient children should have nothing to eat but bread and water. I hope she doesn't mean forever."

"Bread and water, eh?" Morgan gave some thought to what was concealed by the napkin in his hand. Yes, he was becoming indulgent. But how the devil had the old woman gotten into this? "Does Daj talk to you?"

Jeremy looked surprised. "Of course."

"In English?"

"Well, yes." The boy favored Morgan with the look reserved by children for unintelligent parents and guardians. Apparently, Morgan reflected, he was the only member of the household not to meet with Mrs. Veshengo's approval. At that point, Morgan noticed something else. On the lower shelf of the table rested yet another plate.

"And that?"

"Miss Lalia came later. She said she was afraid I might get sick if I didn't eat something hot. She brought me some stew."

Morgan raised an eyebrow. "I see." So his nephew had dined on stew as well as bread and water. Damnation. He had specifically told Lalia not to interfere. And she surely had told her grandmother about his edict, otherwise the old lady would not have contributed the bread and water. And both of them had defied him and undermined his discipline. A serious discussion was called for.

But in the meantime… "Here. You may as well have this, too."

"Blackberry tart! Thank you, Uncle Morgan." Jeremy set to the task of consuming this offering with a will.

Morgan shook his head. "Tell me, Jeremy, a little more about someone calling to you from the cove."

"I thought I heard someone, Uncle Morgan, I really did. They said, 'Jeremy, bring your boat.'" At his uncle's doubtful look, Jeremy reconsidered. "Well, I thought so, anyway. I didn't hear it very well."

"Jeremy, I don't want to believe that you would lie to me, but you don't sound very sure about this."

Jeremy paused in his chewing for thought. "It just wasn't very loud. The waves were making too much noise. Do you think it was my 'magination?"

"That is a good possibility. We tend to imagine what we want to hear, and you wanted very much to sail your boat."

"Maybe. I guess." Jeremy finished his tart and handed Morgan the plate. "Thank you very much, Uncle Morgan."

"You're welcome. Do you understand that even if someone you don't know calls you, you are not to go to the beach? Nor to go *anywhere* with *anyone* you don't know?"

"Oh, yes, sir. I'm sorry I didn't mind you."

Morgan tousled his hair. "You still have to stay in bed. Hand me those other dishes. I'll take them, too. Good night."

Morgan closed the door and headed down the hall.

Thank goodness Morgan did not blame her for the day's misadventure, Lalia thought later as she attempted to brushed the crinkles out of her hair.

Her relief shocked and alarmed her, but it did not surprise her. She had been coming to want him and depend on him more and more every day. What foolishness! She could not afford to let herself fall in love with any man so far above her. Earls married young debutantes. They did not marry twenty-four-year-old widows. They certainly did not marry half-Gypsy nursemaids, let alone one who had been the wife of his sworn enemy.

Yes, he found her attractive, perhaps even liked her company. And yes, widows had affairs at their pleasure, but those were seldom a matter of love. And Lalia did not want to find herself in the role of a mistress. It made her feel... She sighed. It was all so complicated.

The knock brought her out of her reverie. She set the brush on the dresser and went to the door. "Yes?"

"May I speak with you a moment?"

Oh, dear. Another test of her willpower. "Of course."

She turned the key and stepped back, startled when Morgan thrust a stack of dishes into her hands. When she realized what they were, she flushed and guiltily ducked her head. His lordship leaned against the doorway, regarding her with narrow eyes.

"Uh-hh..." Lalia cast about for something to say, but of course, there *was* nothing to say. She glanced hopefully at his face, but he continued to watch her without comment, arms folded across his chest. "My lord, I... Well..." She gave it up. "Would you like to come in?"

She backed away, and after two heartbeats he came into the room and closed the door behind him. Lalia walked backward as he advanced on her, until the backs of her knees encountered the hearth chair. Losing her balance, she plunked down into the seat. Morgan loomed over her for another pair of seconds, then took the crockery away from her and wordlessly set it on the floor beside her.

Lalia began to giggle. She covered her mouth and

strove for decorum. Morgan put his fists on his hips. "Apparently you are well aware of the source of my displeasure."

Lalia nodded, not daring to move her hand from her lips.

"It is *my* place to discipline my nephew."

She nodded enthusiastic agreement.

"You think this funny? Have you nothing to say for yourself?"

Lalia gulped back her laughter. "Forgive me, my lord. It is just that I believe I discern the remains of blackberry tart on the uppermost plate."

"Damnation!" A grin began to break through Morgan's glare. "How is a man to be master in his own house when the women continue to order things as they see fit—not only you, but your grandmother?"

"But, my lord, I *have* endeavored to do as you ask. I just was worried about Jeremy, and I didn't think you'd mind…"

"Ha!" Morgan sat in the chair across from hers. "What you thought is that I would not find you out."

"Well, nor would you have, except that *you*…"

He held up a hand. "Except that I brought him the tart. I know. I spoil the boy, just as I spoiled his mother. But he is *my* nephew. I may spoil him if I wish to."

"True. Perhaps I should not have…"

"No, you should not, but I have quite given up hope of having things as I command in this house. And perhaps you are right. He needed food, and at least you did not bring him dessert." He grinned ruefully. "I fear that I am not as hard a man as I like to fancy myself."

"No, my lord." Lalia smiled. "I thought at first… Well, no, you are not a hard man, especially where Jeremy is concerned." She just hoped that he had given up his hardness where *she* was concerned, that her heart was no longer in danger from his desire for revenge.

Morgan stood and paced a turn around the room. "The thing is, Lalia, that I am not sure now that Jeremy lied. I think he either imagined what he wanted to hear or..."

"Or that someone did call him?" A very disturbing thought. "But who could that have been? There was no one—" She broke off, the warmth draining from her face. No one of this earth.

"Now, stop that," Morgan ordered, coming to a halt in front of her. "It was *not* a ghost. If someone called him, it was for some reason which at the moment escapes me. But I believe I will ask you to be even more diligent in your guardianship than before." After a pensive moment he reached out and traced a scratch on the side of her neck. "I do not like the fact that you were hurt."

Lalia drew in a sudden breath. "Nothing to signify, my lord."

"It is significant to me." He drew the lock of hair lying beside the cut into his hand, running his fingers through it to smooth it. Then he let it fall on the silk of her negligee, watching as it spread out across her breast. Pulling a tress from the other side of her face, he turned it around his finger. Her heart began to race and a treacherous heat spread through her lower body.

Slowly he knelt on one knee before her and threaded the fingers of both hands through her hair. He held her face still while he gazed into her eyes for a long, silent moment. Then his lips descended on hers.

Lalia felt her soul being drawn into that kiss. Her soul and her heart and... Now his arms were around her waist, pulling her close against him. In one motion he stood, lifting her out of the chair and locking her body against his. Of their own volition, it seemed, her arms closed around his neck. Her head fell back as his mouth moved to her throat, and she moaned when his warm hand clasped her taut breast.

"Ah, Lalia." Morgan's tongue touched her ear. His fingers gently closed around her nipple, and she pressed her hips against him, feeling his growing hardness. He lifted her breast and lowered his tongue to taste it. Lalia's knees buckled, and her mind swirled away, leaving nothing but an exquisite awareness of her body. His hand brushed away the silk at her shoulder.

And a resounding crash smashed the silence.

Morgan released her and spun around, searching for some possible menace. Without his support, Lalia collapsed into the chair. She clutched the armrests convulsively. Both of them held their breath, listening. A gust of wind howled into the room, whipping the draperies madly. She gasped and closed her eyes.

"Damnation!" Morgan stalked to the window. "It's naught but a squall blowing up. The shutter blew loose from the catch and slammed shut." As if to confirm his words, a peal of thunder echoed through the room and lightning lit the sky. He closed the other shutter and latched them both.

Lalia stood, her hands pressed to her pounding heart. "I—I best go see if Jeremy's windows are open."

"Never mind. I'll do it." Morgan's words were clipped short, but he stopped beside her and smoothed her hair. Then his hand tightened in it and he brought her lips to his. The kiss was brief, but searing. He gazed steadily into her face for another heartbeat, green eyes demanding.

"Soon, Lalia."

And he left her standing there, breathless and bereft.

* * *

That had been the narrowest of escapes, Lalia thought later as she climbed into bed. Without the interruption Lalia would have committed herself irrevocably to a course of action she knew would be unwise in the extreme. But her heart and her body were conspiring to betray her into his lordship's warm, strong hands. Would it be so terrible to surrender—to him and to herself?

Rebellion stirred in her soul. She was no longer married. If her husband's angry ghost had slammed that shutter, so much the better! He could no longer imprison her unless she let him. She hoped, wherever his spirit was, that it *was* enraged and jealous. That seeing her with his enemy would add to the torment he so completely deserved. What harm to her was a dripping cloak? Or a whiff of cigar smoke?

These sturdy thoughts fled in an instant when a soft thump sounded in the corridor outside her door. Lalia lay still as a stone and strained to listen. What came to her was the sound of Morgan's door opening and closing softly. So he had also heard it. At the prospect of reinforcements, Lalia's courage returned. She pulled on her wrapper and carefully opened her own door. Morgan stood just outside it, studying the floor by the light of his candle. A pistol glinted in his hand. Her gaze followed his.

Footprints.

Wet footprints. Lalia's hand flew to her mouth to silence an exclamation. Heaven help her. Morgan put a finger to his lips and walked down the corridor to Jeremy's bedchamber. He disappeared inside, but after a minute returned. He handed her the candle. "Keep your eye on Jeremy. I'll be back shortly." He slipped down the stairs, silent as a shadow.

It seemed that she stood in the doorway for an age before he returned. "I can find no one, but someone has been in this house. Ghosts do not leave wet footprints, even in a rainstorm."

The rain! Of course. Lalia first felt foolish that she had imagined seawater, then alarmed that an unknown stalked the halls. "But who can it be?"

Morgan shook his head. "I have no idea. The house is too large to search tonight, but I believe I shall spend the rest of the night in Jeremy's room. Be sure your doors are locked, and do not come out unless I call you."

Lalia nodded.

There was little danger of that!

The skull cracked under the blow, the sharp report echoing in the small room. That one should have done the final work. The others had simply been for the pleasure of it, just to hear the music of bones breaking, the song of pleas for mercy. A treat to make up in part for the failure of yesterday's plan.

He licked his lips, savoring the fading satisfaction. That would do—for a while.

Chapter Twelve

"If I provide you with a pistol, will you promise not to shoot me during one of our midnight alarms?" Morgan seated himself across from Lalia at the breakfast table and poured himself a cup of coffee.

"A pistol?" Lalia frowned at him across her plate. "Then you think a real person has been coming into the house?"

He grinned at her. "A pistol would hardly be useful against a *muló*."

"No, I suppose not. But why would anyone be invading the house? Nothing has been stolen, has it?"

"Not to my knowledge. I don't have an answer to the other question, though it has occurred to me that someone may be using these episodes as a ruse to get into the house—perhaps to search for something."

"But what?"

"Another question for which I have no answer, and when I have questions without answers, I am not pleased." Morgan frowned. *And I am also not pleased to have my lovemaking interrupted just as I am achieving a long-desired success.* Had that damned shutter not broken loose he would soon have had the torment of his dreams out of those dreams and safe in his bed. Still, he felt reasonably cheerful this morning. Her response last night confirmed that his desires would soon become reality.

Morgan viewed the subject of those dreams over the rim of his coffee cup. She looked none the less desirable for the fact that she was a bit pale. The pallor served only to set off her delectable skin. But he didn't like knowing that it had probably come about from lack of sleep. She was still frightened, and anger grew in him that, for reasons unknown to him, someone was apparently causing her fright deliberately. One of those unanswered questions that so displeased him. "Have you had this sort of occurrence here in the past?"

Lalia shook her head. "No, nothing mysterious. Of course, there were only a few of us in the house. Do you think it might be one of the staff?"

"That's a possibility." A nasty one. Why would any of his new employees be the agent of these visitations? Unless someone with an ominous purpose had enlisted them. "I am concerned that, if someone did, in fact, call to Jeremy yesterday, that he might have been their objective last night, also. Perhaps the hauntings have been intended to throw us off the track and allow them to scout the house."

"A kidnapping attempt?"

"Possibly. There are pirates at work, and the size of my fortune is well known. But that does not explain why someone has chosen to terrorize you." Lalia's paleness increased, and Morgan scowled. "And I do not accept the *muló* conjecture for one minute, so remove that notion from your mind. Have you ever fired a pistol?"

"No, but I am willing to learn. I would feel safer if I had one in my bedchamber at night—even though it will avail nothing against a ghost.'' She set down her cup resolutely. ''I have decided that I will not be so cowardly. If my late husband wishes to afflict me from beyond the grave, he will have to do better than a puff of smoke or dripping all over my floors!''

A crack of laughter erupted from Morgan. ''Good girl. I suspected that your soft exterior hid sterner stuff. We will have some lessons this afternoon.''

''Very well. By the way, I told Mrs. Carthew that it would be satisfactory to set dinner a little early. Most of the staff want to go to the Midsummer Night bonfire. I hope you don't mind.''

''Ah, the fire. I had almost forgotten.'' Morgan grinned. ''I imagine that I have no more say about that than about anything else around this house.''

''My lord, really—if you don't wish it...''

He stopped her with a gesture. ''No, we have always allowed the staff at Merdinn to attend the bonfire. Might as well, otherwise they slip off and go anyway. Have you ever been?''

''No.'' Lalia looked a bit wistful. ''I always wanted to, but my father said that it was far too rowdy an occasion for a young lady...and I was sure that it would not do for me to go alone later.''

''No!'' Morgan was shocked at the thought. ''Would you like to go tonight? I'll escort you and keep you out of harm's way.''

Lalia sighed. ''I would love that, but what about Jeremy? We must keep him under strong guard.''

''I have already arranged for that. Zachary and Andrew—the footmen who came here from my London establishment—have been with me for years. I know I can trust them. In London it is necessary to keep children much closer than it ordinarily is in the country, and they have served as escorts for him frequently. I am having an extra bed placed in Jeremy's room. One of them will sleep there while the other watches—and I assure you, they will be well armed.''

"They will be disappointed to miss the fire."

"Their disappointment will heal when they pocket the bonus they will earn. But what of you? It would be better if we were not recognized. Do you always wear a braid with that…that thing on your head?''

At his disapproving expression, Lalia move a hand to her kerchief. "My *diklo?* Married Romani women always cover their hair.''

"You are not married, and you are not Romani. You should do away with it. Has anyone in the area ever seen you with your hair loose?''

Lalia considered. "Probably not. I usually wear a bonnet when I go out.''

"Good. Then find some informal clothing that no one has seen you in, and let your hair be free. No one is likely to recognize you then.''

He wanted her to be able to see her first Midsummer bonfire and hear the ceremony. She had had few enough pleasures in her life.

"Well! It seems that I am to accompany a Gypsy siren to the bonfire.''

Lalia smiled shyly as she came into the drawing room. "My grandmother gave me these. I believe they were hers when she was with the Roma.''

Morgan stood back and gazed appreciatively at her. She wore a puff-sleeved, white cotton blouse. A skirt of blue, green and black embroidery swept almost to the floor, and the ruffles of numerous white petticoats brushed her feet. The toes of dainty, black silk slippers could be seen now and then among the ruffles. A long, bright green scarf wrapped her waist, the tassels falling to her knees.

"Enchanting." That was the word for her. She had stepped from another world. Silver necklaces of coins circled her neck, and similar earrings were visible where she had pulled her mass of shining black hair away from her face. "Certainly no one will know you."

Excitement sparkled in her eyes. "Nor you, my lord. We do look a pair of Gypsies."

In spite of the protests of Dagenham, Morgan's valet, Morgan had also given up his usual formal attire in favor of an open-collared shirt with a Belcher handkerchief tied at his throat. He had firmly left his coat in his dressing room. The night would be hot enough with the fire and the press of bodies. With a wide, shallow-crowned hat, he would indeed be a fit escort for the lady at his side. He offered her his arm.

The dusk dropped its violet veil over a warm, balmy evening. Morgan drew the curricle to a stop at the edge of a grove of trees near the bottom of the hill that would be crowned by the Midsummer fire. "We best leave the carriage here." He lifted Lalia down and tucked her hand into the crook of his arm. "Then we can stage a strategic retreat if the going gets rough."

They made their way through the fringes of the wood, emerging on a grassy slope. Already a large crowd gathered around the hill, surrounding a gigantic pile of wood at its crest. Laughter and talk filled the night, the loudness of the voices attesting to the presence of the bottles that were passing from hand to hand. The lively tunes of Gypsy fiddles could be heard from the neighboring hillside.

Considering his lady's short stature, Morgan set about

slowly maneuvering them to the front of the throng. Just as Morgan decided he had penetrated the mob as far as was wise, a series of collisions confirmed his decision. The celebrants swarmed around them, pushing and shoving. Lalia was being buffeted on all sides, and when a sturdy farmer, a bit the worse for drink, staggered into her, he all but knocked her off her feet.

"Here now! This won't do." Morgan pulled Lalia in front of him, her back to him, and wrapped both arms tightly around her, shielding her. He spread his legs and braced his feet against the surge. "Is that better?"

She smiled up at him over her shoulder. "Yes, thank you. This is so exciting!"

Morgan could only agree. His position gave him an excellent view into the front of her bodice, and her round derriere was pressed against his thighs. His body swelled and hardened. She stiffened in his arms, and he feared she would move away. Fortunately, at that moment a hush fell on the assembly, distracting them both.

The master of ceremonies' voice sent the old Cornish words flowing across the meadow. "Herwyth usadow agan hendasow…" *According to the custom of our fathers…*

As the refrain resounded across the breathless throng, the air grew thick with potency, still with expectancy. The spirit of the ancient rite moved in Morgan and he felt the answering force in Lalia as she relaxed against him.

The Lady of the Flowers took up the chant. "Let good seed spring, wicked weeds fast withering…"

Seed, increase, growth. The true purpose of the old custom. All around him Morgan could feel it—breaths quickly indrawn, a muskiness in the air, bodies poised. The sensual tension rose to a bursting point. A moment of hungry silence. The Lady flung her bundle of herbs into the fire and the flames roared to the heavens. An answering shout burst from the spectators.

Suddenly everyone was laughing and talking again. The fiddle music swelled and people began clapping and dancing. The man standing next to them handed Morgan a bottle. Morgan nodded his thanks and took a healthy swig. And then another. Not bad. The fiery liquor was one with the fire in his blood. He wiped the mouth of the bottle on the palm of his hand and held it to Lalia's lips. She hesitated, then took a cautious sip. Choking and giggling, she pushed the bottle away.

Not so fast, my delicious lady. Morgan leaned close to her ear, speaking over the noise. "Have another. A little won't hurt you." *And it might help me.* He tipped the bottle, pouring a mouthful past her lips. She sputtered a bit, but swallowed, laughing and shaking her head at his offer of more. He helped himself to another gulp and passed the bottle back to its owner.

"Thank you, my friend."

Around them the night was becoming raucous with shouts and guffaws. The bottles passed faster. A couple near them threw themselves into an enthusiastic kiss, an activity being repeated all around them. When one of the men began to pull his partner's dress away from her breast, Morgan concluded that the time had come for their departure. Soon the whole gathering would descend into the fertility rite that it was. That scene would be a bit much for a shy lady, and very probably, not safe for her.

He began to back through the crowd, pulling Lalia with him. At last they stumbled clear and, catching her hand, Morgan led her, running and laughing, into the small wood. They emerged breathless on the side near the curricle. Morgan swept Lalia into his arms and kissed her hard. But he dared not linger in the embrace. He needed to get her home, lest he drag her down into the grass under the stars. That would not do with so many people about.

Before he could lift her into the carriage, she spun away from him and began to dance to the music still to be heard from the next hill. She turned and twisted in the sensuous dance while he watched, bemused. Her hair floated out behind her as she whirled, caught up in the spell of the song. At times she swept near him, but when he reached for her, she twirled away, laughing, tantalizing. His groin ached with need.

"Lalia, come." *Have mercy, cruel lady, sweet torment.*

She seemed not to hear him, but at last the music paused. He caught her around the waist and lifted her onto the seat before she could elude him again. "Come, you wicked temptress. We are going home."

They had little to say on the drive home. Morgan set an easy pace so that he could use one arm to draw her close. Pulling into the stable, he was gratified to see a somewhat disheveled groom emerge from the shadows. Morgan suspected that the lad had a companion hidden in the dark, but made no comment. The effects of Midsummer were pervasive. At least Morgan would not have to unhitch the horses himself.

"I want to go to the tower." Lalia snuggled her head against him as they walked to the house.

"Very well." That sounded like an excellent, very private, idea. They paused in the front hall long enough for Morgan to bar the door and pick up a candle. She led him up the rickety stairs, pointing out hazards as they went.

At the top of the stairs Morgan, entering Lalia's bower for the first time, stopped dead in his tracks. Rich colors glowed from every side—from the exotic silk hanging from every wall, from plump pillows piled on an alcove bed, from a soft rug beneath his feet.

He lit the candles in the sconces and turned in a slow, appreciative circle. "This looks just as I have always imagined the inside of a Gypsy wagon."

Lalia smiled her slow smile, her chin lowered, eyes lifted shyly to his. "Yes. Daj obtained these things for me when I decided I needed this room. I have always felt very safe here. At least until—" She resolutely bit off the sentence. "But listen. I believe there is a storm blowing up."

She led the way out the second door to the watch platform. Indeed, clouds and lightning could be seen moving rapidly toward them from the ocean. The wind blew in erratic gusts, first from the mainland and next from the sea. When it swung to the hills, scraps of the Gypsy music could still be heard, slower now, more haunting, more seductive. Lalia began to dance again. Morgan clapped softly, filling in the rhythm when the breeze whipped the song away.

Lalia moved before him as in a dream, silently as if drifting on the water, her arms above her head, her breasts rising and falling, her hips pivoting slowly. His breathing deepened and the blood pounded in his ears and in his body, aching, demanding. Enough!

Morgan moved to take control of the dance. Stepping beside her, facing her with one arm around her waist, he circled Lalia in the manner of an old country dance, modifying the steps to the Gypsy air. The storm blew harder from the water, but the music drifting to them between puffs led them around and around and around.

Gradually the song slowed, and gradually he drew her closer—now hip to hip, now leg to leg, now belly to belly. Still he moved them in lazy circles.

The rain swept over them in a rush, and Morgan swept Lalia through the door into the security of her retreat. The thunder from the skies was only a weak echo of that in his body. He wrapped her in his arms and took her mouth, moving his tongue over her lips in the rhythm of the now silent music. They parted under his and opened to him. He slid into the warmth of her mouth, absorbing the wine of the feast he had so long desired.

Moving the kiss to her throat, Morgan tasted her in tiny, moist kisses, breathing in the aroma of her skin as he worked his way lower. Lalia's head dropped back and a small sound in her throat spurred him. Kneeling before her, arms locked around her hips, his teeth fastened on the drawstring that controlled the neckline of her blouse. He pulled the bow loose and the fabric began to slide off one shoulder. Again he used his teeth on the garment and the blouse slipped to her waist. Her plump, generous breasts glowed in the candlelight.

Morgan devoured them. Pressing his lips to the smooth, pearl-hued skin, Morgan ran his tongue over the warm flesh in ever-narrowing circles. When at last he allowed his mouth to close around the nipple, Lalia was moaning. The pressure in his lower body threatened to burst through, but he sternly denied it. He wanted to savor every inch of her. Moving his tongue from breast to breast, from nipple to nipple, he commanded more and more from her while he unwound the sash and unfastened the skirt and petticoats.

They pooled around her feet, and he moved his feast to the soft curve of her belly, but left his hands to stoke the fires in her breasts. She writhed under his assault now, her hands braced on his shoulders, her hips pulsing faster and faster. He placed one thumb on the straining flesh between her legs and pressed, moving gently, but firmly.

Morgan watched Lalia's face as he grasped her bottom with his free hand and increased the pressure with the other. Her eyes widened, as dark blue with passion now as the deepest ocean. Her mouth came open. Her head flung back and her eyes closed. A surprised cry issued from her and she convulsed in his arms. He extracted every morsel of her moaning climax from her, until her knees began to give way. Standing, he gathered her into his arms, holding her close as the last shivers subsided.

Then he laid her on the bed and waited only until he could get the flap of his britches undone before covering her with his ravenous body. As he slid into her soft sheath, she gasped again and moved under him. He increased his rhythm and heard her moan again, and yet again. Inflamed beyond control now, he drove himself into her faster and faster until her soft shriek and a sob forced him over the edge, his hips pumping his seed into her with the rhythm of the sea pounding the cliffs and the power of the storm. His own voice filled his ears. His mind fell through blackness, swirled, soared. At last he plummeted to earth, landing softly in the warmth of Lalia's body.

They lay together, breathing raggedly. Morgan didn't want to move. Ever again. But gradually the awareness of his weight on his small partner prompted him to roll to the side. He didn't want to *actually* crush her. He pulled her against his chest, the softness of her hair sliding over her back beneath his arm. He dropped a silent kiss into her ear. "Are you all right?"

Her head nodded against him. A drowsy silence ensued. At length she murmured something against his shirt. At his inquiry she repeated, more loudly, "I didn't know it could be like that."

Come to think of it, Morgan hadn't known it, either. Something in him had moved in a way that he had never before felt. He would have to think about that, but at the moment he didn't want to. He'd rather think about her. To throw the protecting shield of his presence over her. To heal her wounded spirit. To teach her that all men were not like Cordell Hayne.

That he was not.

Brushing her hair from beneath her, he laid her against the bright coverlet and raised himself on one elbow. He began to smooth the silky strands over her silky breasts. "Since the moment I first saw you, I've wanted to see you clothed in nothing but your own hair."

Lalia relaxed into the cushions, lulled by the stroking. Had he really wanted her then? He had seemed so threatening, so menacing. She saw him very differently now—kind and warm, playful and humorous. Strong. Desirable.

And probably still very dangerous to her.

She looked up into the green eyes, the tousled curls, and another wave of longing flooded her. Danger to the contrary notwithstanding, she still wanted him. Having come this far, Lalia was determined to experience every moment of intimacy available to her.

Tentatively she ran her hand over his chest, tracing the muscles beneath his shirt. He paused in playing with her hair long enough to sit up and pull his shirt off over his head. When he again lay beside her, Lalia slid her fingers through the crisp curls, memorizing the sensation, the sight. What did the rest of him look like?

The only other man she had ever known had dragged

her clothes from her, leaving her naked and vulnerable while he remained armored by his own. "I—I have never seen a man completely unclothed."

"Never?" Morgan sounded astonished. When she shook her head, he sat again and wrestled off his boots. They and his britches soon joined his shirt in a heap on the floor. He stood beside the bed and looked fixedly at her face. Lalia struggled to move her gaze from his. Slowly she was able to let it slide down his body, noting the ripples of muscle across his stomach. Exerting an effort, she made herself look at the rest of him. A flush washed over her and she quickly looked away. Morgan laughed and lay down beside her.

"Perhaps a little much all at one time. We must let you become accustomed by degrees." He nuzzled her neck and guided her hand back to his chest.

Lalia stroked him, slowly letting her hand drift down to the tense ridges across his belly, studying the shape and feel. At last, she let her fingers touch his shaft and tangle in the coarse black hair that spread across his groin. He began to swell and grow hard. His mouth sought her breasts and she melted under his siege.

The world began to fade. All that was left were his lordship's lips and hands and her body, helpless with passion. When she was trembling with need, he came into her slowly, stroking and caressing until she dissolved into wave after wave of sensation, calling out, sobbing aloud. His own release subsided and he gathered her to him, buttressing her against the storm. He held her until her tears faded, leaving the sound of raindrops spattering on the stones outside the door.

The rays of sunlight filtering through the door told Lalia that she had slept later than usual. Little wonder.

It had been an eventful day—and night. She rolled over and pushed her face into the pillow beside her, taking in the scent of Morgan that lingered there. He had risen before dawn, leaving the little room so full of his presence that she had slept on unafraid while he returned to the respectability of his own bedchamber.

Lalia appreciated his consideration. No one would question her sleeping in the tower retreat. She had done so often enough. But gossip would have been rife had the staff awakened and found them both there. She had no doubt that speculation was boiling through the house as it was. This way she retained at least a few scraps of privacy.

Lalia gathered the pillow into her arms. Now she understood the poetry of love. She knew that passion must have its attractions, but never before had she had the opportunity to taste them. Her husband had not bothered with her pleasure. Now that she had experienced ecstasy, it would be very difficult to give up. It had claimed her whole soul—devastating. Shattering.

And beautiful beyond belief.

Chapter Thirteen

"Would anyone like to go for a sail in the *Sea Witch?*" Morgan strolled into Jeremy's bedchamber, where Lalia was helping choose the boy's clothes for the day, and casually tossed this grenade. The predictable explosion followed immediately on its heels.

"The cutter? Yes, Uncle Morgan, yes, yes, yes!" Jeremy bounced wildly around the room.

"One of your ships? Here?" Lalia stopped in her task to gaze at him. That was possibly a mistake. The heat smouldering in his eyes transferred itself to her and crept up her neck to her face. She drew a quick breath.

"Yes, yes. The cutter. Hooray!" Jeremy bounced onto the bed.

Pulling her gaze away from Morgan's, Lalia shook an admonishing finger. "Jeremy! Calm yourself. That is enough."

"Yes. The cutter. Yes." The chant subsided to a whisper, the bounce to a bob.

Morgan laughed. "More than enough. Leave off, Jeremy."

Peace restored, Lalia looked questioningly at his lordship. "I thought it unlawful for private citizens to own a cutter."

"Not if one has a license from the Admiralty, but since I do not wish to become the object of hatred in this vicinity, I've chosen another path. This craft varies from the definition of a cutter in a few minor points, thus scraping by the law." Morgan smiled wryly. "But she is as fast, or faster than anything of her size on this coast."

"You are going to hunt the pirates." Lalia's heart dropped into her stomach. Pirate hunting was a dangerous business.

"Yes." The hot green gaze focused on her again. "They should not have attacked my people."

Lalia looked at him solemnly for a moment. The thought of·him in danger frightened her so much that the very intensity of the feeling frightened her even more. She mustn't let him become so important to her. The feelings between them could be no more than temporary. She must remember that.

She licked dry lips. "I—I suppose you must."

Morgan almost extended his hand to touch her face, then, apparently remembering Jeremy, withdrew it. "I am not without experience, Lalia. Why do you think I own a cutter? Do not be worried about me."

"Do you think it safe to take Jeremy…?"

"She mounts fourteen guns, Lalia."

"I see." Fourteen cannon. A fighting ship.

"Are you going to fight the pirates, Uncle Morgan?" Jeremy bounded around the bed, energetically slashing at imaginary foes with an equally imaginary cutlass.

"If I have to. More likely I will assist the Preventive Service. They get paid for doing it."

Lalia was not deceived. That answer had been de-

signed to discourage Jeremy's more daring fantasies and
to calm her fears. From the look on the boy's face, it
had done neither. But what could she say? She had no
right to restrict his lordship's actions. She was
only…what? The governess? Nursemaid? His lover?
Or…? She winced at some other possible designations
that came to mind.

What had she done?

Not prepared to sort out the ramifications of the new
status of their relationship or the probable consequences
of her actions last night, she took refuge in flight. "My
lord, will you help Jeremy dress while I change my own
gown?"

She hastily closed the door, leaving him to gaze after
her with hungry eyes.

Morgan pulled the curricle up at the pier in the village
harbor. James jumped down from his perch behind to
take charge of the horses while his lordship lifted Jeremy
and Lalia down. The *Sea Witch* stood at anchor some
distance out, her dinghy awaiting passengers beside the
dock.

Morgan turned to his retainer. "James, would you like
to accompany us? We can leave the horses at the inn."

"Nay, my lord." The older man shook his head emphatically. "I ain't much of one for the water. Never
took to fishing. Give me my horses and dry land any
day."

"Very well." Morgan laughed. "We'll be gone quite
a while though, so make yourself comfortable."

Lalia held tightly to her charge's hand. She had her
own doubts about this expedition. How they were to
keep the energetic Jeremy contained aboard ship was a
subject she didn't even want to consider. Already he was

wild with excitement. Presumably, his uncle had a stratagem in mind. She hoped.

His uncle's plan proved to be simplicity itself. The end of a stout piece of rope tied around his nephew's waist was secured to the mast. The rope was long enough to allow him to approach the rail, but not to fall into the water.

"A trick I learned from my father's captains when I was Jeremy's age." Morgan grinned at Lalia. "It will also keep him out of the upper rigging." He took her arm in a firm grip. "I will personally see that *you* do not go over the side." In the warmth of his eyes on her, the sun's rays paled in comparison.

Lalia flushed. How was she to maintain her composure before thirty sailors with Morgan so near, touching her, his scent washing around her? She tried to step away a little, but he playfully pulled her nearer.

"Oh, no, you don't." His voice was pitched for her ears only, husky, caressing. "I want you as close to me as I can have you. You may pretend to be afraid of the water if you need an excuse."

"That requires only a little pretense." She smiled up at him and gave up trying to escape. "I have not been on a ship since my father died, and the idea of really deep water has always unnerved me a bit. I love watching the sea, or wading in the tidal pools, but... Of course, I never admitted that to Papa, because a sail aboard his yacht was such a treat."

"I don't suppose you can swim?"

"Only a little. Papa thought it would make me safer, living so near the sea, but there is very little opportunity for young ladies to swim. My grandmother nearly had a fit at the very thought."

"So you see...I must hold you close to provide for your safety."

It occurred to Lalia that anyone seeing the expression on her guardian's face would know his true motives in an instant. She decided to bask in the heat and enjoy it.

"Where are we going today?"

"I just want to sail along the coast for a little distance to reacquaint myself with how it lies. I have not sailed here for nearly twenty years."

"I doubt that is something you would forget."

"No, but precise knowledge often makes the difference between life and death. I want to be sure."

Chilling thought. Lalia thrust that one away and watched as one breathtaking expanse after another of gray cliff hung with moss and fern swept by them. Gulls swooped and dived as they passed, but whirled away when no food fell from the craft. The cutter sliced the waves easily, throwing a fine spray over Lalia and Morgan where they stood in the bow. Drops of water beaded his dark curls, his face now strangely content, his gaze focused on something only he could see.

"Look." He pointed at the headland just ahead of them. "Those are the Merdinn towers. Soon we will be able to see them clearly."

As they approached, Lalia spied figures on the cliff top just short of the castle. A Gypsy caravan camped there, and gayly dressed figures waved a greeting. Lalia waved back. "That reminds me, my lord. Daj told me to tell you that the only reason your horses were not stolen last night is that my uncles intervened."

"Your uncles?" Morgan gave her a startled look. "You have Gypsy uncles?"

"Yes, of course. They are my grandmother's sons."

"I—I suppose I have only thought of you as English—in spite of making love to you in your Gypsy bower.''

''Shh! Someone will hear you.'' Lalia glanced around furtively, and Morgan grinned. ''The Roma also consider me English, but they still respect and include my grandmother, and they are kind to me.''

''In any case, I must send your uncles my thanks.'' He winked wickedly. ''I shudder to think of our being required to walk home last night—that would have been a very disappointing end to a promising evening. But I'll take this as a lesson in vanity. I had assumed that my position in this area kept my property safe. In the future…''

A squeal from the far side of the deck caused them both to turn. Lalia beheld Jeremy's rope stretched to its full length and disappearing over the port rail. Both of them dashed across the deck, but one of the crew was before them.

''I've got him, me lord.'' He hauled on the rope and a slightly damp Jeremy appeared. Morgan grasped the boy and lifted him over the rail.

''Oh, Jeremy! Are you all right?'' Lalia knelt beside the boy and gathered him into her arms, her heart pounding with fright. ''You are all wet. Did you go into the water?''

''The rope was not long enough for that. Only the spray wet him.'' Morgan's hand closed over her shoulder, squeezed and guided her back a bit. His unspoken message was clear. *Don't fuss over him.* Lalia got to her feet.

''The purpose of the rope, Jeremy, is to allow you to learn from experience safely.'' Morgan considered his nephew sternly. ''I expect you to take the lesson.''

"Yes, Uncle Morgan, I will." Jeremy looked up at them ruefully. "I lost my shoe."

Morgan shook his head and sighed.

They spent a remarkably commonplace evening. No observer would have suspected from their careful demeanor that they were new lovers—much to Lalia's relief. They even took tea together in the newly refurbished drawing room, talking of swimming lessons for Jeremy and his need for new footwear. The lost shoe made two pair ruined within a few days. They sounded like an old married couple, Lalia thought. Like parents.

Another moment to treasure for lonelier times.

She wasn't at all sure what would happen next. It was possible that his lordship, having attained his goal, would be satisfied. But he hadn't sounded that way this afternoon. Uncertain as to how to proceed, she excused herself and went to her room alone. While she was brushing her hair, a light tap sounded on the connecting door.

She opened it to find him standing there, bare-chested, boots discarded. "Would you like to have a glass of wine with me?"

Lalia nodded, and he stepped back, ushering her into his bedchamber. Two glasses and a decanter rested on the table that stood beside the large chair near the hearth. She would have taken the other chair, but Morgan stopped her with a hand on her arm.

He sat and drew her into his lap. "I don't want you that far away from me tonight." He poured the sherry and handed her a glass. His free hand stroked her hair. "There are some things we must discuss."

Lalia's stomached tightened. She had no idea what

"things" he might find it needful to say. She nodded again without answering.

"Actually, there are many things we must discuss eventually, but most of them are better kept for later." He sipped his wine, then looked directly at her. "Do you know any ways of preventing conception?"

Lalia shrugged. "Only what Daj has told me—that a couple should make love only in the light with their eyes open—and never look away from one another."

His lordship raised one eyebrow. "Hmm. That sounds like a very weak reed on which to lean. Did you keep your eyes open?"

Lalia smiled. "You know I did not."

"Yes, I know." He placed a light kiss on her cheek. His voice close to her ear grew rough. "You are breathtakingly lovely in your passion. I would not miss a moment of it."

"You closed yours, too."

"Later I did. It seems we had best not depend on that method." He wound her hair around his hand.

"I will ask Daj…"

"Uh…" Morgan interrupted hastily. "I had rather not involve your grandmother in this."

Lalia giggled. "She will know, anyway. I've told you that."

"Perhaps, but I do not wish to confirm her suspicions. There are devices that a man can wear. I will obtain some."

"That doesn't sound very comfortable."

Morgan grimaced. "Nonetheless… I do not wish to subject you to any preventable difficulties. But nothing is completely effective." He set down his glass and lifted her hair to his lips, kissing it softly. Lowering it again, he gazed steadily into her eyes. "Lalia, I want you to have no doubts about this. No matter what the future brings us, I will not desert you. And I would certainly not abandon my child. Have no fear of either.''

Lalia sighed. She didn't doubt him. He had proved that he did not abandon those for whom he felt responsible. Yet, in spite of herself, she wished for more. She wished for—somewhere in a distant time—a future she could see. With him. With children. Foolish. He had told her he regarded Jeremy as his heir. He did not expect to have children. Which meant he had no intention of marrying.

Another reason to live for the moment.

He took the glass out of her hand and set it aside. With a hand in her hair he pulled her mouth close to his, his breath against her lips. ''But now, come what may, I have a blazing ambition to see how you look in my bed.''

He released her hair and stood, lifting her in his arms. Feeling suddenly shy, Lalia buried her face against his shoulder as he carried her across the room. Morgan sat on the edge of the bed with her on his lap and, with a hand on her chin, gently turned her lips to his. The kiss was soft, tender.

''Sweet lady.'' His lips trailed to her throat, murmuring against her skin. ''There is no need to be uncertain with me. At this moment I want you more than I want my next breath.'' He slowly and carefully brushed the silk of her nightclothes aside and lowered his head to her breasts. His mouth left little damp kisses in the valley between them.

Lalia drew in a sudden breath as a delicious warmth began to grow in her lower body. Morgan responded by moving the kisses nearer to her nipples, his tongue just touching her skin. She arched her back, bringing her yearning nipples closer to his mouth, but he continued to circle them with hot, tantalizing touches. When she began to tremble, he stood her before him and let her gown drop to the floor.

In the next second she found herself lying on her back on the bed with Morgan, standing beside the bed, spreading her hair out around her, his hungry gaze feasting.

"Beautiful." His hands found her breasts, stroked her quivering legs. "God, Lalia, you are unbelievably beautiful." He stepped out of his britches and rolled across her to the other side of the bed. Stacking the pillows under his head, he lay on his back and reached for her. He lifted her to straddle his body and then carefully eased her onto his straining shaft.

Lalia felt only a moment of puzzlement before his hands cupped her breasts, drawing her closer. She leaned forward on her hands, her hair falling to create a curtain around them, shutting out everything but the two of them. His lips resumed the teasing kisses, moving ever closer to the touch her body demanded. When, at last, his mouth closed over her nipple, she moaned aloud, and her body clenched around him. He gasped and thrust into her hard.

For Lalia, the world dissolved into a cloud of sensation—Morgan's mouth and hands on her nipples, the pulse of his hips under her, stroking her desire. Her own hips moved in the ancient, mindless manner of feminine passion, a force unto themselves, rotating, lifting, falling. The rough sound of her breathing and his echoed in her ears.

Suddenly darkness overwhelmed her. Her body began to shudder, closing around him tighter and tighter. She cried out—some meaningless sound—and heard the cry echoed in his deeper tone. When it seemed that she must surely die, the tension exploded into a thousand points of light, and she collapsed into Morgan's arms, sobbing.

His arms closed around her, holding her hard against him while the world returned and she found she could breathe again. One of his big hands stroked her hair.

"Ah, my beautiful, generous lady." Morgan's lips found her ear. "Stay in my bed tonight."

And she did.

The next morning Dr. Lanreath surprised Morgan with a visit as he was inspecting work newly done in the guest bedchambers. Morgan hurried down to the library and shook the older man's hand warmly. "How are you, Doctor? To what do we owe this pleasant surprise?"

"Have some news that I thought would interest you." The doctor accepted a glass of Madeira and sat. Rather than barricade himself behind the desk, Morgan took a chair facing him and waited expectantly. The good doctor was one to waste neither time nor words.

"Found some bones."

"Indeed?" That did interest Morgan. "Where were they found?"

"Under the bonfire."

"The bonfire! Bloody hell, man. How did that happen? I was there myself." Morgan set down his glass, his mind racing. While he had laughed and drunk and lusted after Lalia, someone's body had been burning before his eyes. A chill raced up his spine. "Whose bones are they?"

"Don't know yet. I can't tell from what's left. We'll have to wait and see who comes up missing." Lanreath crossed his ankles and sipped his wine. Apparently grim sights did nothing to disconcert him. "Again, I can't be sure, but I believe the skull was cracked before the body burned. There were several broken bones, but the body being under the fire might have done that.''

"How did the damn things get in the fire? Someone must have put it there while the wood was being gathered.''

"I would say so. Building the pile required a couple of days. I would guess that the corpse was placed there the first night.''

They sipped wine in thoughtful silence. Morgan hoped that somehow Lalia would not hear of the gruesome discovery. He would like to think that she had fond memories of that night. He did not want them tarnished. But what did this imply? Another murder clearly.

He looked back at the doctor. "That suggests to me that the recent piracy is locally based.''

"Never doubted it.'' Lanreath nodded. "I've suspected these several months that something is afoot. Never liked the cut of that fellow Killigrew's jib. He came here for a reason, and it wasn't running an inn, but I've heard nothing to the point.''

"Have you heard anything about Poleven?''

"Sir Roger? No, can't say that I have. The district doesn't see much of him—no loss to us.''

"He's been here several weeks now.''

The doctor's brows drew together. "Is that a fact? Unusual for him. Must be under the hatches.''

"Probably. Is he friends with Nascawan?''

"The parson? I wouldn't think so. What are you after?''

Morgan shrugged. "Nothing. Just speculating.''

"In that case, I best be on my way.'' Suiting the action to the word, the doctor rose.

"Thank you for coming.'' Morgan walked with him to the door. "I appreciate knowing about the bones.''

Although he couldn't say he liked it above half.

* * *

Afternoon found Morgan atop the wall once again, scanning the horizon with his glass. He might see more from the tower, but he did not want to trespass on Lalia's sanctuary, and the second tower no longer had any steps at all. Perhaps he would have it repaired for his own retreat. There was nothing in view except the *Sea Witch*, cruising the area. Tomorrow night, if it was clear, he would personally be aboard her in pursuit of his prey.

Coastal pirates, like all rats, preferred to operate at night, and the moon should be bright. When he got them in his sights, they would soon be drowned rats, their craft resting on the sea bottom. Unlike the preventives, Morgan did not have to capture a prize intact to be paid for his trouble.

A hail from the ground below him caught his attention and he turned to see James at the foot of the wall. Morgan climbed down and settled himself on a large stone that had fallen centuries since. James found himself a similar perch.

"Something I think it needful for you to know, me lord."

Hmm. Now what? Morgan hoped that the news was less grim than the last bit he had received with that introduction. "What's that, James?"

"Been a young fellow from the village hanging around here talking to the stable lads—goes by the name of Breney—George Breney."

"Looking for a position?"

"Nay, not that one. He ain't that much in favor of work." James spat on the ground in disgust. "One of the young'uns what got took up by the press gang to fight Bonaparte—probably found that life more exciting than a little honest labor. But they don't need him no more.''

"So now he is back.'' Morgan regarded his groom patiently. "Well, then, what does he want?''

"I'm not rightly sure, and that's what bothers me. There's something havey-cavey about that lad—very. Hangs about at the Pilchard most days.'' James repositioned his spare rump on the hard seat. "With all this talk of pirates and such…''

Morgan scowled. "You think Breney is recruiting?''

"That's what worries me. Not that I think any of our lads would go with him into that sort of meanness. I been knowing them all since they was breeched. Still…''

"It's well that you are keeping an eye on him.'' Morgan stood. "See if you can find out from one of the boys what he wants. I guess you heard about the find under the Midsummer fire?'' No doubt of it, the way news traveled around the district.

"Aye. A right bone fire—ain't that what a bonfire really is?'' The old man cackled.

Morgan regarded him with narrowed eyes. "Do you know who it was?''

"Not I.'' James shook his head. "But I reckon we'll figure it out before long. Can't no one go missing around here without it gets noticed.''

"Just so.'' Morgan stared into the distance. It all fit together somehow. Just how, he couldn't yet fathom. But sooner or later, it would come to him.

He knew how to wait.

After dinner both Lalia and Morgan announced—to the household—their intention of retiring early, and with much show of formality, Morgan escorted Lalia to her bedchamber. She wondered if they had deceived a single member of the staff. Very likely not. Their intentions were probably writ large upon their faces.

But true to the pretense, Morgan opened Lalia's bedchamber door and stepped aside to let her through.

She had no more than entered the doorway when she froze, her hand clutching her chest. "M-Morgan. Look."

He moved her aside and stepped into the room. "Damnation!"

All of the garments that had been stored neatly in the wardrobe lay in a tangled heap on the floor. The smell of seawater was strong and a piece of muddy seaweed lay on top of the pile. Lalia went to her knees by the soggy clothes, a pain jabbing her breast.

After so many years of privation, of having nothing new or pretty to wear, the beautiful things had meant far more to her than any material thing should. She knew that. She should be ashamed of herself. They were just dresses. Still, all she could do was sit on the floor and stare wordlessly up at Morgan, tears trickling down her cheeks.

He knelt on one knee beside her and brushed the moisture away. "Don't cry, Lalia. The gowns can be replaced."

"I know." But she could never afford it and she drew back from allowing him to do it. It spoke too strongly of the kept woman.

Morgan gathered up the top layer and moved it aside. "See, the bottom of the stack is still dry. The water did not have time enough to soak through. Where is Sarah?"

"She was not feeling well. I sent her to bed."

"So there was no one up here?" Morgan strode into the hallway and looked both ways. "Surely we would have seen someone had they been in the corridor. But Andrew and Zachary are both in Jeremy's room. Whoever did this had ample time to make good their escape while we were at dinner, if they were silent about it. Is the priest's hole securely fastened?''

''I certainly hope so.'' Lalia trailed him across the room, drying her cheeks with her handkerchief. ''I always keep it locked.''

Morgan reached for the hidden mechanism that opened the panel. But he never touched it. ''It *is* open. The door is ajar.''

Lalia gasped.

''And there are damp footprints. It appears that...'' Morgan's voice faded as he made his way down the stairs. ''Yes... Yes...here... There is little doubt they entered this way. Here is spilled water.'' His voice got louder rapidly.

He erupted from the tunnel and dashed passed her. Moments later Andrew and Zachary ran into the room and disappeared into the opening. Morgan followed with an excited Jeremy in tow.

''Oh! A hidden door. This is above anything, Uncle Morgan! Is there one in my room?''

Morgan collared his nephew, preventing him from following his guards. ''I fervently hope not. Jeremy, do leave off the questions for a moment. Go sit down. I will explain in a moment.''

Minimally subdued by the unaccustomed impatience in his uncle's voice, Jeremy obeyed, perching on the edge of the hearth chair and obviously containing his curiosity with some difficulty.

Eventually the shuffle of footsteps was heard from the concealed passage and Andrew and Zachary reappeared through the small door. ''We could find no one, my lord.'' Zachary frowned. ''He had too great a start on us. We saw nothing in the cove, either.''

Morgan nodded. "Never mind. I did not expect you to find him, though I hoped you might. You may take Jeremy back to his room."

But Jeremy had caught sight of Lalia's pale face. "Are you all right, Miss Lalia?"

Lalia heard the anxiety in the boy's voice and started to answer when Morgan cut her off. "Some one has played a wicked trick on her and ruined part of her clothes."

"That was mean of them." Now the voice was definitely disapproving.

"Indeed it was." Morgan nodded at his footmen. "Keep a sharp eye. This may have been intended as a diversion."

"Aye, my lord." Andrew gathered up Jeremy while Zachary made sure the hidden door was fast. "Come on, Mr. Jeremy. It's bed for you."

Jeremy waved at Lalia. "Good night, Miss Lalia. Don't worry. Uncle Morgan and I won't let anyone play any more tricks on you."

"G-good night, Jeremy. Thank you." She had to struggle to get it past the lump in her throat.

After the three had left the room, Morgan went to close the hall door, but stopped short as he spied Watford standing in it. "Yes, Watford?"

"It is Mrs. Veshengo, my lord. I intercepted her trying to climb the stairs. I persuaded her to let me come and see what the commotion is. It seems very difficult for her to negotiate steps."

"Oh, thank you, Watford." Lalia shook her head. "I cannot persuade her..."

"You may tell Mrs. Veshengo that her granddaughter is well and safe. And that I will see to it that she stays that way."

* * *

Lalia was so busy with her own thoughts at breakfast the next morning that she missed hearing Morgan enter the room.

"Lalia. Lalia! What are you thinking on so hard?"

"Oh!" Lalia started and looked up at him. "Nothing... I... Nothing."

Morgan's brows drew together. "Humph. You don't expect me to believe that, do you? Allow me to hazard a guess. You still half believe that, even though we found tracks in the priest's hole, that Hayne's ghost is somehow behind last night's visitation."

Lalia studied her plate. "No... Well... Not really. I saw the footprints. It is just that Daj keeps insisting that he is angrier than ever because of...because we... Well, you know."

"Indeed I do." Morgan's smile took on a seductive quality. "And I am very happy to say it. But his posthumous interest or lack of it is not what concerns me. I want to know how the door to that tunnel got opened."

"Yes. I do, too. I'm positive I did not leave it that way—especially since the other disturbances we have had."

"Perhaps the catch has broken. It has been there for centuries, after all. I want to test it."

Morgan laid aside his napkin and rose. The two of them mounted the stairs and entered Lalia's room. The pile of clothes had been spirited away by Sarah, who promised to work miracles of restoration. Lalia had her doubts—the cottons, certainly, but the silks? Unlikely. Unless, of course, Sarah was conspiring with his lordship for their replacement. Lalia didn't know whether to smile or to frown at that possibility.

Morgan operated the hidden catch and slid the secret

panel back. "Close it behind me. Let me see if I can open it."

Lalia followed these instructions. After a few moments and some scraping noises, his muffled voice sounded again. "Very good. Let me in."

A devil of mischief momentarily overcame Lalia. "Say 'please.'"

"Lalia! Open that... Oh, very well. Please." He did not sound amused. Lalia quickly opened the panel.

Morgan stepped through the secret door, giving her a grimace. "This is not funny. That door did not open itself—nor was it opened by a bucket-wielding ghost. I believe the time has come to nail that opening shut."

Dismay washed over Lalia. "Oh, no!"

"What?" Morgan looked perplexed. "Why not? It clearly presents a danger to you."

"But...but... It is..." Lalia stammered to a stop, not knowing how to explain.

"Ah. I think I see." Morgan brushed a hand down her cheek. "It also represents a means of escape to you."

Lalia nodded. "Yes, that is it. I always knew I could get out if...if he cut me off from the corridor. But now, of course... He is..."

"Gone but not forgotten." Morgan wrapped his arms around her. "It will no doubt take years for you to feel safe again. Very well. I will set guards in the cove near the entrance. Perhaps it will serve as a trap. I intend to find whomever is terrorizing you. But you must check it carefully each time you come into the room. Will you do that?"

"Oh, yes. You may rest assured on that point."

Morgan placed a lingering kiss on her lips, at last

lifting his head and gazing into her eyes. "I can't stay. I have appointments today. I'll see you at supper."

Lalia sighed and clung to him, reluctant for him to leave. She was coming to depend on his comfort more and more. That did not bode well for her heart.

Morgan had to see her alone for a moment, had to offer his desire at least a crumb of comfort. Just before dinner was served, he tapped on the hall door to Lalia's bedchamber. Sarah opened to him, so Morgan bowed and addressed Lalia with the utmost formality. "Excuse me, Mrs. Hayne, may I speak with you for a moment?"

Lalia gestured at the maid. "Thank you, Sarah. That will be all for now."

Morgan waited for the girl to leave. Then he carefully closed the door behind her. And turned the key. Lalia stood up from the dressing stool and he quickly crossed the room to her and took her in his arms. He intended to kiss her carefully, so as not to muss her artfully arranged hair and one of the few gowns that had escaped the dunking. But his restraint proved to be unequal to the task. Her mouth was too warm, her breasts too soft upon him.

And she melted against him with far too much heat.

He did manage to keep his hands out of her hair, but they, apparently with no instruction from him, found other things to do. Morgan slid them across her bottom, relishing the sensation of curves barely concealed by clinging fabric.

"Ah, sweet torment." He lifted his head and was gratified to see that her eyes had taken on the deep-sea blue of her passion. Now her gown and her jewels echoed it exactly. He bent and kissed his way across the skin re-

vealed by the open neckline, blessing the clever modiste.
With just a little more effort…

Morgan slipped a finger under the fabric and the
slightest tug revealed one taught nipple. He closed his
mouth over it and Lalia sighed. At the sigh the ache in
his groin threatened to undo his control completely. He
lifted his head. "I must leave off, else I will not be able
to. Besides, I am leaving marks." With a possessive satisfaction he gently touched her swollen lips and the red-
dened patches his carefully shaved beard had created on
the fine skin of her breasts. "That won't do." He restored the gown to its proper place. "We must go down
to dinner shortly."

"I suppose we must." Lalia smiled a bemused smile,
a hint of regret in her tone.

Morgan placed his hands on her arms and looked into
her face. "I'm afraid so, and I also must tell you that
this will have to satisfy me for now—though I believe
it has only whetted my appetite." He smiled ruefully.
"I am going aboard the *Sea Witch* as soon as I've eaten.
I will not be back until perhaps tomorrow afternoon—
longer if we engage in a chase. I don't want you to worry
at my absence."

Lalia covered her mouth with both hands. Not worry?
How could she possibly not worry? She could find nothing to say and so gazed up at him silently.

"Now, Lalia." Morgan lifted her hands away from
her mouth. "There is nothing to concern you. I have a
well-armed craft and experienced men at my back. Besides, I would be much luckier than I expect to be to
find the blackguards at work the first time I look."

Still no words came to Lalia. How could she tell him
how she felt? He would not want to hear it.

"Lalia?"

She dredged a weak smile up from somewhere in her depths and grasped at the tatters of her calm facade. "Of course, my lord. I do hope you will be cautious." Another thought occurred to her. She turned and lifted a small cloth packet from the dressing table and handed it to him. "Keep this in your pocket."

Morgan turned the little bundle in his hands. "What is it?"

"A…well, a good luck charm. My grandmother made it." She struggled for another smile.

"A Gypsy talisman?" He started to lay it back down.

Lalia stopped him with a hand on his arm. "Please, my lord. To ease my mind."

"What's in it?"

"Just some herbs and a small piece of bread. Won't you keep it for my sake?"

"Very well, if it will calm your fears." Morgan shook his head indulgently and slipped the amulet into his pocket. "I suppose you have one for yourself?" She nodded. "Good. I want you to be very careful until I return. I also worry."

She nodded again, and he pulled her closer. "Now, give me a proper goodbye kiss. We will have no opportunity after we eat."

At the rate she was going, Lalia knew her poor heart stood to be shattered into a million pieces when summer ended and Morgan sent her away.

He could do nothing else. His mother would return and it would become completely impossible for her to continue living in the mistress's bedchamber. Already Daj grumbled about that arrangement. Besides, when Jeremy's new tutor arrived, she would no longer have a role in the household. At least she now felt sure that his lordship would help her find a place for herself and her grandmother. He had promised not to abandon her and she believed that.

But, oh, the ache in her soul.

How had she allowed herself to fall in love with him? To depend on him? She who had relied on no one but herself for so many years? She must pull back before her feelings made her helpless to do so. But how? How could she tear herself away when the very sight of his square shoulders made her ache with longing? When the sound of his voice made her heart leap into her throat? It was so easy to go on leaning on him, lying with him. Loving him.

But it was time to stop.

Time to take control of her life while she still could.

Chapter Fourteen

The night's search had proved fruitless and Morgan came home tired and irritable. But the thought of Lalia awaiting his return lightened his spirits. He had no intention of going to sleep early after they had eaten—not when he could have Lalia's sweet sighs to inflame him, her soft, round hips to cradle his own. No, tonight was no time to catch up on lost sleep.

Morgan stepped through the connecting door into Lalia's bedchamber and dropped the talisman onto her dressing table. He had divested himself of everything but his trousers, and the sight of Lalia sitting fully clothed in the chair by the hearth startled him. He knelt beside her and took her hands in his, kissing first the backs of them and then the palm. "I have returned your charm. Apparently it did its work well. I am quite unscathed." He looked up into her solemn face. "Did you miss me?"

She freed one of her hands and pushed the tousled curls off his forehead. "I missed you very much, my lord."

Something was wrong. She was not smiling. Morgan sat back on his heels, still firmly gripping her hand, and studied her. "What is it, Lalia?"

She sighed, then took a long breath. "I need to speak with you."

Hmm. Not a good portent. "Very well." Morgan stood and drew the other chair close enough that he could maintain his hold on her hand while he sat, leaning forward. "I'm listening."

She continued to sit in silence. Morgan waited. He was just about to nudge her into speech when she began. "I'm concerned, my lord, about what is happening between us. I—I don't think it is in my best interests."

Definitely not a good sign. His brows drew together. "What do you fear, Lalia? I told you that you have no need to worry. I will see that you are taken care of."

"I do not doubt that, my lord, but…I… I am coming to care for you more than is wise." She kept her gaze on her hands.

Now what did that mean? Morgan felt too tired for riddles. He leaned back in the chair. "What is unwise about that? I care for you, also."

"Perhaps…but what I mean is… We know that this affair must come to an end in a few more weeks, and I must go away. I'm afraid, by then, it will be very painful for me to do that."

Ah. That could remedied. "But there is no need for your departure to be distressing. I have been thinking that I might perhaps find a pleasant cottage for you. Something nearby so that I may continue to see you. Wouldn't you like that?"

"I don't know, my lord."

She didn't know? Morgan frowned. "I thought you would like a place of your own—something with a garden to tend. Is there something else you want?"

Lalia thought for a long time before answering. Morgan's fatigue and irritation grew. Most women would jump at a chance like that. When she did speak, she surprised him.

"My lord, you cannot understand what my life has been. Since I was born, I have been hidden away. I used to think that my father was ashamed of me. Now I understand that he was protecting me from snubs and slights. But my husband—he left me at Merdinn so that he would not have to trouble himself to show me how to go on in London—and so that others would not know he had taken a Gypsy to wife. And Roger wanted to rid himself of me for much the same reasons. I have been despised also by the local folk for my association with the two of them. Nor am I acceptable to the Roma."

"I am not ashamed of you, Lalia."

She gazed at him for a long, assessing moment before she nodded acceptance. "Thank you. I appreciate that." She stared at the empty fireplace for several more heartbeats. "What you are offering—a home, a garden, a place for Daj—would be heaven for me if… If it were my own. If it were permanent. If I held a respectable place in the community. But a mistress kept by…"

"I would not allow anyone to show you disrespect."

"You could not stop them. And what will happen to me later—a woman with no reputation? Another man? And another?"

"No! Not that. I told you—I will not abandon you. There will be no need for other…" Morgan took a calming breath. "Besides, Lalia, what else will you do? Where will you go? How will you live?"

"I don't know."

This was becoming ridiculous. What other choice did she have? Couldn't the woman see how much he was willing to give her just for the delight of being with her? How much he wanted her? He slid out of his chair onto one knee again, catching her around the waist and pulling her to him. "You are being absurd—flinging a secure future back in my teeth. I won't listen to any more of this."

Morgan began to taste the skin of her throat, moving his lips lower as he spoke. "Come now, sweet torment. Tell me, if you can, that you do not want me. Tell me you wish to leave me. Tell me that while I take your breath away, while I make you moan. Come, make me believe it if you think you can."

He stood and pulled her into his arms, bruising her lips under his. She collapsed against him and Morgan thought the victory won.

But suddenly she pulled back from him, holding him off with her palms, her eyes the ominous gray of a lowering storm. She spoke quietly at first, but her voice rose steadily with growing emotion. "You say I want you. And I do." She wiped angrily at her eyes. "And you know it. And you are taking advantage of it, and..." She wrenched away from him. "And you are trying to make me..." She was shouting now, tears trailing down her face.

"I will not be your whore!"

She ran for the door as Morgan stood stunned. "Lalia! Wait!"

The door slammed and he heard light footsteps flying down the stairs. He started after her, then remembered his bare feet and torso.

"Damnation!"

By the time he had tugged on boots and found a shirt, Lalia had already disappeared into the tower. Morgan had run out without bringing a candle, so he dared not try the stairs alone. Confounded woman! Once again, he climbed the wall and made his way around the outside of the tower to the watch platform, only to be disappointed to see the door to the old guard room closed. He pulled on the handle, but it refused to budge.

"Damnation!"

Morgan threw his weight against the door. Nothing happened. Of course not. That bar had been designed to forbid an invading army. Confound her! "Lalia! Open the door." Silence from within. Morgan lowered his voice. "Please open it, Lalia. I only want to talk to you. You don't understand."

He waited while the silence stretched.

And stretched.

He heard not a sound from within. Not one word.

She wasn't going to open it.

"Damnation!"

Bloody hell!

He'd be damned if he would beg. Morgan climbed down the tower and stomped into the house. The brandy decanter in the library needed refilling, so he stalked to the family dining room. Luckily there were several bottles of wine on the sideboard. This evening was going to require a generous supply.

Morgan sprawled in his chair and poured himself a glass of port. He had eschewed his after-dinner port because he was tired and he wanted to be in good condition to make love to Lalia. Bah! That had been a waste of restraint. He gulped down two swallows and refilled the glass. Propping one boot on the adjacent chair, he made himself comfortable to brood.

What did the woman want? He refused to believe that she didn't want *him*. Nor did she deny it. She said she wanted respectability. He could understand that. Look at what the lack of it had done to Beth. Perhaps Lalia wanted marriage. Morgan pondered that thought for a moment. But she knew how he felt about Jeremy. Morgan loved him as though he were his own—had always thought of him as his heir.

But if he married and had children, would he want to put Jeremy ahead of his own son? That gave him pause. He had never felt inclined to marry, so it had not seemed to be a problem. But did he want some obscure and distant relative to become the next earl of Carrick? Never before encountering a lady to whom he was willing to be married for life, he had not given the matter much thought. Perhaps it was time to think about it.

These reflections were interrupted by the thump of a walking stick on the flagstones of the hall. What the devil was Mrs. Veshengo doing abroad at his time of night? Well, it was hardly a wonder that she had heard so much slamming of doors and running up and down of stairs. She undoubtedly intended to ring a peal over his head. As he turned toward the door, the old woman hobbled into the room. Without a word she approached and sat down across the table from him. In no mood for a scolding, Morgan raised a questioning eyebrow and waited silently.

From out of her voluminous skirts she produced a deck of cards and handed them to Morgan. He glanced at them. Tarot cards. So—he was about to be treated to some Gypsy fortune-telling. He almost dismissed her, but curiosity got the better of him. He shuffled the cards several times and handed them back to her. If she had stacked the deck, that should disrupt her plot—whatever it was.

She cut the cards again and turned the topmost face up. A dark-haired, stern-faced man holding a sword with arms crossed on his chest peered back at him.

The woman spoke at last. "The King of Swords. You."

Morgan considered. A reasonable likeness. The picture conveyed strength of will, determination, and a good bit of anger. He shrugged. She turned over another card.

A grinning skeleton with a scythe greeted him. The Death card. She was trying to frighten him. She must have contrived to control the cards, after all. A sneer threatened to curl his lip, but she surprised him by nodding sagely, but calmly.

"Yes. You have brought about great change. The old is swept away, the new is forming."

Morgan raised both eyebrows. He certainly couldn't deny that. A promising beginning.

The next card showed an older woman in the robes of a priestess. "The influence of your distant past. A strong, wise woman."

Well, he couldn't argue with that, either. That would be his mother, always steadier and more perceptive than his father. He waited with increased interest for the next card.

"The more recent past." The card revealed a jeering thief, stealing the swords of men who stood with their backs to him.

Morgan scowled. He had no trouble identifying the trickster. And that man with his back turned and his eyes closed was certainly his father. An old rancor stirred in him, taking him unaware. How could the man have been so blind? How could he have permitted the shipping interests to deteriorate to the point that he must allow the entail to expire and mortgage the land? And let himself be gulled by the damned Haynes? Morgan's fist clenched convulsively.

The old Gypsy said nothing more on that head, but turned up the next image. "The Devil. You are barred from reaching your next goal."

That was a masterpiece of understatement! Barred, shut out, furious and frustrated. And, if he admitted it, hurting. Lalia had run away from him to hide in the safety of her retreat, just as she had run from her drunken, abusive husband. Morgan gritted his teeth. Damn it. He did not deserve that. How could she do that to him?

"Your present goal."

Morgan leaned forward. The new card showed a naked man and woman, arms entwined. The Lovers. He looked up, startled, at his companion. She gazed steadily back at him with canny black eyes. Morgan flushed.

She said nothing, laying another card on the table. "As the world sees you."

A man leading a triumphal procession. He had felt like that man only a few hours before—exultant, all his goals attained. But now... A harsh laugh escaped him when he saw the next card. A man holding three gold cups grasped unavailingly for a fourth just out of his reach, his face discontented. Morgan sent the lady a questioning glance.

"As you see yourself."

How true. Morgan grimaced and leaned back in his chair as she showed him the next picture, puzzled at the representation of a wolf and a dog howling at the moon.

She fingered the card for a moment. "The Moon card. In this place it stands for your emotions. You will not trust. You will not give your heart."

Morgan glared. That struck a little too close to home. Was that indeed the case with him? Was he refusing to trust? Reluctant to love? Was that why he had never wanted to marry—never even had a long affair? He would have to think about that.

"Your last card, the outcome of your present course of action—if you choose not to change it." Ignoring his troubled expression, she turned over another card. "The Falling Tower."

Morgan picked up the drawing. Bodies fell from a flaming tower into the sea. He looked into the old woman's face. "You mean I will lose everything I have worked for—all I desire."

She shrugged. "Only you know what the cards mean for you in your present situation. I do not tell the future. I only advise."

Morgan digested that information in silence for several heartbeats, sipping his wine. Then another thought occurred to him. "What about your granddaughter? What does this situation auger for her?"

Lalia's grandmother turned over one more card and silently laid it before him.

It showed a heart, pierced through by three swords.

There seemed to be an actual ache in Lalia's heart. For the next few days she went through her daily routine blindly. She knew that Morgan had gone out on the *Sea Witch,* but did not know exactly when and did not ask anyone. She had done the best thing for herself, Lalia knew. Her love for his lordship had already caused her more pain than she felt she could bear. If only the agony would abate, she might be able to think about her future. As it was now, she could think only of the next heartbeat, the next minute, the next task.

She cared for Jeremy mechanically until he complained that she was no longer any fun. At that Lalia rallied herself and tried to throw off her depressed spirits for his sake. She was not being fair to the boy. Together they enticed James into whittling a new boat. They chose a suitable scrap of cloth and Lalia made a sail while Zachary painted the craft for them.

After much debate Jeremy settled on *Wave Witch* as a name. ''For she's cutter-rigged, Miss Lalia, just like Uncle Morgan's ship.''

Ignoring this considerable exaggeration, they set off late one afternoon, with Zachary and Andrew on guard, taking advantage of the low tide to christen their masterpiece. A stout cord ensured that the *Wave Witch* would not depart for the open sea and that her master would not plunge into the depths after her.

They had been uneventfully engaged in their sailing for some half hour when the real cutter rounded the adjacent headland. Jeremy danced in excitement as she reefed her sails outside the rocks of the cove and put the ship's boat over the side. Lalia's heart constricted so hard that she could scarcely get her breath as Morgan climbed over the rail and down the ladder into the small craft. He was coming ashore.

She could not retreat. Jeremy skipped back and forth in happy anticipation, and the footmen stood to welcome their employer. How could Lalia turn her back on him? She reached deep into herself and somehow found enough calm to don her serene manner. As the dinghy reached the shallows, Morgan, with a casual salute to his crew, vaulted over the side and splashed ashore. Lalia stepped back and waited with folded hands as Jeremy ran to his uncle.

''Look, look, Uncle Morgan. I have a new cutter. Her name is *Wave Witch*.''

''And a fine one she is, too.'' Morgan lifted the boy

into his arms and peered at the toy. "Have you been behaving yourself while I have been away?"

"Oh, yes, sir. Haven't I, Miss Lalia?" Jeremy sought corroboration as Morgan set him back on his feet.

Nodding to the footmen, Morgan turned his attention to Lalia, uncertain as to what to say.

She gave him an equally uncertain smile. "He has been a veritable paragon of virtue, my lord."

Morgan stopped beside her and looked into her face— a face altogether too pale and hollow-cheeked for his liking. Especially as he felt sure that the cause of those conditions lay squarely at his own door. Her wonderful eyes were tinged with red at the corners. Had she been crying the whole time that he had been gone? He barely contained his impulse to reach out to her, remembering just in time their audience. He took a step back.

"I am delighted to hear that." How the devil was he to make things right between them? He couldn't stand this separation much longer. He ached for her even as she stood staring at his feet.

"Your boots are wet." She glanced up at him for a second.

Morgan chuckled to himself. Apparently she knew no more what to say to him than he did to her. "They are old ones."

Jeremy broke the awkward moment. "May I go out in the *Sea Witch?* May I? Please?"

"Another day, Jer. Now she must move away before the tide comes in, as we should also do." Morgan took his nephew's hand and started up the trail. Jeremy accompanied him, chattering, while the footmen followed a much too quiet Lalia. Morgan looked back just in time to see Andrew take her hand to help her up a small incline. Morgan's hackles rose. How dare that insolent…

Stopping himself just in time to prevent violence, he broke off the thought and called himself to order. The footman was only doing his job. But did he have to enjoy it? The sight of another man's hand on her was almost more than Morgan could stand.

He could not allow her to leave Merdinn without his protection. She would be too vulnerable to… No! He would never allow her to sink into the demimonde. But she might marry someone else. He ground his teeth, shocked at his next thought.

Over my dead body!

Chapter Fifteen

Now what? Morgan propped his feet on the desk and sipped his brandy. Rather than appearing for supper, Lalia had sent regrets, claiming a headache. He had knocked on the door of her bedchamber, only to discover that she wasn't in it. A trip up the tower had revealed the door again shut. He hadn't bothered to knock on it. He would think of something else.

No need to repeat that scene. At the thought of her fleeing from him, locking him out, the hurt and anger welled up in him. How could she fear him? Granted, his behavior early in their acquaintance had left something to be desired... Well, a great deal to be desired, if he were honest, but he had apologized and he had not forced her into anything. Seduced her, perhaps.

Maybe that was what she feared.

The house lay shrouded in quiet darkness, everyone else having sought their bed. He must find his own soon. Pirate hunting was exhausting work. He swallowed the last of the brandy and was about to rise from his chair when something in the doorway caught his eye.

A man stood there.

"What...?" Morgan jerked open the drawer of his

desk and grasped the pistol within. "Who the devil are you?"

The man held up both hands in a placating gesture. Middle-aged and of medium height, he wore a wide felt hat over dark curling hair and a red scarf around his neck. "Do not be alarmed, my lord. I am Yoska Veshengo. I came to visit my mother, but I would like to speak with you."

Morgan laid the gun on the desk and motioned the man to a chair. So—the Gypsies had access to the house through Lalia's grandmother. Interesting. "I see. Are you the person to whom I owe thanks for preventing the theft of my horses?"

A small smile flitted over the man's face. "I may have spoken with a few people."

"If so, I am in your debt." Morgan held out the brandy decanter, his eyes questioning.

"Yes, thank you." Veshengo settled himself and accepted a glass. "I understand that you would like to apprehend those who are responsible for the destruction of your ship."

"You understand correctly. I *will* apprehend them."

Veshengo nodded. "Some of my people have noticed that a certain churchman stores a surprising number of goods in his cellar."

Morgan's eyebrows rose. "Oh? Spirits?"

"And other things." Veshengo sipped his liquor. "Things that might more properly be stored in the hold of a ship. They seem to appear there at night."

"Hmm." Enlightening, indeed. Morgan twirled the liquid in his own glass. "How do your people know this?"

Again the man smiled, but said nothing.

"Ah." Clearly better not to ask. "Are we discussing the Reverend Nascawan?"

"Just so."

Aha! Now he had more than a hunch and a dislike of the clergyman to go on. Morgan sighed with satisfaction. "I'm much obliged for that information. I'll think further about how to pursue it."

"There is another subject, my lord, which worries me and my mother—the affair of the *muló*. This is not a matter to dismiss lightly." Veshengo leaned forward and placed two small cloth packets on the desk.

Morgan picked one up and studied it—another talisman. He looked inquiringly at the Gypsy.

"The *gadje* do not take the presence of a *muló* seriously enough. They can be very dangerous. My mother sent for us when it first appeared."

"Oh? How did she do that?"

Veshengo shrugged. "We have arrangements for passing messages."

"I see." Morgan spoke noncommittally. He now had several more candidates for the identity of the specter. "I hope you understand that when I find the person responsible for frightening your niece, I shall be extremely displeased with them."

The enigmatic smile reappeared on the Gypsy's face. "As you should be. But I do not think you will find them, my lord. Not on this earth. Those—" he indicated the amulets "—are for you and the boy." His expression became serious. "Do not underestimate your possible peril, Lord Carrick—or his."

Morgan nodded. He did not want Jeremy exposed to such superstition. Morgan would not give him the charm, but he decided to accept the gift in the spirit he hoped it was given. "Thank you. I appreciate your concern."

Veshengo rose and started for the door. In the doorway he stopped and turned to face Morgan.

"I think you should know, my lord, that I am very fond of my niece. *I* should be extremely displeased to find she had been treated badly." Another moment and he was gone.

Morgan leaned back in his chair studying the empty doorway. Apparently Lalia's uncle had come to deliver warnings of several types.

The question of how to proceed on the information given him about Reverend Nascawan troubled Morgan's sleep for the rest of the night. The simplest thing would be to pass it on to Hastings and let him pursue it. He rejected that notion on several grounds. In the first place, the preventive water guard was not well paid, but often they were well bribed. Hastings didn't seem the sort, but you could never be sure. In the second place, he did not want to attract more animosity toward himself than was necessary. The most important place was that he wanted to catch the actual perpetrators, not just their onshore confederates.

Accordingly, he decided to do a little looking around himself. He had James saddle Demon, his favorite black, and set out on a tour of the countryside the following morning. The parson's cottage lay a little distance outside the village, but as it gave every evidence of being occupied, he could see nothing that looked suspicious.

Morgan grinned, brushing his curls away from his forehead. After his last encounter with the reverend, paying an afternoon call hardly seemed the proper course of action. He would have to return after dark and lurk about, where he might see a load brought in or perhaps even find a way into the basement, as the Gypsies must have done.

He rode back along the cliffs, trying to decide which was the likeliest cove in which goods could be brought ashore. The possibilities were endless. The pirates might choose a different location every night. His best chance lay in catching the knaves red-handed.

Morgan turned Demon away from the sea and made his way back to Merdinn's lane. Just before he emerged from the wooded motte, the view of the house and lawn opened up before him. Near the flower beds Lalia and Jeremy were engaged in a noisy game involving a ball, while their bodyguards lounged in the shade near the main doorway of the house. He paused to admire the scene.

Suddenly, movement from the woods across the cove caught his eye. A huge hound had cleared the trees and the gully and was now bounding across the grass toward the players. Morgan stood in his stirrups for a better look. The dog was not one of his. Alarm flooded him, and he set his heels to the horse's sides. At the same moment he glimpsed Lalia's grandmother hurrying toward her from the housekeeping wing, making surprisingly good speed in spite of her heavy walking stick.

As the hound came into their line of sight, Andrew and Zachary began running to intercept it. They were going to arrive too late. They were too far away. Morgan kicked Demon again, and the stallion charged across the lawn at a full gallop. Lalia looked up from her preoccupation with her game, flung the ball at the animal, and quickly stepped in front of Jeremy. The dog leapt at her.

Her grandmother jumped between them, shrieking, "*Muló!*" She swung her stick, but the hound dodged away. The footmen had pistols in their hands now, but could not shoot into the group around the dog. Lalia looked toward the sound of thundering hooves and seized her grandmother's arm, pulling her away from the hound. The old woman continued to flail with her cane.

The snarling beast also heard the oncoming horse. Surrendering to a superior force, it spun away from the fray and fled back toward the cove. Both footmen fired, but the dog ran on, unharmed. Several of the stable-hands, alerted by the commotion, pursued it toward the trees, brandishing various implements. Morgan was turning his mount to follow when he was stopped by a scream from Lalia.

"Daj!"

Turning, he spied Mrs. Veshengo crumpled into a heap on the ground. Leaving the chase to the grooms, he reined in and sprung out of his saddle. Lalia knelt beside her grandmother, sobbing and calling her name. One glance told him that Jeremy's bodyguards had wisely stayed with their charge, so he turned his attention to the women, gently moving Lalia aside so that he could lift her grandmother to a sitting position.

The old woman's face was gray with pain and she clutched her chest, gasping for breath and muttering, "*Muló*. Wolf. *Muló*."

Morgan shouted for James. The older man came hurrying from the direction of the stable. "Take Demon and ride for Dr. Lanreath. Go!" As James climbed into the saddle, Morgan scooped the fallen woman into his arms and stood. "Zach, you two get Jeremy into the house. Lalia, show me her room."

Lalia ran ahead of him and pulled the door open. As Morgan strode across the lawn with his burden, the old woman continued to murmur, "*Muló, muló.*"

* * *

Dr. Lanreath straightened up from listening to Daj's heart, patting her comfortingly on the shoulder. "You will be all right after a little rest, I think. This was just a spasm, but it *is* your heart, you know. You must not go racing to any more rescues. It won't stand much more of that." He turned to Lalia who covered tears of relief with both hands. "I will give her a composer, so she should sleep for the rest of the night. Keep her in bed with light food, if you can, tomorrow, also."

Lalia sniffed and nodded. "Thank you, Doctor. I have tried to get her to consult you before, but she will not. She prefers her own remedies."

"Hmm." The doctor smiled. "They may be as good as mine." He turned to Daj. "Do you use foxglove?" She nodded. "As I thought, nothing better. But you take *my* tea tonight." He handed Lalia a packet.

"I'll see that she takes it." Lalia walked Lanreath to the door of the room. "Thank you so much for coming. She...she is all I have."

"Of course." He squeezed her hand. "I'll see you again in the morning."

The door closed behind him and Lalia turned to Morgan, who stood back in the shadows. "And thank you, Lord Carrick. I'll stay with her tonight."

Morgan nodded and reached for the bellpull. "I'll order us some supper brought in, and some hot water for her medicine."

Us? Good heavens! Did he mean to stay? Lalia glanced up at him with alarm. She couldn't bear to have him so near. Already she ached inside. "You...you don't need to stay. I can take care of her."

His lordship pulled up two chairs. "I'm sure you can. But who will take care of you?"

*   *   *

Lalia awoke, still in the chair that Morgan had pulled near Daj's bed for her. A blanket covered her. Where had that come from? At some time near morning she had obviously fallen asleep. She looked at Daj anxiously, but her grandmother snored peacefully, having accepted the doctor's medicine with a minimum of protest. Lalia stretched.

"Good morning."

"Oh!" Lalia jumped at the greeting. His lordship sprawled in another chair a few feet away from her, the black shadow of his beard darkening his chin. "Have you been here all night?"

He yawned. "Yes, I have decided to give up sleeping. I seem to be doing very little of it lately."

"I—I'm sorry. There was no need for you to stay. I would have awakened if she had called out."

"Don't look so guilty. I'm sure you would have." He stood and stretched. "But I would not have heard *you* call had I been above stairs in my room. I—"

A knock on the door interrupted him, and Lalia hastily smoothed her hair and straightened her skirts. Dr. Lanreath came in and, after listening to Daj's heart, confirmed his opinion that she would recover from yesterday's excitement. "And now I want the two of you to get some sleep, before I have two more patients."

Lalia opened her mouth to insist that she felt well enough to watch Daj through the day, but Morgan firmly grasped her arm and ushered her and the doctor out of the room. He did not relax his grip after they parted from Dr. Lanreath, but guided her tired steps up the stairs to her room.

Once inside it, he turned and spoke sternly. "I will send Mrs. Carthew to care for your grandmother.

So…will you ready yourself for bed, or must I do it for you?''

A spark of rebellion flared in Lalia's exhausted brain. ''You will do no such thing. I will go to bed if and when I wish to.''

''Have it your own way, then.'' He seated her on the side of the bed, knelt and removed her shoes.

Lalia tried to pull her feet out of his grip and, when he reached under her skirt for her garters, indignantly swatted at his hands. ''My lord! That will be quite enough, I thank you!''

He kept his hold on her ankles and grinned. ''Will you promise to go to bed? I find this very pleasant. I would as lief continue.''

Lalia gazed at him in exasperation. The wretch would do it. ''Go away and leave me alone.''

His lordship sobered and released her. ''Is that what you truly want, Lalia?'' He stood and smoothed her hair back from her face. ''For me to leave you alone—forever?''

A lump rose in Lalia's throat. ''Y-yes.''

''I don't believe you.'' Morgan sat beside her on the bed and put his arm around her shoulders, pulling her close.

Tears of fatigue and misery trickled down her face. Lalia sniffed determinedly, but to no avail. The dratted tears continued fall. She swallowed a sob.

Morgan pulled out his handkerchief and, after wiping her face gently with it, gave it to her. ''I don't want that, either. I can't bear the thought of giving you up. I just don't know at this moment what is right for me to do. I understand your misgivings about living as my mistress, but I have never before formed a lasting attachment, Lalia, so I am afraid to predict my future feelings. I don't know if I am capable of constancy—and you deserve no less. And marriage…marriage would badly complicate my plans for Jeremy's future.''

''I never expected marriage from you, my lord.'' Lalia choked back another sob. ''Nor from anyone else.'' She was feeling sorry for herself—something she should not allow. At the moment, however, worn out and forlorn, it seemed perfectly justified.

''A lonely prospect.'' He studied her quietly for a few moments. ''I don't want that for you.''

''But I know I am not the sort of woman…''

He laid his hand over her mouth. ''Don't say that. You are a very desirable woman whose circumstances are very difficult. Any man would be fortunate to have you as a wife—including me. It is just that… I must consider a number of things.''

Lalia sniffed and gazed into his eyes. ''I know that, Morgan. I will not ask anything of you.''

''I hope you will not ask me to leave you. Not now. This may be the only time we have.'' He stood, regarding her soberly. ''And please… Please, don't run from me and lock me out. There is no need for that. I would never hurt you or force you. Nor will I press you now. You also need time to think. And you need sleep.''

He pulled her to her feet, turning her to unfasten the back of her dress. He briefly touched his lips to her bare back, then turned her to face him.

''Now go to bed.''

Morgan slept for the better part of the day. Late afternoon found him once more atop the wall with his spyglass. Today, in addition to scanning the ocean, he also scrutinized the woods along the cliffs. The hound had disappeared into them yesterday, and its pursuers

had lost it. Nor had a search today turned up any sign
of it. Where had the bloody thing come from? And
where did it go?

One opinion on the subject was shortly forthcoming.
Hearing his name called, Morgan looked down to find a
familiar figure standing near the wall. So Yoska Veshengo moved about in the daytime as well as at night.
Morgan climbed down.

"Good afternoon, my lord." The Gypsy bowed politely.

"Good day, Veshengo. Have you come to see your
mother again?"

"Of course. Word reached me of her collapse yesterday. She was so frightened, I feared her poor heart might
stop." He shook his head sadly. "One dislikes seeing
his parents declining, but unfortunately, the process is
inevitable." He brightened a bit. "But I believe she has
survived this encounter."

"So the doctor assured us."

Lalia's uncle studied him, eyes narrowed. "You still
do not believe in the *muló.*"

"I fail to see what that dog had to do with our noc-
turnal visitations."

"Ah. But the *muló* can take another body—often a
wolf. And as England no longer has wolves…" The man
shrugged. "This spirit is very vindictive. You must give
the boy the talisman—he is a target as well as my niece.
The dog might have seriously injured both of them. My
mother is too feeble to protect them. That is why she
sent for us."

Morgan rubbed his chin, but decided not to comment.
Lalia's words came back to him. *Daj always knows.* So
it seemed. Every time their ghost walked, she appeared
as if by magic.

Veshengo accepted his silence, shrugging again. "Very well. I cannot compel you. I appreciate your care of my mother, my lord. I assure you, whatever happens, I will provide for her, but it is better that she has a quiet home."

Morgan nodded. "I am happy to furnish her one. She is an interesting lady."

"Indeed she is." Veshengo nodded his agreement. "Did you know that a new keeper has been appointed for the lighthouse? A man named Breney."

"George Breney? What happened to Old Tom?" As if he didn't know. Bones under the bone fire.

"No one knows. He has not been seen for some time. I think we can guess."

"Almost certainly." Morgan frowned, his anger flaring in his chest. An old man—murdered and burned. "Now what does that mean, I wonder?"

"Who can say? But it seems to me that the lighthouse bears watching, as well as the parsonage."

"And…?" Morgan raised an inquiring eyebrow.

The Gypsy smiled. "We hear things. If I have further news, I will bring it."

He bowed his farewell and strolled off toward the lane. Morgan hoped that meant that the Roma would be doing the watching.

And that he could trust them.

She would have to be the one to do it. As difficult as that might be, Lalia knew she must. Morgan would not approach her again. She had heard in his voice, when he'd helped her to bed, how hurt he had been when she'd fled from him, yet he had explained his feelings and respected hers. When she arrived for dinner, he had been cordial, polite, absolutely correct in his behavior. Leaving it to her, as he promised, to decide.

Well, she had decided.

She couldn't be any more unhappy at the end of the summer than she was now. She might as well enjoy what time fate had given her to feel at least wanted if not loved. To feel the warmth of another body against hers. To feel the rush of desire through her blood. To see the heat in his lordship's emerald-green eyes. Memories to store away against leaner times.

Memories of more than two nights of passion.

Lalia let Sarah help her out of her dinner gown and sent her away without allowing her to brush her hair. Hands shaking, she donned a white, silk nightgown and robe heavy with lace, both much too sheer, too revealing. Oh, heaven. Could she actually do this? Perhaps if her hair were down she would feel more covered. Yet she somehow felt braver with it up, the elegant coiffeur creating a fragile shield of propriety.

It took three tries before she could actually let her knuckles fall in a light rap on the wooden panels of his door. Part of her hoped he was not in his bedchamber, after all, although she had distinctly heard him enter it. A vain hope.

He opened the door.

Lalia looked at her feet.

She heard a quiet sigh of relief and satisfaction, and a warm hand closed around her arm and drew her through the door. She heard it close behind her. Slowly she let her gaze travel to his face. The fire in the green eyes rivaled that in the emerald pin holding his cravat. Only deeper, hotter.

"Lalia."

One word. One word imbued with all the longing of

the ages. He led her to a spot beside the bed where the flicker of the reading candles fell full on her.

"Sweet torment." He framed her face with his hands and gazed into her eyes. Lalia stood silent, her voice frozen somewhere in her throat. "Gentle lady."

Morgan traced her throat with one finger, letting it trail down the neckline of the gown, his eyes following the finger. It lifted the robe off first one shoulder, then the other. The wrapper fell unnoticed at their feet. Something somewhere in Lalia's lower body tightened. She felt the slide of silk down her body once more as he guided the gown over her arms. His gaze never left her breasts. She sensed it like a weight against her skin, as she stood naked before him. Her breasts began to ache.

Morgan's eyes returned to hers. Without looking away, his hands slipped into her hair, finding a pin, pulling it free. Lalia felt the arrangement slide. He found another pin, dropped it to the carpet. A lock fell over her shoulder. Another pin. Another strand tickled her back.

One more pin and the whole heavy mass tumbled down around her.

Morgan continued to gaze into her eyes, and the heat warmed her. With both hands he drew her hair over her shoulders and smoothed it over her breasts. Sensation coursed through Lalia, increasing as his hands found her nipples through the shimmering veil, his fingers applying gentle, pulsing pressure. She sighed and closed her eyes. His breathing roughened, and his mouth found hers, his tongue demanding entrance.

When she opened to him, he did not plunge into her as she expected, but teased her lips and the tip of her own tongue with his. His hands carried on their mesmerizing work, and Lalia grasped his arms to steady herself. The whole room seemed to be swaying. But it was not the room. Her own hips moved to the rhythm of his lordship's hands and mouth.

Her whole body moved, brushing against his. He spread his legs and she felt his answering movement against her, his hard shaft pressing against her. Her knees failed, and Lalia sat suddenly on the bed. Morgan followed her down, covering her with his body, kissing her hard now. His scent welled around her.

She never quite knew when he had gotten his clothes off, but now he was standing between her legs, holding her thighs with strong hands as he forged into her. Lalia moaned as the room circled around her and clasped his body with her legs.

"Yes. Yes, Lalia." His hands were now back on her nipples. She could not stay still. She writhed and moaned as he thrust faster. Now there was a strong pressure against the taut nub straining against him. A strong, insistent pressure, demanding response. It wound the tension in her tighter and tighter, until suddenly, like a spring breaking, she flew apart. Lalia swirled away into a whirlpool of peacock colors, Morgan's voice dimly heard mingling with her own cries, his grip on her thighs scarcely felt as he surged into her urgently.

She settled back to earth, gasping, to find him collapsed across her, his breathing ragged, his solid weight filling her with a sense of wholeness.

Lalia drifted off to sleep in a cloud of peace and comfort.

Somehow he managed to straighten them on the bed. Morgan drew Lalia into his arms and cradled her against him as she slept. Back in his arms at last. Safe. His.

At least for the moment.

No! Morgan refused to consider the possibility that they might be separated soon. He would not let her go. She needed protection. *His* protection. She needed someone to care for her. She *needed* him.

He needed her.

What? That thought struck him on his blind side. When had he started feeling that? And why? Why did he need anyone? And why Lalia? For the sake of passion? There was that, of course. He could not remember ever being so caught in the toils of desire before. Nor had he ever been aware of this compulsion in him to shelter and comfort a lover. To hold her forever as he wished to do at this moment.

Forever?

Morgan stiffened. Forever was a very long time. That was indeed a disconcerting thought to a man who, but a few months ago, had found it always easier to move on than to stay. Would this feeling fade in a few months, as his other infatuations had? It didn't seem likely at the moment. But how could he know?

Never mind. For now he would keep her close and hope that time would tell. She had come back to him. He did not have to let her go yet. Convulsively, Morgan pulled Lalia to his chest.

Not yet.

Chapter Sixteen

The next evening the *Sea Witch* stood just off the headland, awaiting Morgan and the tide. The dinghy was already in the cove. Lalia had kissed him goodbye in the
privacy of her room and now bravely climbed the stairs
to her tower. She had not thought she could let him go,
but necessity had thought otherwise. She had no way of
stopping him. And would not have if she could. How
could she keep him from his duty? She could only pray
for his safe return, for more than three nights of passion.

Just as she gained the watch platform, Morgan
emerged from the back of the house and gave her a
casual wave. Lalia waved back, grateful that in the gathering twilight he could not see the tears on her cheeks.
How many of his ancestresses had stood as she did on
that tower, seeing their men off to the sea? How many
had waited there in vain for a return that never came
about, never knowing what the fate of her love had
been? Lalia took a sustaining breath and turned her attention to the view as Morgan sauntered across the lawn
toward the ship.

Lights were beginning to be lit along the coast. The
fire of the lighthouse flickered and then burned brightly.

Lalia let the familiarity of the scene comfort her. He *would* be home again. He would.

She cast another glance across the cliffs. Now it seemed to her that the lighthouse light did not burn as steadily as it should. Nor was it, now that she studied it, exactly where she thought it should be. Lalia measured the distance with her eye and scanned the coast for the well-known landmarks. She could not be mistaken. She had gazed at this vista far to often. Something was wrong.

"Morgan! Morgan wait!" Lalia commenced waving frantically, but the wind whipped her words away and Morgan continued toward the cove. "Morgan! Morgan!" Her voice took on the desperation she felt. But he could not hear her. And she could not get down the tower before he climbed down to the dinghy. "Morgan!"

As though something of her feelings had communicated themselves to him, Morgan paused at the head of the path and looked back at her. Gasping with relief, Lalia renewed her gesturing, beckoning him to the tower. He hesitated, glanced at the sea consideringly, and turned toward the tower. Striding toward her almost at a run, he dived into the tower door. Lalia hurried to fling open the door at the top of the damaged stairs to provide him with enough light to climb them.

"What is it, Lalia? I must not tarry long."

"The light. Morgan, the light is in the wrong place."

A bit out of breath, he pulled out his spyglass and followed her pointing finger. "How? Wait…I see. It is too near— Probably this side of Sad Day Cove instead of… Damnation!" He whirled and raced down the steps, shouting back "I must go. I'll speak with you later."

He tore across the lawn at a full run and bounded down the trail, quickly being lost to Lalia's anguished gaze.

Morgan was shouting orders before he was even on board. The cutter's master brought her about and, mounting full sail, they glided downwind toward the spurious fire. Dark had fallen now and there was no moon, and though Morgan alternately paced the deck and peered through the spyglass, the starlight showed him little save the treacherous light on the headland.

Morgan's heart sank. A ship would be expecting to hug the coast once it cleared the lighthouse. That fire would lead them directly into the jaws of Sad Day Cove. As the *Sea Witch* rounded the last headland, he saw the lanterns of a shipping vessel, a brig, just entering the cove. The ship's master had perceived the danger and was attempting to steer his vessel out to sea, but another ship, a lugger, blocked his way, forcing him toward the reefs.

Training his glass on the lugger, Morgan could see the steel of many cannons glinting in her running lights. She had her quarry neatly trapped. The captain of the first ship must either choose the rocks of the inlet, or come near enough to his attacker to be boarded. Preparations to fire could now be seen aboard both crafts, but the brig was clearly outgunned and being pulled by the currents much too close to the jagged stone teeth.

"Fire a shot!" Morgan snapped out the order, and within seconds the *Sea Witch*'s first cannon sounded. At the sound, the lugger began to pull away, running with the wind past the cove. Morgan prepared to give chase until a cry from the rigging stopped him.

"It's the *Lark!*"

Morgan directed his glass to the distressed brig and a

string of curses burst from him. The ship was his. And she was in trouble. Although her master tried valiantly to pull out of the cove, the cliff blocked the wind, creating unreliable eddies. The currents forced him inexorably toward the rocks. Morgan cursed again.

He could not bring the *Sea Witch* to the aid of the *Lark* without catching himself in the same predicament. Somehow he must help her from a distance. A glance at the fleeing lugger told him that he could not do so and have any hope of catching the predator. Morgan didn't hesitate.

"Ready a harpoon. We'll shoot her a line." He kept his eye fixed to his glass until he heard the report of the harpoon gun. The range was long, but he dared not bring the *Sea Witch* into the clutches of the adverse currents. A shout went up from both vessels as the harpoon buried itself in the wood of the *Lark*. Eager hands grasped for the attached line. Morgan shouted another order and the *Sea Witch* turned several points, heading out to open water.

The *Lark*'s master adjusted his rigging for the new heading, calling on the wind for every ounce of assistance. A hard jerk told Morgan that the line, now tied fast, had come taut. The *Sea Witch* slowed, but the wind was almost directly astern now. With a little luck, he might succeed in bringing the *Lark* out. She gained headway a few lengths at a time. If he could only get her out of the lea of the precipice...

A flurry of shots from the top of the headland caused Morgan to spin around and look upward. Against the backdrop of the deceptive fire he could see figures running. As he watched, the fire began to break apart. Someone was putting it out. Now who...?

Suddenly the *Sea Witch* sprang forward, the *Lark* following in her wake. The wind was solidly behind them now. Another cheer went up.

"She's free, my lord."

Morgan heaved a sigh of relief at his captain's words. The crew of the *Lark* cast off the line and the men of the *Sea Witch* turned the windlass to bring it in. Morgan glanced up again. The headland was now dark, the fire extinguished. He searched for the lugger with his glass. She had long since disappeared, her lights doused.

"Bloody hell!"

Lalia had been dozing fitfully, too anxious to really sleep. The first pale light of day had barely made its way over the horizon and into her window when a soft sound from Morgan's bedchamber roused her. She slid out of bed and opened the connecting door a crack. Morgan turned quickly at the sound, a smile breaking over his face when he saw her. She entered the room tentatively, and he opened his arms. Lalia flung herself into them.

"Oh, Morgan." She clasped him tightly around the waist. "I was so worried."

He held her close, stroking her hair with his free hand, his smoky masculine scent enveloping her. "Very flattering, but as you see, I have come to no harm."

"Thank God." She looked up at him, tears of relief burning behind her eyelids. "What did you find?"

"I found that your alarm came just in the nick of time." He bent briefly to kiss the tears away. "Without it I would have wasted my time searching in the wrong place. The pirates had trapped another of my ships at Sad Day Cove. We drove them off with a shot, but I was obliged to aid my ship back into open water. The damned blackguards got away in the dark." One big hand slid down her back to her hips, pressing her closer.

"Had I not come upon them when I did, I'd have lost the *Lark* and probably all her people."

Lalia found herself torn between disappointment and relief. At least Morgan had not been involved in a sea battle. "Could you identify their ship?"

"*I* couldn't, but we escorted the *Lark* into the harbor, and I spoke with my captain. He said the name on the bow was *Harpy.*"

"An apt name." Lalia shuddered. "But why would anyone wish to name their ship after such a hideous being?"

"Why does anyone wish to become a pirate in the first place?" Morgan had backed them across the room as they spoke and now sank into a chair, pulling Lalia into his lap.

She snuggled into the secure warmth of his shoulder. "They must have hideous souls."

"Indeed they must." He tipped her chin up, and Lalia luxuriated in the long, soft kiss.

When he lifted his head, she sighed and rested her head against him again while he gazed off into the middle distance. At last she asked, "A penny for your thoughts."

He smiled down at her. "I was giving some thought to the subject of coincidence. Tell me, Lalia, how many ships do you think pass along this coast each day?"

"Good heavens. I couldn't begin to guess, but there must be a great many." She gave him an inquiring glance. "Why?"

"With so much possible prey, what are the odds that our marauders should choose two of my ships in such rapid succession?"

Lalia sat up in his lap, her eyebrows drawn together.

"I couldn't say precisely, but they must be very much against such an occurrence."

"Just so."

"You have an enemy." Lalia's heart sank. Another danger.

"I probably have several in the pirate trade. As I told you, I have dealt with them before."

"Revenge, then?"

"Very likely." Morgan lifted her braid and began to undo it. "But whoever it may be, I disposed of them before, and I shall do so again. Now I know where to start hunting. I must concentrate on my own ships." He combed his fingers through the liberated tresses and lifted a lock to his lips. "Your hair smells so good. Let us forget, for the moment, about these outlaws." He brushed his mouth against Lalia's throat and she sighed at the rasp of his unshaved chin, closing her eyes and dropping her head back.

By the time he had worked his way down to her breasts, she was gasping for breath. An unwelcome thought intruded. "But, my lord, your valet will…"

He stood with her in his arms and started toward the bed. "Dagenham will not disturb me before noon."

"But Sarah…"

"Will believe that you are in the tower." He laid her on the neatly turned-back sheet. "And all our doors are safely locked."

It took only the feeling of his lips around her nipple to effect Lalia's complete surrender.

Lalia looked up with surprise as Morgan declined his after-dinner port later that evening and rose from his chair. "You are going out again tonight? It feels to me that a storm is building."

"Yes, I am aware of that, too, but as the blackguards missed their prey last night, I feel it likely that they will make another attempt. It is also likely that we will be driven back in. I can but try."

Lalia nodded and walked him to the door, her heart sinking. It was bad enough that he must deal with vicious men. Now she must also worry about the storm. But like all dutiful women of seafaring men, she would not tell him that. Not while he was leaving. "Do take care, Morgan."

"I will. Don't worry." He kissed her quickly and trotted across the lawn toward the cove.

Lalia sighed and made her way to the staircase. After carefully locking her bedchamber doors, both to the corridor and to Morgan's bedroom, she tried the panel that concealed the hidden stair. It was firmly fastened. She checked her pistol for priming and laid it on the bed table.

Then she went to the window and studied the sea. Yes, the weather was definitely brewing something. The sails of the *Sea Witch* were no longer in sight. The offshore winds had carried Morgan away in the brief time that it had taken her to climb the stairs and secure her room.

As she stood there in the dark, the wind suddenly died. An eerie calm descended over the castle, heavy, oppressive. Even the roar of the breakers seemed quiet, subdued by the hush. The room grew very warm.

Lalia shivered.

She loved storms, but this sense of brooding disturbed her. A film of perspiration coated her face, and the beating of her heart grew loud in her ears. It was as if some unseen but powerful menace lay in wait for an unsuspecting world. Perhaps it did. Her fears for Morgan surged up in her breast. He and the *Sea Witch*—wherever they were—would lie becalmed, drifting out with the tide, until the wind picked up. Until the storm broke. Then he would be at its mercy.

And she could do nothing.

Like the dutiful women of all seafaring men.

Nothing at all.

Lalia sighed and turned away from the window. Well, at least if Morgan could not move, neither could the pirates. She undressed in the dark, unwilling to add even the small flame of a candle to the damp heat of the room. A gibbous moon, veiled by thin clouds, allowed enough light for her to sponge her face and breasts. Even the water in the basin was warm.

She turned back the covers of the bed and lay down on the sheet. Heavens, she was tired. The disturbances of the past weeks were taking their toll on her. Not to mention many nights with a great deal of lovemaking but very little sleep. Lalia yawned. But she would probably not sleep much tonight, either.

She must have done so, however. When the sound roused her, she had been dreaming. Something vague and fuzzy, but far from comforting, dispersed into the dark as she came to herself.

Lalia sat up. A stiff breeze from the sea now flowed through the window and thunder rumbled in the distance. Perhaps that is what she had heard. Lightning danced on the horizon. The air was cool now and smelled of sea and rain.

She heard the noise again.

Lalia froze, waiting, listening. Again. It came from Morgan's room. Perhaps he had come home. She slid off the tall bed and started for the door. Another bump

stopped her. It sounded as though someone was blun-
dering about in the dark. Morgan knew his own room
much too well to be doing that. She turned back and
picked up the pistol. Should she call for help? Would
the guards in Jeremy's room hear her? If not, or if they
were slow to respond, the intruder would get away at
the sound of the alarm.

She needed to be able to see. Lalia lit the night candle
on her bed table and took a deep breath to steady her
hand. She quietly turned the key in the connecting door.
As she pushed it open, a figure leaning into Morgan's
wardrobe spun around, then stopped abruptly, arrested
by the sight of Lalia's pistol.

"Roger!" The pistol wavered. "What are you doing
in here?"

"Good evening, little sister." The crouching form
straightened. "I thought you were asleep."

"Obviously." The shock made Lalia's voice sharp.
"And you also clearly thought his lordship was away."

"His lordship *is* away." Looking relaxed now, Roger
took a step toward her. "I made sure of that before I
came in."

Lalia brought the pistol up. "Don't, Roger. Don't
come any closer. You are frightening me."

Roger shoved something into his pocket—a paper.
"Why, Lalia, you don't think I'd hurt you, do you?"

"I don't know what you would do." Anger and suspicion stiffened her resolve. "I hardly know you at all."

He moved another foot closer. "But I, on the other
hand, am quite certain you will not hurt *me*. Gentle little
Lalia? Rescuer of kittens and the downtrodden? Shoot
your own brother?" He took another step. "You won't
do it."

"No, but *I* will."

Chapter Seventeen

At the sound of Morgan's voice, Lalia and Roger both whirled. His lordship stood just inside the door to the corridor, his own pistol leveled at Roger. Roger moved to lunge for Lalia, but the steely voice stopped him in his tracks.

"Don't."

Roger didn't. Morgan gestured with the pistol. "Take off your coat. Now."

Lalia's brother struggled out of the tight coat, finally dropping it near his feet. Morgan shook his head. "Don't try it, Poleven. You forfeited your life when you broke into my house. Only your kinship to Lalia is keeping you alive. Back up and sit in that chair."

Roger slowly complied, keeping a wary eye on Morgan.

Morgan held out a hand for Lalia's pistol. "Lalia, see if there is a weapon in his coat."

She gave him the gun and knelt by the coat, soon pulling out a small pistol. She laid it aside. "Morgan, I saw him put a paper in his pocket... Ah, here it is."

She stood and perused the document. Morgan kept his eyes firmly on Roger. "What is it?"

"I—I don't know. It sounds very legal." Lalia wrinkled her brow. "I don't understand it. It has my name in it and…" She turned the paper over. "That is my father's signature."

"Hmm. That's interesting. What is it, Poleven?"

Roger glared at him sullenly. "Read it yourself."

"I shall. But not right now. You and I have a score to settle." Morgan moved up to loom over Roger, anger in every line of his body. Roger pulled back into the chair. Morgan's voice rose. "You bastard! Why have you been tormenting your sister? Didn't you hurt her enough by marrying her to Hayne in the first place? Now you have to frighten her half to death with these hauntings, ruin her gowns. What were you hoping for? To drive her away?"

"What? Now just a bloody minute. You better pull in your horses, Carrick. I don't know what the devil you are talking about."

"No?" Morgan shoved the pistol against Roger's forehead. "Perhaps I can refresh your memory."

Roger, apparently perceiving that his brains were likely to be decorating his lordship's chair in the immediate future, sat very still. Sweat broke out on his forehead. "No! Have you taken leave of your senses? Do I look like a ghost?"

"Morgan." Lalia's voice was soft. She touched his arm lightly.

Morgan stepped back, obviously trying to get control of his anger. "Lalia, don't defend him. He doesn't deserve it. This scoundrel deserves to be thrashed to within an inch of his life, just for what has done to you, let alone…"

"I damned well *don't* deserve that, nor all these absurd accusations, either." Roger glared indignantly.

"You haven't been breaking in to search for whatever that is?" Morgan nodded at the paper in Lalia's hand. "You haven't been playing ghost while you were at it? To terrify your sister—for your amusement, apparently. Convince me." He pulled the gun up again.

"Hold on, now. I *have* been in the house hunting several times since Hayne died. You almost caught me going through your desk the first time. After that I came at night."

Morgan looked skeptical. "Who let you in?"

Roger held up a pacifying hand. "No one had to, Carrick. A place this large always has something unfastened—especially with all the workmen coming and going. I just came in to have a look around. I haven't done anything to my sister, you have my oath."

"For whatever that is worth." Morgan relaxed slightly and took the pistol out of Roger's face.

Seeing that Morgan's rage was momentarily checked, Lalia shifted her attention back to the paper in her hand. "Hold a minute, Morgan. Let me read a little more."

Silence ensued while she lit Morgan's night candle and pored over the document, sitting on the bed. After a few tense minutes Lalia lifted her head. "I am not perfectly sure, but I think that Papa left me some money—there's something about a trust."

"Oh?" Morgan raised an eyebrow. "Let me guess who the administrator of the trust is."

"Yes. I think it is Roger, but there is something about my husband, also."

Morgan glowered at Lalia's brother. "Is it worth your life to keep this secret, or will you explain it to us? You have been looking for this?"

Roger eyed the weapon still inches from his face. He nodded. "Hayne made me give it to him. He knew...well, he threatened to tell the preventives that..." He broke off and Morgan bristled. Roger hastily added, "I *had* to, Carrick. I was to be the trustee until she married, then it would be her husband, so Hayne insisted on marrying her. Once he died..." He shrugged.

"You again became the administrator of Lalia's money. But why all this secrecy? Why hide the document?"

Poleven wiped his brow and watched Morgan through slitted eyes. "I never told her about the trust—nor did Hayne. As it was set up, neither of us could touch the principal. As trustee, we were supposed to pay her an allowance out of the interest. Hayne gave her a little of it to keep up the castle and told her it was from his rents, but he spent all those. She will have control of all the money when she is twenty-five, but he intended never to tell her about it."

He winced and pulled away as Morgan leaned over him, his voice little more than a growl. "You bastard! You spent Lalia's allowance yourselves—first you and then Hayne. And now you want to do it again."

"I'm deep in the River Tick, Carrick. I need the money badly. If I had it for another year, I might come about."

"And if you were lucky, she might never learn of its existence and you would have the income indefinitely?"

Roger shrugged again, but did not try to refute the charge. "The rest—this nonsense you are on about, ghosts, haunting, ruined clothes—you're fair and far off. I have nothing to do with that."

"And nothing, I suppose, to do with the piracy in our waters?" Morgan sneered.

"God, no!" Roger looked genuinely appalled. Morgan looked unconvinced. As he lifted the pistol, his eyes narrowed and he spoke very softly.

"And who gets the principal if Lalia dies?"

Poleven gasped in horror, throwing up a hand and cringing away from the threat in Morgan's voice. "No, Carrick! It does come to me, but I wouldn't hurt Lalia! With God as my witness. You must believe that!"

"Oh? Must I? Why?"

"Because I'm not a pirate nor a murderer! The money…the money is different. It should have been mine in the first place. My father should never have married that…" He glanced up at Morgan and stuttered for a moment. "That…that woman."

"That Gypsy, you mean." Lalia slowly lowered the paper, the import of what she was reading gradually becoming clear to her. "Is there any money left in the trust?"

"I don't know. Hayne took it over eight years ago, but I should think so. He couldn't touch the principal, only the income."

"Do you mean…" Anger began to rise in her chest. All the drudgery, the need… "Do you mean that I might have had my own money… That… You and he have been stealing my money while I all but starved! Wore used clothes… Struggled to maintain *his* property… Endured his abuse… I might have been able to leave him." Words failed her and she dropped the document into her lap.

She stared into space for several heartbeats, then covered her face with her hands.

"Papa did not forget me after all."

Morgan just wanted to get the man out of his house before the desire to kill him grew too great. He marched

Poleven downstairs and had him reveal the unlocked door. By now the storm had broken in earnest. Thunder crashed and lightning blazed. Wind pounded the house and whipped the trees. Rain cascaded from the heavens in sheets.

"You best see to your craft, Poleven." Morgan opened the door. "I saw your dinghy tied in the cove."

Roger looked out the door in dismay. "You aren't going to put me out in this, are you? I can't sail in this weather."

Morgan considered the man who had sold Lalia into virtual slavery and now had attempted to steal her inheritance for the second time. Perhaps he was not their ghost. Perhaps he would not stoop to murder. Still...

Without warning, he drew back his fist and planted the facer he had longed to administer flush against Poleven's nose. Roger stumbled backward out the door and sprawled in the mud, his nose gushing blood.

"Good night, Poleven." Morgan closed the door and locked it before proceeding to send Watford with a contingent of footmen to ensure that every opening on the first two floors of the building was secure. Then Morgan hurried back to Lalia. He found her sitting cross-legged on the floor in front of his wardrobe.

"What are you doing?" He crossed the room and lifted her to her feet, taking her into his arms.

"I was wondering where he found this paper. The envelope was glued under the bottom shelf." She pointed, and Morgan bent to examine her find.

"So." He pulled the envelope loose, glanced inside and, finding it empty, crumpled it and tossed it into the cold fireplace. "I wondered how I had not found it before."

"What did you do with Roger?"

"I showed him to the door. Or rather, I had him show *me* the door through which he entered. I showed him out of it."

A tiny chuckle emerged from Lalia. "In this storm? I guess he deserved it. Do you think he was our ghost?"

Morgan pondered the question. "I wish I knew. He sounded convincing enough, but he is probably an accomplished liar. I would say the issue is still unresolved. He *has* entered the house clandestinely, several times by his own admission. What bothers me the most is that he would benefit by your death."

Lalia frowned. "I can't believe he would try to kill me. He is dishonest, yes. But I doubt he has the resolution to kill someone in cold blood. Besides, no one has done me any physical harm."

"True." *Yet.* "Nevertheless I intend to set a guard in the hallway in addition to the ones in Jeremy's room." Morgan let the statement go at that. He didn't want to frighten her any more than necessary.

"Is he with the pirates, do you think?"

"I think that question also is still unanswered. He is certainly a good enough sailor to captain a lugger. I think we may know when I catch them, certainly not before, and possibly not then."

"Did you see any sign of the *Harpy* tonight?" Lalia snuggled closer into his shoulder.

Morgan held her a little tighter. "No. When I saw the size of the storm that was developing, I decided to come in. We might have ridden it out, but I had a strange feeling that I should return. I sent the *Sea Witch* to harbor."

"I am so grateful you did come in when you did. I don't know what would have happened otherwise."

"Otherwise, he certainly would have made off with

that document. You would never have shot him. I'm glad I heeded my hunch. How do you feel now?''

Lalia sat silent for several heartbeats, staring at the envelope in the fireplace. At last she sighed. ''Very strange. And very relieved. I hadn't realized how hurt I felt that Papa had not arranged for my future in any way, that he had apparently abandoned me completely. I guess I didn't let myself think about it. Now that I see that he did provide for me, the hurt…'' Tears welled up in her eyes, and a sob escaped her. ''Now I f-feel it.''

Morgan cradled her head against his shoulder and stroked her hair. He let her cry, hoping the old and painful emotions would dissipate. He knew nothing else to do, nothing useful to say. God, he felt helpless. Tears burned behind his own eyelids. How could anyone be so cruel to a spirit as sweet as Lalia's?

At length her sobs ceased, much to Morgan's relief. He continued to smooth her hair while the two of them sat quietly listening to the howl of the wind around the house. Eventually, another question began to nag at him.

''What will you do now that you know you have an income?''

Lalia sat up and looked at him thoughtfully. ''I'm not sure. I may find that there is nothing left in the trust, after all. Or not enough to help me. But if there is… Well, I will have more choices than I have ever had. I will have to think about it.''

More choices. She could now choose to go away. To leave him. Morgan's arms tightened around her, pulling her back against his body. God! He didn't want her to do that. But if she chose to stay…then what? All of his previous goals were whirling around him, demanding realignment. His future, once so clearly defined, now appeared murky and indistinct. He half wished that they had never discovered that damned document.

But they had.

"Your half brother will still be the administrator of the trust until you are twenty-five, but now that he is found out, he should have no recourse but to pay the allowance. Would you like for my man of business to look into this for you? He can alert the bankers." He let his hands stroke her body, her warmth assuring him that she was still in his arms, still his.

"Yes, if you please. I have no way of doing that." She snuggled closer.

"Very well." Morgan cupped the shape of her bottom, so soft, so round and womanly. His hands moved over it as though of their own accord. Down over her thigh, so welcoming. Up her side to the gentle swell of her breast. His body began to manifest his need, hardening under her legs.

She sighed. With an arm under her back, Morgan lifted her so that he might reach her breasts with his mouth. Lalia moaned and her head dropped back, exposing her throat. He devoured it, her sweet sounds driving him. When he lifted his head for a moment, she opened her eyes and he saw the deep blue of her passion.

With a choked groan, he slid off the chair, carrying her to the floor with him. He needed her. God, how he needed her. He fought his britches fastening, wrested her nightgown upward. She opened to him. He came into her with more urgency that he could remember ever before feeling. She closed around him, sheltering him. They gazed into one another's eyes for a long moment before he began to move.

Then his desire took him, took them both, fusing them into one body, one spirit. Her cries rang in his ears, his own deeper voice entwined with hers into one harmony, rising, rising, the crescendo climaxing with them.

They drifted downward slowly. Morgan rested his forehead against hers, unwilling yet to give her up. The anguish in his voice startled him. "I don't want you to go away, Lalia."

Her arms held him close.

"We must know, Morgan. We both need to know what our feelings will be in this new situation."

It must be some sort of feminine conspiracy. Much later in the day Morgan propped his feet on his desk, hands behind his head, and stared at the ceiling. The letter rested neglected in his lap. But surely his mother had never made Lalia's acquaintance, let alone that of her grandmother.

He picked up the missive again, staring at the elegant script.

My dearest son—
I received your letter of last week with great happiness. It is good to hear that my old home is being restored to its former grace and beauty.

It warms my heart that you wish for me to come there to make my home with you. I am indeed blessed to have such a loving son. But, Morgan, my dear, I must tell you that coming to Merdinn is not my wish. I am very happy in London.

But more importantly I must tell you that today Sir William Tavistock has done me the honor of asking me to be his wife. We both beg that you will look favorably on the union and give us your good wishes. Morgan, dearest, you cannot know what a comfort it is to me to have a companion for my declining years.

As for you, my cherished son, I can only hope that you will consider the benefits of matrimony for yourself. It is time to put aside the hurts of the past and move on. As much as we both love him, Jeremy can never be the earl of Carrick, and it is neither wise nor right to separate the title from the estate. I know that you will provide richly for him in any event. It is my daily prayer that you will soon find the lady to become the mother of your own children and make you as happy as I am today.

Always your affectionate,
Mother

Morgan sighed and dropped the paper on the desk. Somehow his crowning achievement was falling short of expectation on all counts. No chains, no horses, not even a boat. The crushing was going quite well, but had somehow taken on a very different significance. And now his mother no longer *wanted* to be restored to her long lost home.

Damnation!

She no longer needed his support. His mother was to marry Tavistock. Morgan pondered that fact. Sir William was a good man and blessed with a large fortune. Morgan trusted him to provide handsomely for his new wife, but… The responsibility for her that Morgan had held for fifteen years was difficult to relinquish.

For all those years, and more, he had but three goals. The restoration of his family's fortune. The utter destruction of Cordell Hayne. To regain Merdinn and to put his mother back in the home that had been torn from her. He had succeeded in all three.

Except that now his mother didn't want her home back.

She was looking forward to a new life.

And Morgan was looking back at an old one.

Jeremy and Andrew sprawled on the floor of the morning room, each maneuvering a wooden boat, while Lalia worked at some sort of fancy needlework. Zachary, a bit older and more dignified than Andrew, watched the scene indulgently from a position opposite the door. He glanced up alertly when Morgan stepped through the door, coming to his feet and bowing as his employer entered. Andrew scrambled up for a belated salute and Jeremy called out gleefully, "Look, Uncle Morgan. Andrew is the pirates, and I am you, and I am going to send his boat to the bottom."

"Very ambitious, but suppose Andrew's pirates do not wish to go the bottom?" Morgan signaled for the footmen to relax and tousled his nephew's hair.

"Oh, then we shall have a famous battle, but I am sure our side will win."

"I would think that highly likely." Morgan winked at his pirately henchman. The young man grinned.

Lalia set aside her work and smiled at him. "Good afternoon, my lord."

She had wound her braid into a tall crown atop her head, and little wisps of hair whispered around her exquisite nape. She was not wearing the concealing scarf. By dint of strong effort Morgan prevented himself from trailing a line of kisses along her neck, tasting the sensitive skin behind her ear. "Good afternoon. I am riding to the lighthouse. Would you like to accompany me? We could discuss some matters on the way."

Her face lit with pleasure, but quickly puckered into

a frown. "I would enjoy that, my lord. But I haven't ridden since…" She paused, a new expression crossing her face. "For many years," she amended.

James had told Morgan that Hayne had sold her favorite mount not long after she had married him. The cur. "Never mind, it is not something you forget, although…" He smiled ruefully. "It might not be as comfortable as it once was."

Lalia laughed. "Delicately put. I shall no doubt suffer for it tomorrow, but I would love to ride, if you have a suitable horse."

Morgan did indeed have the perfect horse. He had known as soon as the mount was brought down from London that the dainty black mare would be perfect for Lalia's petite frame. He had bought it originally for his mother who still loved to ride, but… Well, that was no longer his duty. Now he looked forward to Lalia's smile of delight when she saw the mare.

She didn't disappoint him. "Oh, Morgan. She's lovely." Lalia smoothed the horse's nose. "Do let us go immediately."

Morgan tossed Lalia into the saddle, gratified to see that she clearly knew what she was about. They talked of trivialities on the road, Lalia acquainting herself with the mare's gait and Morgan drinking in the sight of her as she did so. Her every gesture was grace itself. The subtle movements of her soft curves made his mouth water. How was he to wait until the cover of darkness and bedtime to taste them again? Morgan shifted in the saddle, suddenly uncomfortable. Better keep his mind on his riding.

As they trotted up the lane, he scanned the cottage attached to the lighthouse. Seeing no one about, he dismounted and pounded on the door. Several minutes passed without an answer. "No one seems to be here."

"Perhaps the new keeper is in the tower tending the light." Lalia shaded her eyes and gazed upward.

"Perhaps." Morgan felt no surprise. He had not expected to find anyone. Most likely Breney had abandoned his post when the false fire was lit. Or when parties as yet unknown extinguished it. Just the same... Morgan slipped his pistol from the saddle holster and climbed the stairs to the top of the lighthouse. No one. Returning to the ground, Morgan tried the door of the cottage. It opened readily, but revealed nothing except a disorderly room.

"I best send someone to mind the light tonight." He vaulted back into his saddle and turned his mount's head. "Let's ride home along the cliffs."

The whip crashed to the deck, spattering blood. Panting, he rubbed his arm. Now that his rage and lust were spent, his shoulder ached with fatigue. His target hung limply from the mast. The ragged form had long since ceased to scream excuses or even to moan. It was no more than the fool deserved. Had he followed orders, the *Lark* would now be flinders on the rocks, its cargo in the hold of the *Harpy,* its crew food for the fish.

The young men assembled on the deck watched him warily. Good! Let them see what happened to the man who cost him his prey. He flung one more order at them as he stalked away.

"Heave him over the side."

Chapter Eighteen

They rode companionably side by side along the cliffs, enjoying the changing colors of the ocean and the countryside as the sun sank slowly toward the waves. Morgan made a quick examination of the area where they discovered the ashes of the deceptive fire, but found nothing to tell him the identity of the culprits, nor who had put out the blaze.

A little farther along, he pulled in his mount, indicating a convenient boulder with a nod of his head. "Would you like to dismount for a while?"

Lalia nodded. "Yes, I confess that I am already a little saddle sore, but I am enjoying my ride too much to go home yet."

"Poor Lalia." Morgan grinned and lifted her down. "I do hope you are not too sore to…well, perhaps I should not be greedy." He glanced around them, and seeing no one else, wrapped her in his arms for a leisurely kiss. A few breathless moments later he led her to the boulder and sat beside her. They watched the breakers in silence, and Morgan gathered his thoughts.

At last he spoke. "I had a letter from my mother this morning."

Lalia looked at him with lifted eyebrows. "She's well?"

"Apparently so. She's getting married."

"Married?" Lalia turned in surprise. "Is this unexpected?"

Morgan shrugged. "It was to me, but perhaps… I don't know why I never thought of it. Sir William was certainly in her company a great deal."

"You sound a bit disappointed."

He considered that in silence for several heartbeats. "Yes, if I am honest, I must say I feel that, but I don't understand it. I'm happy for her. Tavistock will make her a good husband. It is just that… She has been in my care since I was nineteen."

"A heavy responsibility for a man so young."

"I suppose. I didn't think of that at the time. I was just determined to do a better job of it than my father had. Then, when Hayne shot me in the back, I became determined to ruin him and reclaim her home and bring her back here to her proper place." Morgan grimaced. "Now she doesn't want to come."

Lalia laid her hand on his wrist. "So your dream will not be fulfilled. I can understand your feeling dispirited."

He covered her fingers with his other hand. "This has caused me to realize something else. I have achieved my great goal. I have done what I set out to do. I have recovered my family's fortune. My home is being restored. My enemy is dead. What do I want for my life now?"

"I don't know. What *do* you want?" Lalia looked attentively into his eyes.

"That's where the devil's in it. I never gave it any thought, other than to bring my land back to prosperity.

My mother recommends marriage, and of course, my association with you has also made me think in those terms, but…''

She covered his mouth gently. ''You don't have to explain. I doubt very much that your mother would consider me a suitable bride.''

''It isn't that!'' Morgan turned and looked at her sharply. ''She would welcome you as you deserve, and even if she didn't, it is my decision.''

''And mine.'' Lalia regarded him soberly.

He glanced at her, startled. Had he, in his vanity, been assuming that she would jump at an offer from him? Yes. Yes, he had. What made him so cocksure? Before he could answer, she continued.

''Even if you were sure of your feelings, I am not sure of mine. I—I cannot hide from you how much I care for you. I have been in love with you since the first night you came here, I think. But I am by no means certain that I am ready for another husband. I need time to heal. And drifting into another marriage because I have no better choice would fair to neither of us.''

Morgan had not considered that. It was certainly not what he wanted. But he believed she did love him. That was evident in the wholehearted way she gave herself to him, worried about him. But was her love based on her need? He liked being needed. This business of his mother's marriage had shown him that. He *resented* no longer being needed. And he liked being loved.

But was need an adequate reason to love? To marry? He didn't like the sound of it. He wanted to be loved for himself, not because he was the solution to someone's problems.

At the same time another realization was taking form in his mind—the greatest reason that his revenge against

Hayne must always be incomplete. He would never see tears for Hayne on the faces of his loved ones.

The man had had none.

Hayne had loved no one, and no one had loved him.

Morgan was suddenly damned sure he didn't want that outcome in his own life.

Lalia expected him to argue with her, but he only held her hand and gazed into her face, his expression searching. She didn't know what else to say. Somehow, suddenly, she had known that even if Morgan asked her to marry him, she must not, not yet. Somehow, somewhere she must create a life for herself, become her own person, to become a whole person, before she could give herself to anyone. Even to someone she loved.

Especially someone she loved.

She lifted one hand and stoked his hair back from his face, then rested her palm against his cheek. "Do you understand?"

"I think so." Morgan mirrored her gesture with his own, cupping her face in his big hand. They sat thus, silent for several heartbeats, gazing at one another. "It seems we have much to consider." He slid his hand behind her neck. Drawing her to him, he placed a lingering, thoughtful kiss on her lips, then looked deep into her eyes. "These desires will not be denied, Lalia, but we must learn more of what they mean for us."

She nodded, and he stood, helping her to rise.

They took their time riding toward Merdinn, enjoying just being together and the twilight as it crept in from the eastern sky. From time to time they paused to gaze at the sea, watching the breakers of the incoming tide crashing against the rocks. They were almost back to Merdinn when something on the crest of a wave caught Lalia's attention.

"Look, Morgan, what is that?"

His gaze followed her pointing finger. "Where? Oh, I see." He scowled and nudged his stallion a little closer to the edge.

Lalia pulled her mount up beside him and squinted for a better view. In a flash of intuition recognition struck her. "Oh, God, Morgan. It is a person."

He grasped her bridle and abruptly turned the horses away from the sight. Both the mare and Lalia protested this cavalier treatment, the mare with a toss of her head, and Lalia with an exclamation.

"This is not something I want you to see." Morgan urged them into a canter. "I will take you home and come back."

And none of Lalia's objections moved him one iota from that intention.

Lalia ordered dinner held back until Morgan returned from the expedition to retrieve the body they had seen from the cliff. He had taken several men with him and, also, had sent for the doctor and Hastings. Several hours passed before he came into the drawing room, weary and disheveled.

"I'm sorry to be so late. You must be perishing from hunger." He sprawled into a chair and loosened his cravat. "Let me but catch my breath, and I shall go and change for dinner."

Lalia poured out a glass of sherry and handed it to him. "I see no reason that you may not be comfortable in your own house. Catch your breath and drink your wine, and we shall go directly to the table. I gave the order when I heard you come in."

He captured her hand as he took the sherry from her, smiling up at her. "Can you stand me in all my dirt?"

She scrutinized him with mock severity. "Perhaps. Just this once I may be able to tolerate you."

After a grateful swallow, he set the glass down, pulled his cravat off and, with her help, shrugged out of his fashionably tight coat. "You are a very gracious lady."

He slipped an arm around her shoulders and brushed a kiss across her lips. The warm scent of his body wrapped around Lalia, causing her to take a sudden breath and reflect that she could tolerate him very well with his collar open and his sleeves rolled up. Apparently taking her sigh as encouragement, he took her in both arms and kissed her more thoroughly.

When they were both gasping for breath, he lifted his head and cast a guilty look over her shoulder. "I best leave off before we are discovered."

Lalia nodded and hastily shook out her skirt and patted her hair. He offered her his arm and they strolled toward the dining room.

"But tell me, my lord, what you learned."

Morgan's smile disappeared and a crease formed between his eyebrows. "I hesitate to tell you. The implications... It was George Breney."

"The man who was supposed to be watching the light?"

"The same." They entered the dining room and Morgan held Lalia's chair for her to be seated before taking his own. "I suspected that he was in league with the pirates, but I had not expected to find him dead. Now I wonder if they killed him in order to put out the true light. But why would they have—" He broke off frowning.

Something in his expression sent a chill through Lalia. "Why would they what?"

"They... I should not tell you more. I'm glad I brought you away before you saw him."

"Come now, Morgan, you cannot say that much and not finish." Lalia sent him an exasperated glance.

Morgan considered for a long moment, but finally answered. "He had been beaten until the bones of his back... Suffice it to say, he was probably dead before he hit the water."

Lalia covered her mouth with both hands. "Dear God."

"I'm sorry." He reached across the table and clasped her hand. "I should not have said as much. I would not have, but that it preys on my mind. You didn't know him, did you?"

She shook her head. "No. I didn't, but how could any human do that to another?"

"They have ceased to be human." He gave her a wary glance. "And don't think I am talking of ghosts."

"No. No, I know what you meant. Isn't there something in the Bible...something about, 'they are as ravening beasts'?"

Morgan grinned. "You have me there. I'm not all that well informed on biblical quotations. But of course, that is very apt. They have become beasts. But we knew that. We have seen their work before. I have *my* work cut out for me to stop them."

Lalia's heart sank. "Will you go out tonight?"

"No. It is too late now." A sly smile curved his lips. "Besides, I do not feel like hunting pirates tonight."

The hour being late, they made short work of dinner and retired. True to their carefully maintained fiction of propriety, they made their way to their bedchambers, nodding a greeting to Eric, the new guard, where he sat in the hallway. Morgan opened Lalia's door and glanced quickly around the room, his eyes concentrating for a long moment on the priest's hole. Satisfied, he turned back to the corridor. "It looks as if the coast is clear." Then in a whisper, "I'll come in as soon as I've washed up. I've already sent Dagenham to bed."

Giving her a hasty kiss, Morgan stepped back into the hall and entered his own room. Just as he sat down to pull off his boots, a small strangled sound from the next room, almost too soft to hear, caught his attention. He went to the connecting door and peeked in.

"Lalia? Did you call?" Another choked sound emerged.

Lalia stood by the bed, clutching the post for support.

"Lalia!" Morgan dashed across the room and slipped an arm around her waist. "What's the matter?" She silently pointed to the bed, then jerked around and buried her head in his shoulder. His gaze followed her gesture. "Good God!"

On the carefully arranged pillow lay two bloated, severed fingers.

"Eric!" Morgan sprang to unlock the door, half dragging the wilting Lalia, shouting orders as he ran. "Rouse Andrew and Zachary, but don't let them leave Jeremy. Then look around. Someone is about." He tugged on the bell cord with enough vigor to summon several servants at a run. In the moments before they arrived, he settled Lalia in a chair.

"My lord, you rang?" Watford hurried in, puffing for breath. Just beyond him Sarah could be seen over his shoulder.

"Watford, send someone to the cove immediately. Find out if anyone has tried to use the escape tunnel tonight. And take these away." Morgan scooped the fingers up in his handkerchief and thrust them at the startled Watford. "Sarah, your mistress needs a dose of hartshorn. Quickly. And send Joseph to help Eric."

Having dispatched his forces, Morgan turned back and knelt before Lalia. She had slumped forward with her head on her knees. "Lalia?"

She lifted her head and leaned back into the chair, weakly muttering. "I will *not*…faint…again."

Morgan eyed her pale countenance closely. "That remains to be seen. Ah. Here is Sarah." He took the glass from the maid and held it to Lalia's lips. She sipped and turned away with a wry face. "Oh, no, you don't. You must drink it—all of it."

Lalia did as she was bid, her color returning slightly. She tried to give him a brave smile. "Alas, I have fallen back in my determination not to be frightened. I may be courageous in the face of dripping water and puffs of smoke—even a soaked wardrobe—but disembodied fingers…" She shuddered. "I just can't…"

"No." Morgan pulled her to him in spite of the presence of her maid. It was highly unlikely that the girl remained in ignorance of their liaison, in any event. "Severed digits are another matter. I'm sorry, Lalia. I didn't even think to look at the bed. But rest assured, those fingers came from the body of George Breney—not the hand of Cordell Hayne. We also found that injury on Breney's corpse. Damnation! This is a direct threat. The pirates are involved in this."

"But how could they possibly know that I dreamt of his hands and the fingers falling…" Lalia leaned back in the chair and covered her mouth with one hand. "And why would they care?"

"Another of those very persistent but unanswered questions." Morgan rubbed his chin, his eyes narrow.

"Servants' gossip, very likely. But… I wonder if your brother saw Hayne's body."

"My *half* brother," Lalia corrected automatically, her eyes dark gray with distress. "But even if Roger *did* intend to make away with me, why would he do something like this?"

"Why would anyone do something like this? When I find the answer to that question, I suspect I'll find the answer to several more. In the meantime Joseph will also watch in the corridor. I want someone outside this door every minute, as well as in the tunnel." He strode to the priest's hole and confirmed that the door was fast. "Until now I have thought that the target of these mysterious occurrences was Jeremy—that the rest was diversion. Now I begin to doubt that. I wish I could have someone in the room with you when I am at sea, but that is a privilege I intend to reserve to myself—even if I must trust the pirate hunting to the captain of the *Sea Witch* for a time."

Lalia's head still swirled with images of rotting flesh and disintegrating corpses. Her stomach clenched and bile threatened to rise into her mouth. Shaking, she covered her eyes with one hand. "Oh, Morgan! Who hates me so?"

He returned to her and pulled her to her feet so that he could hold her close. "Hush, now. No one could hate you. They are choosing to torment you for some reason of their own—one that a sane person cannot fathom."

"But I must have made an enemy." Lalia shook her head. She could feel the aura of hatred twining around her. "Do you think that Reverend Nascawan could be so angry at me that…"

"I don't know. Jealousy can bring about some very strange actions, and he did have the cloak. But this studied cruelty…it is hard to know who would be capable of it. He might be.''

''I never thought of him as cruel—just unpleasant—although I must admit I don't know him very well. And Roger has never been *cruel* to me.''

''Except when he married a young girl to an animal like Hayne.''

''Well… Perhaps he didn't know how it would be. My husband, of course…'' Lalia let the comment trail away. She didn't want to remember life at her husband's hands.

''Is gone now. Mercifully. Do not think of him. I am here now, and I *will* keep you safe, Lalia. And I *will* find out who is doing this to you. And he *will* regret it.''

Morgan had held her in his arms throughout the night—at first simply to stem her terror, but slowly they began to respond to the ever-present spark of desire between them. The passion, riding on the crest of the wave of fear broke over them both, submerging them in a whirlpool of emotion that swept them almost to dawn. He left her sleeping later that morning and rode out to find her uncle.

He could only hope that his presence had reassured her and his lovemaking had distracted her. It certainly distracted him. But in spite of his distracting memories, he could not get the anxiety for Lalia's safety out of his mind. And he could see her own fear in her haunted eyes every time he looked at her. The sight created a wrenching ache in his heart and the fire of anger in his gut. His fury toward the author of this anguish was perhaps greater than that he had held toward Hayne.

Morgan found the Gypsy camp with little trouble. He reined Demon in at a respectful distance from the brightly painted wagons and waited. A few moments later Yoska Veshengo came around the side of a bright red vehicle with wheels and scrollwork picked out in green. He raised a hand in welcome and came to stand by Morgan's stirrup. Morgan dismounted.

"Good day to you, Veshengo." He extended a hand.

Lalia's uncle shook his hand, but not before he bowed politely. "My lord. How may I serve you?"

Morgan glanced at him with narrowed eyes. "Perhaps you have already done me a service."

"I can only hope that this is so."

Hmm. Why I did I think he would volunteer anything? Morgan smiled ruefully and decided to abandon subtlety. The Rom was definitely better at it than he was. "Did your people extinguish that misleading fire night before last? Or did you build it?"

Demon sidled a bit, and Veshengo stroked his nose with the practiced skill of his kind, calming him. He smiled at Morgan. "That would be a very poor place for a camp, my lord. Indeed, it was a very poor place for any fire."

As elusive an answer as usual. "Well, I thought it was. I almost lost another ship." Morgan considered for a moment before asking his next question. He was never sure whether Lalia's uncle was being honest with him, dishonest, or merely evasive. He decided to ask. "We had another threatening episode at Merdinn last night." Morgan related the incident in detail, watching the man's reaction. "Did your people observe anyone about?"

For once Veshengo's answer was direct. "No, my lord." His brows drew together thoughtfully. "I thought that you have men watching the house."

"I do, but someone eluded them."

"I fear, my lord, that your men are looking in the

wrong world.'' The Gypsy sighed and shook his head. ''But I cannot convince you of that.''

''No, those fingers definitely came from this side of the grave. They belonged to George Breney.'' He sprang into his saddle. ''In any event, accept my thanks for any services you may or may not have rendered.''

Veshengo grinned and saluted. Morgan put his heels to his mount's side and cantered away. He rode back along the cliffs, deep in thought. He found it hard to believe that Veshengo would do anything to hurt Lalia, yet he wished he could be completely sure. The Gypsy could certainly get into the house, and he was rarely anything but indirect.

As he approached Merdinn, Morgan would not have seen the two people emerging from the small copse had one of them not suddenly pulled away and started running. He slowed his horse and turned to look. The running figure was a young girl, vaguely familiar. Even at a distance Morgan recognized the muscular man as Killigrew, the tavern keeper. He took several steps after the girl, saw Morgan, and abruptly retreated into the trees.

The girl ran agilely down the side of the defile leading to the cove, and Morgan watched as she reappeared on the other side and hurried toward the house. At that point he realized who she was. He had seen her the day he came to Merdinn.

''What is the name of the young woman who was working here when I first arrived? Penny...? Polly...?'' Morgan asked, turning to Lalia.

''Peggy.'' Lalia forked a bite of asparagus. ''Why?''

''Is she still employed here? I haven't seen her.''

''Yes. You don't see her because she is so afraid of

most people. She works in the scullery and tries to keep out of everyone's way.''

''I saw her today talking to Killigrew. Or possibly running from him.'' Morgan looked at her questioningly.

''Oh, dear. That is quite possible. He is her father.'' An angry scowl puckered her face. ''The cause of her fearfulness lies at his door. He abused her terribly—both mentally and physically—and she is terrified of him.''

''Then why would she meet him in a lonely place? She should be avoiding him at all costs.''

''That's why, of course.'' Lalia gave him one of those looks that women had been giving him since Beth had been about ten years old. ''If he sent for her, she would be afraid not to obey.''

''Ah. I see.'' Well, maybe he saw. He, at least, saw that women had many more fears than men. Justifiable fears, it seemed. And he also saw that the innkeeper must be more than capable of deliberate cruelty. ''So it is likely that she might be giving him information about what occurs here.''

''Oh, yes. I'm afraid it is. But what could he possibly want to know?''

''Now that is another interesting question. We seem to have no end of them.''

Chapter Nineteen

The girl sat in the chair, trembling, and looked down at the hands clenched tightly together in her lap. Morgan could see the whiteness of her knuckles from where he sat behind the desk. He would get nowhere this way. She was much too frightened. When he stood and walked around desk, she cringed back in her chair.

"I'm not going to hurt you, Peggy." God! What had the man done to her to terrorize her so? Morgan sat in the chair opposite her and leaned forward, his forearms resting on his knees. Now his face was level with hers. She still kept her gaze on her hands. He made his voice as gentle as he could. "You have my word, Peggy. I only want to ask you a few questions. Will you look at me, please?"

Her head remained bowed, but she lifted her eyes enough to see him. Well, that was a little progress. Morgan would have taken her hands in his, but he feared she would panic if he touched her. He smiled what he hoped was a soothing smile.

"First, Peggy, I want you to know that I will not let your father hurt you anymore. As my employee, you are now under my protection. I will not allow him to come here. I shall tell Mrs. Carthew and Watford that he is not to be admitted to the house. Neither will I allow anyone in the house to harm you. If anyone does so, I want you to tell me immediately, and I will put a stop to it. Do you understand?''

Peggy nodded, but didn't look very reassured. Well, it would probably be a long time before she felt safe. Her fear was obviously ingrained in every fiber of her being. Now for the difficult part. ''Now, Peggy, please pay close attention. I do not want you to see your father again for any reason.'' The girl's head came up, but she did not reply. ''I mean that, Peggy. If he sends for you, you are not to go. Is that plain?''

She nodded and looked again at her clasped hands. Would she obey him? Morgan had his doubts. She was still too afraid of Killigrew. He made his voice firmer. ''If I find you have gone to him, I will be very annoyed.'' Damned angry, in fact, but he didn't want to alarm her further. Peggy leaned as far away from him as her chair would allow. Morgan sighed in frustration and changed his tack. ''Has he asked you questions about what happens in Merdinn?''

Peggy's gaze shifted away from him, moved to the door as if seeking escape, veered back to him. Morgan nodded. ''Very well, Peggy, I know you are afraid to answer. I am not going to punish you for anything you may have done at his behest in the past, but understand me clearly—you are not to tell him anything more, and under *no* circumstance are you to open the hidden passage into Mrs. Hayne's bedchamber.''

Peggy flashed him a startled look, but continued to sit silently, guilt in every line of her body. Morgan looked sternly at her for a moment before continuing. ''I want you to think carefully about this—if you are not under my roof, I cannot protect you. Also, if your father is in gaol, he cannot abuse you again. If you know anything about him that will help me put him there, you need to tell me.''

He stood. ''You may go now.''

Peggy sprang to her feet and darted to the door. Morgan watched, shaking his head. Her actions would boil down to a question of whom she feared most, him or her father. What a pity.

He was going back to his desk when she stopped in the doorway and turned toward him. Her murmur was so soft he had to strain to hear her. ''He takes things to the parson.''

Morgan's attention focused fully on her. ''What things, Peggy?''

''Things he gets from the man on the beach.''

''What man?'' She shook her head.

''I don't know. A mean man. My father is scared of him.'' Her tone reflected utter amazement that anyone could frighten so terrible a being as her father. Morgan was impressed by that himself.

''He transports these things to Reverend Nascawan's house?''

She nodded, inching toward the door.

''Wait, Peggy. What beach?''

The girl again shook her head. ''Sometimes the one just the other side of the lighthouse. Sometimes—I don't know—other places. And sometimes he takes the things back to the beach.''

''Thank you, Peggy. You have helped me very much.''

Peggy turned and dashed away down the corridor toward the kitchen.

Morgan rubbed his jaw thoughtfully. Now he knew

where the booty was stored until it was reloaded to be sold. It was time for him to have a talk with Officer Hastings.

True to his word, Morgan had written to Horsham, his man of business, and at length a reply was received from that worthy. Lalia did, indeed, still have a trust. Horsham had held a conference with the bankers, and they were shocked to learn that she had never been paid the allowance her father had intended for her. As soon as they could write to Sir Roger and receive his reply, she might expect a payment from them. Lalia would soon be able to establish a suitable home for herself and Daj.

Morgan, of course, would not even discuss the thought of her moving away from Merdinn while so much danger threatened, but she could at least make plans.

In the watchful company of Joseph and Eric—and Morgan, as often as he could leave his duties—she traveled the neighborhood until she had found the perfect spot—a comfortable cottage situated near a wide creek, with the large garden flowing down to the willows along the bank. The previous occupant, an elderly spinster, had died, leaving behind enough furniture for her to begin housekeeping. She could add to it later. Having reached an agreement with the executor as to the rent, Lalia looked forward with anticipation to the day she could move in.

Excitement, sorrow and fear mingled in her heart. How could she leave the only home she had known for eight years? How could she remove herself from Morgan's protection? How could she bear to be so far away from him?

The pain of the impending separation gave way from

time to time when she reminded herself that she needed to know that the love she felt for him was real, not just a product of her need for love and protection. And she needed to know if his feelings for her went further than desire, that they were of a lasting nature, that they were not based on her all too convenient presence and his need for a new goal.

But, oh! How her heart ached at the thought of losing him, even temporarily.

At the same time, the thought of having no one to answer to, to be responsible for, of having a home that was truly her own, with her own garden, her own furnishings, brought joy to her step. At last, something that belonged to her, not just a place granted her by some man who held authority over her. The joy made it possible to look forward to the day she might claim them.

And for now, she still had Morgan.

A few nights after his talk with Peggy they had an unexpected guest for dinner. In fact, Lalia reflected, for many years any guest at Merdinn had been unexpected. But that was changing. Since Lord Carrick was again in residence, she suspected that visits from neighbors and perhaps even dinner parties would again become commonplace.

The visitor of the evening was Dr. Lanreath, explaining in his gruff way that he had delivered a baby nearby earlier in the evening, and thought he might presume on old acquaintance to drop in and eat his mutton with them. How pleasant it was, Lalia thought as she listened to the men's conversation, occasionally adding a comment, to again preside at an elegant table.

True, she was not really a suitable lady to act as Morgan's hostess. In fact, her continued presence in his house was nothing short of scandalous. Happily, if the doctor had any suspicions of impropriety, he kept them to himself and treated her with all the courtesy he would extend to a real countess.

When the covers were removed and the port brought in, she excused herself and left the gentlemen to their wine and their talk. She went to the library and searched out a book with which she had been meaning to reacquaint herself, thinking that Jeremy might enjoy looking through it with her some afternoon. Lalia remembered it as a huge volume of maps and pictures drawn by travelers to exotic climes. If her recollections were correct, the boy would be entranced by it.

She carried the unwieldy tome up the stairs clasped in both arms. Intending to read in her bedchamber on the morrow, she would leave the book there and carry her sewing into the drawing room to await the gentlemen and the tea tray. Joseph and Eric, on guard in the corridor, came to their feet, and Eric opened the door for her. Lalia thanked him with a smile and stepped into her room. He had only closed it behind her when she realized something was wrong.

The room was dark.

Why hadn't Sarah lit the night candle? A gust of wind blew in from the casement, ruffling her hair. Perhaps it had blown the candle out. Still, she wanted to be sure immediately that the escape tunnel was latched.

Lalia walked around the bed, shifting the big book so that she could hold it against her chest with one hand. Feeling for the hidden door, she had just satisfied herself that it was fast when a scuffling sound somewhere behind her caught her attention. As she whirled around something struck the book with a loud thunk.

Someone was in the room with her!

"Joseph! Eric!" Lalia dropped the book and scrabbled frantically for the hidden catch, her voice a whisper choked with fear. The door sprang open even as the slither of unseen feet started toward her. She slipped through the opening and pulled it shut behind her. The scratch of fingernails on wood told her that the intruder was searching for the catch.

God grant that he did not know where to find it!

But Lalia did not intend to rely on God's grace alone. She turned and flew down the stairs, stumbling and clutching for handholds in the dark. Every time she tried to run, she tripped and narrowly missed falling. Sliding along with her shoulder to the wall, she batted at the cobwebs that clung to her face, refusing to think of the small, stinging creatures that had spun them and even now might be crawling inside her clothes and into her hair.

Stopping now and then, Lalia held her breath and strained her ears. Nothing. But her assailant had been very quiet. Was he still behind her, slipping silently through the gloom toward her? She held her breath. Her heart pounded so hard in her ears, she might not hear him at all. Could he hear her? Lalia redoubled her efforts at stealth.

A few yards farther on Lalia stopped again. She knew that the passage made several turns before emerging into the cove, but on previous trips to familiarize herself with the way, she had always carried a candle. In the darkness she became completely disoriented. There was only one path. She couldn't be lost. Could she? How far had she come? Would Morgan's men be waiting for her at the end? Or would the pirates have taken control of the exit? She couldn't stop to think. She could not go back through the hidden door, in any event.

And then she felt it. The rush of air could mean only one thing.

Someone had opened the door from her bedchamber.

She could hear nothing but the sound of the breakers filtering in from cove. Oh, God! He was coming.

Rounding the last turn, Lalia could see the lighter area where the guards's lantern glowed in the exit. She ran pell-mell, slipping on damp moss, catching herself, running, running...

"Who goes there?"

Thank God! A well-known voice. Lalia burst breathless from the tunnel and flung herself at the familiar figure with a cry of relief.

"James!"

Morgan was just reaching to refill his guest's glass when a loud commotion from above shattered the peace and Watford dashed into the room.

"My lord, my lord! Come at once. We have another intruder."

Morgan sprang from his chair so abruptly that it went crashing backward onto the floor. Taking the stairs two at a time, he raced into Lalia's bedchamber to find it lit only by the candles in the corridor and Joseph leaning out of the window gazing up the wall to the roof. Morgan put his own head out and perceived a rope swinging beside the window. Joseph swung a leg over the sill and seized the rope.

"No!" Morgan grasped the young man's shoulder. "You are too exposed. Try to overtake him on the ground." He glanced around the room as Joseph bolted for the door. "Where is Mrs. Hayne? Somebody strike a light."

Watford, who, with the doctor, had come puffing into

the room behind him, reached for the flint. As the candle flared, Eric appeared in the connecting door to Morgan's bedchamber, pistol in hand. ''She came up, my lord, but she's not in there, either.''

Morgan flung a hand the way Joseph had gone, and Eric sprinted after him. Morgan, looking toward the priest's hole, spied the book where it had fallen. He crossed to it and picked it up.

In it a deadly looking knife stood embedded to the hilt.

''Damnation!'' A smear of blood darkened the point of the blade where it protruded through the tome. ''Lalia!''

Morgan pushed the hidden panel open as Dr. Lanreath shoved a candle into his hand. He dived into the opening, taking the stairs at breakneck speed. Only when he heard the crash of the waves in the cove did he extinguish the candle and draw his pistol from his pocket. Creeping along the wall, he peered cautiously out of the tunnel.

Lalia stood surrounded by his men, James with one arm comfortingly around her shoulders. A huge sigh of relief welled up in him, only to be cut off when she turned toward him.

The front of her gown glowed red with blood.

Morgan had thought his own heart would stop at the sight of Lalia's bleeding breast, but Dr. Lanreath assured him that the cut was not serious. Still, he had paced the floor of the corridor like an expectant father while the doctor, with Sarah's able assistance, placed a few careful stitches and bandaged the wound. When he was at last admitted to the room, Lalia was ensconced in her bed, looking pale and drawn from the pain.

"I've given her some laudanum, so she will probably sleep more soundly than you will." The old physician clapped Morgan's shoulder. "I know you'll watch her carefully. Not hard to see which way the wind is blowing here. I'll return tomorrow." The moment the door closed behind the doctor, Morgan came and sat on the edge of the bed, clasping both of Lalia's hands in his.

"Ah, sweet torment! You frightened me into premature old age this time." He leaned forward, careful not to brush against the injury, and kissed her gently.

She gave him a wan smile. "Had I realized that it was a knife that had hit me, I am certain that I should be completely white haired at this moment. I never felt it until James and his lads began to exclaim."

Morgan crossed to the window and tested the shutters. Both they and the casement were firmly locked. Satisfied, he gave her a strained smile. "We may smother, but at least I think you are safe for now. I'll stay with you, of course."

Lalia gripped her hands together tightly and bit her lip to hold back exhausted tears. Still, her voice came out as a wail. "Oh, Morgan. I'm not safe anywhere."

"Lalia…" He settled on the bed again and covered her hands with his big ones.

"It's true!" The hysteria she had been fighting threatened to end the battle in its own favor. Lalia drew a deep breath and squeezed her eyes tightly shut. "You set guards—in Jeremy's room, in the hall, in the cove… We can't move without an escort. And still they come. Now the windows must be shut. I know that knife was not supernatural, but it might as well have been."

"Lalia, I understand. I have never been so frustrated in my life. As your *half* brother pointed out, it is very difficult to secure a house this large and rambling. But I shall do so. I promise you.''

''You c-can't.'' The sobs were winning. With great care Morgan folded her in his arms. She hid her face in his shoulder and wept—not great, heaving sobs, but the quiet weeping of weakness and hopelessness. ''I might as well just give up.''

After she had cried for a while longer, the tears abated, and Morgan lifted her chin and dried her face with his handkerchief. ''You won't. You have never given up, and I very much doubt that you will now. Your strength has been sapped by being hurt and by the laudanum.''

She leaned back into the pillows, sniffling. Commandeering his handkerchief, she determinedly blew her nose. ''I'm sorry to be such a watering pot. I'm sure you are right. Tomorrow will look brighter. But what are we to do, Morgan? Perhaps I should go away...''

''No! I...''

Lalia lifted a restraining finger to his lips. ''Wait, Morgan. If I went to London, perhaps...perhaps I should be safer.''

He paused, consideringly stroking his chin. ''I don't want you alone anywhere, certainly not in London. The city is danger enough of itself. If Roger is the author of this atrocity, your removing to London will not help matters at all—will probably worsen them. But perhaps there is somewhere...''

''I might move into the cottage.''

''You and your grandmother alone in a cottage? Hardly!''

A real smile broke through Lalia's somber mood. ''Alone? Alone, my lord? I very much doubt that you will ever allow me to live anywhere without hordes of your minions in attendance.''

"True." Morgan grinned, then sobered. "It might be easier, at that, to guard the smaller dwelling. I could better concentrate my forces, and that cottage is old and very stout. It was designed to be defended. I plan also to hire some men from Bow Street. Yes… That might answer. But…I could not stay with you. Not without destroying your reputation completely."

Lalia grimaced ruefully. "I fear my reputation is in shreds, in any case, what with one consideration or another. But no…it would not do for you to stay."

"At least that will allow me to turn my attention to disposing of the pirates. I strongly believe that must be done to alleviate this threat for once and for all. But… I… I will miss you." He brushed a gentle hand across her hair.

Lalia captured the hand and brought it to her lips, tears again trembling on her lashes. "I will be so lonely without you."

"Never fear. You will have your garden, and you will see a great deal of me, I assure you." He grinned. "You will very quickly be wishing me elsewhere. But now your eyelids are beginning to droop. You must sleep. We will make plans for your going tomorrow."

She shook her head, but he firmly pulled all but one of the pillows from behind her and tucked the covers under her chin. "It seems that I must learn a new skill."

"Oh?" Lalia opened one drowsy eye. "And what is that?"

"I must learn how to go courting."

Actually, Morgan knew quite a bit about courting. He had just never before been in serious danger of matrimony. The merry widows and neglected wives who had heretofore provided his amorous adventures were as happy as he to form temporary alliances, moving on when the novelty palled. But he had long since realized that the situation with Lalia had taken an alarming turn for a confirmed bachelor. Not that it bothered him any longer.

Now the alarm he felt came from the fear that his courting might not prove successful. That he might yet lose her.

The experience of having his lady in his house was a new one for Morgan. Lalia had gradually resumed the direction of domestic matters, creating a welcoming home in a way that a housekeeper could never do. He had come to look forward to her gentle presence when he returned to the house, to quiet conversations with her over breakfast. To feasting on the tantalizing sight of her at dinner, to slaking his building thirst for her in her loving, generous body.

Like it or not, he was developing a need for her, and this was beginning to sound suspiciously like love. Was that the way of it? That he needed her because he loved her? Was it that simple?

Yes. It was that simple.

All the impossible intentions of making Jeremy his heir—leaving the boy an estate he might never want, all his unnecessary plans for his mother—plans she didn't want—none of that applied. He loved Lalia. He wanted her. Therefore, he needed her. The question became, would she continue to love him now that she no longer needed his support?

That nasty question froze into a lump of ice in his gut.

But Morgan was not accustomed to losing. *Not at all.* He wanted her, and he would win her.

It was that simple.

Chapter Twenty

Lalia was directing some work on the greenhouse when Morgan came cantering up her lane. Her heart leapt at the sight of his square shoulders and the rakish tilt of his hat. And something a bit farther down also stirred to life. She had left Merdinn with her meager belongings nearly a week ago, as soon as her injury had begun to heal safely, and although Morgan had sent half his army of remodeling workers, Joseph and Eric, three Bow Street runners, Sarah and James and the black mare to her, he had not come himself. She had begun to wonder if...

But no, that couldn't be. And besides, here he was. With an outward serenity she was far from feeling, she strolled out to the lane to welcome him as a grinning James came from the stable to take charge of Demon.

"Good afternoon, my lord. A lovely day for a ride." Lalia winced. What an inane thing to say. Especially when she wanted to throw herself into his arms.

Morgan doffed his hat and bowed. "Yes, I thought so." He favored her with a knowing grin. "With a lovely lady at the end of it."

Lalia felt the blood rising into her face. How foolish

to be blushing just because those green eyes claimed a possessive knowledge of her that... Never mind. He was teasing her. She held out her hand, and he kissed it and tucked it into the crook of his arm.

"Do come in and see my new home, my lord." She led him into the entry and gestured about her with pride. "Do you like it?"

"I like it very much." He wasn't looking at the house. He was looking at her.

Her face got hot again. He moved toward her, but at that moment Eric appeared to take his hat and riding crop. Morgan withdrew to a discreet distance, handing his gear to the footman. Why did she feel so awkward? No doubt it was the awareness that their relationship had changed, and changed to what only time would tell. She indicated a doorway on their left. "Won't you come into the parlor? I'll send for tea."

"Thank you, perhaps later. I believe I would like to see your garden first." Sending a furtive glance around the room, he leaned in close to her ear. "Since I can't see your bedchamber."

"Morgan!" Lalia could feel her face fairly flaming. "Someone will hear you."

"There is no one about. I promise I won't compromise you. But don't be surprised if you find me climbing in your chamber window in the dark of the night. I shall bribe the guards." He brushed a lock of hair back from her face, sobering. "I have missed you, Lalia."

She gazed into his hungry eyes. "And I have missed you."

He started once again to bend toward her mouth.

"Will there be anything else, ma'am?" Eric appeared at the door. Morgan jerked back.

"Oh, uh. Thank you, Eric, no. Not at the moment." Lalia stifled a giggle. The footman withdrew.

"I must have a talk with that young man. He does his job too damned well," Morgan muttered.

The giggle burst forth into a full-fledged laugh. "You wanted me well protected, my lord."

"Not from me. But tell me…" They strolled toward the garden door. "How are you? Is your injury healing well?"

"Oh, yes. It is still tender, but the stitches are out."

"And there have been no more alarms?"

"No. Sarah sleeps on a truckle bed in my dressing room, and there is always one of the men in the hall as well as outside. I feel quite secure."

Morgan patted her hand. "I am relieved to hear that."

They toured the front garden, then made their way behind the cottage across the lawn to the creek. A clump of willows bordered the water at one side of the grass and Morgan steered their steps in that direction. The weeping branches of the largest tree hung to the ground, forming a hidden space. He parted the boughs and looked between them.

"Aha. Some former gardener has taken pity on us poor suitors. There is a bench." He led her through the opening and dusted the rustic bench with his handkerchief.

Lalia regarded him, her head a little to one side. "And is that what you are, my lord? My suitor?"

He sat and pulled her down beside him. "Of course. I told you I would come courting."

"I've never had a suitor before." She smiled. "I rather like it."

"As long as you like the suitor, I am satisfied." He gazed at her for a moment and then declared, "No. No

I am *not* satisfied.'' He pulled her into his arms and kissed her hard. When they were required to breath, he broke off the kiss. "And I am still not satisfied. I want so much more of you, Lalia.''

He slid off the bench and knelt before her, cupping her face in both hands. "I want you to be mine. Mine forever and for always. And be warned. I *will* have you. Enjoy your cottage and your independence for as long as you like. That will make no difference to me. But know this—one day when this trouble is behind us, you *will* be my wife.''

His wife. He wanted her to be his wife. Lalia sat for a moment, letting the fact soak in. She longed to shout, *yes, yes,* but she held back. She would not give up her new life, her respite, her new self just yet. She could not reconcile herself to taking another husband so soon.

But he wanted her.

Smiling, she touched his face. "Is that a proposal or a threat, my lord?''

"Consider it a declaration of my intentions.'' His hands clasped her waist, pulling her to him. "I am prepared to wait as long as necessary.'' He nibbled at her throat. "But I will not wait very patiently.'' His kisses trailed down to her neckline. "And I shall appear and glare ferociously when other suitors come to call.''

Lalia laughed. "I do not expect any other suitors, my lord.''

"I do.'' He tugged at her bodice. "I expect a veritable swarm of them. And I do not promise to fight fairly.'' His mouth brushed the healing wound gently, then closed over her liberated nipple.

She gasped. Then moaned. "Unfair tactics, indeed.''

He did not answer, but teased her breasts with tongue and fingers until she was limp with desire. She leaned backed against the tree and melted. When she thought she could not stand it another minute, he pulled back.

''Unfortunately, that is as unfair as I can safely be with gardeners lurking about. But perhaps it will keep me on your mind. It will certainly keep my mind on you.'' He stood and adjusted the fit of his britches, then sat beside her and enclosed her in his arms.

''I love you, Lalia.''

He loved her. He had said it. Aloud. To her. Suddenly loving him seemed infinitely safer than it had been. She would marry him one day. There was no sense in pretending otherwise. How could she not? But Morgan had promised that he would wait, wait for her to be ready. Lalia would have time to savor her new status, to prepare herself to be a wife again—a real wife this time.

She had not seen Morgan for two days, and although she was going to Merdinn today, she knew she would not see him today, either. Today he would be aboard the *Sea Witch,* on the lookout for the pirates. There had been no more wrecks and Morgan speculated that the *Harpy* had sailed to France or London to sell its ill-gotten booty. But they would return, and he intended to be ready for them.

Lalia made this visit, rather, to see Jeremy. Morgan had told her that the boy missed her, and she certainly missed him. He'd woven himself into her heartstrings as thoroughly as had his uncle. She had dressed herself for the beach and sailing, confident that she could persuade his new tutor, Mr. Grantham, recently brought to Merdinn, to release his charge for a few hours.

In that she was not disappointed, but she was surprised to find Jeremy's attention otherwise engaged. Smoke was among the missing.

"I have looked and looked, Miss Lalia." The despondent expression on the boy's face almost broke her heart. "I can't find her *anywhere.*"

Lalia knelt beside the boy, encompassing him in a hug. "Do not despair, Jeremy. She cannot have gone far. She is probably playing least-in-sight with you. There are thousands of places she might hide."

"Do you think so?" Hope broke over his small face.

"I am sure of it. Why don't we go and sail the new ship your grandmama sent you? When we return, I'll help you look."

"Oh, good. I know *you* can find her." Spirits restored, he sprinted away, returning shortly with his favorite toy.

As Zachary was suffering from a toothache, Eric, Joseph and Andrew escorted Jeremy and Lalia to the beach. The small company had nearly reached the sand when suddenly Jeremy cried out, "Smoke! There she is."

He darted ahead of them and around a curve in the path, disappearing from sight.

"Jeremy, wait!" Lalia flung out a hand to restrain him. "Wait for Andrew."

Andrew picked up speed, jogging down the rough path. Lalia hurried after him, only to be, as she rounded a curve, brought up short by the sight of the footman standing immobile, his back rigid. She peered around him and gasped.

Where the beach met the path stood a man, his hair gleaming gold in the sun, his arm around Jeremy's neck, and a pistol pressed against the boy's temple. Lalia stood wide-eyed and uncomprehending for several heartbeats. Then in a blinding flash the truth struck her.

"You!"

Cordell Hayne grinned wolfishly. "Well, well. If it isn't my faithless wife."

The world threatened to close in on Lalia, but she fought it away, determined to stay on her feet. She could not faint now. Jeremy needed her. Joseph's strong hand closed around her elbow, steadying her. Lalia gulped convulsively, trying to moisten her dry mouth, and drew in a long breath.

At last she managed a ragged whisper. "But you are dead."

Hayne sneered. "Do not confuse desire with reality, dear wife, as much as you might prefer me dead."

"But I saw you... You were dead and rotted and..." She couldn't go on. The image of the corpse danced before her eyes.

"And my fingers fell off." He laughed unpleasantly. "A gruesome sight, wasn't he? You soak a man in the sea long enough, he tends to become so. So gruesome that I have been able to use him to entertain myself with your punishment for some time—you and your stupid Gypsy grandmother. I made a fine *muló,* don't you think? I am told that you were absolutely quaking in terror."

Understanding gradually filtered through to Lalia. "It was you. You are the one who came into the house and... But why?"

"To toy with you and your paramour, of course. I might have killed either of you whenever I wished, but I was not ready to strike so soon. I was enjoying my little game—your fear. Besides, I wish to destroy Carrick a bit at a time, as he attempted to do to me. It is now time to take his precious nephew." He grinned ferally again. "After all, he is really mine."

"I am not!" Jeremy began to struggle, kicking his

captor's shins with his heels. Hayne's grip on the boy's neck tightened. Jeremy stopped kicking and clutched at Hayne's arm, his small face turning red. Andrew and Eric inched forward, bodies tense.

"Back off! I can achieve my purpose as well by killing him. Although perhaps with less enjoyment than seeing his lordship suffer the agony of anxiety." The footmen paused.

"No! Don't hurt him." The cry burst out of Lalia. She took a step forward.

Hayne smiled and tightened his hold on Jeremy's throat. The child's face darkened with blood. *"Don't hurt him,"* he mimicked. "Of course I will hurt him. Be sure to tell his most top-lofty lordship that I will keep hurting him until he grows to be just like his long-lost father. And I will tell him it is all his uncle's fault. In time he will come to hate his dear guardian as much as I do."

He eased the pressure on the boy's throat. Jeremy began to cry.

A rustling suddenly sounded from the trees near the path and several dark-haired men appeared, knives in hand. Yoska Veshengo held a pistol steadily aimed at Hayne. Hayne's lip curled in derision.

"So...your ragtag relatives think to thwart me." He whistled and four more men emerged from behind the rocks at the bottom of the path, also wielding blades. "They won't do it. I will kill this little bastard in a heartbeat, I assure you." He pressed the pistol to Jeremy's temple more firmly and continued to back away. "All of you stay back."

Joseph slipped around Lalia to stand in front of her. The guards shuffled forward by minute degrees, as did the Gypsy men. Hayne's party moved slowly backward toward a small boat that could now be seen clearing the rocks behind which it had been concealed.

"No!" Lalia thrust herself between the footmen and ran forward several steps before they could react, coming to within a few feet of Hayne. "Let him go. Let Jeremy go and take me."

He paused his eyes narrow. "Ah, so dutiful. But do I want a wife who spreads her legs for everyone but me? Now let me think."

Lalia ignored the sarcasm. "Lord Carrick has asked me to marry him. Take me. Take his bride."

"Oh?" He considered her shrewdly. "He is a bit premature. I seem to remember that you are already married to someone else. Still, your value increases—to him and therefore to me. I will take you both. You will write to him, describing my tender care. Get in the boat." Lalia hesitated. "Get in the boat, or I shoot the boy. Your choice." Another step and he could fling Jeremy into the dinghy.

"No-oo!" Lalia launched herself with the banshee shriek. Before the startled Hayne saw what she was about, she grabbed the arm holding the pistol. Clinging with all her might, she collapsed to the sand, dragging the pistol down with her and pulling him off balance. He stumbled and his grasp on Jeremy loosened for an instant.

"Run, Jeremy! Run!"

Jeremy struggled free and fled across the sand. Andrew picked him up and ran up the path for the castle. Joseph started toward Lalia. The Gypsy men also made a dash for her, but all were intercepted by Hayne's men. Knives flashed. She heard the crack of shots. Joseph dropped to the ground.

"Bitch!" Hayne seized Lalia and hurled her bodily

into the boat. He sprang in after her and stood to loose a shot at her uncle. Once more she tried to get control of the pistol, clawing her way up his arm. He swung it around viciously and struck a stunning blow to the side of her head. Lalia crumpled to the bottom of the boat, her senses whirling. She felt the dinghy moving under her, felt the swell of the waves, heard the creak of oars. She struggled to sit up, but Hayne was on her, his knee grinding into her shoulder.

"Don't move, slut." He leveled the gun at her nose. "I do not want to kill you this easily, but I will if you so much as twitch. I should have done it long ago." He locked his fingers in her hair and leaned his hand on the bottom of the boat.

Lalia could just glimpse the Merdinn towers receding as the boat moved away. Her shoulder screamed with the pain of his weight, and surely he would tear her hair from her head. But she would not give him the satisfaction of crying out. She gazed defiantly into the face contorted with rage and hatred.

His lips curled cruelly. "Aboard the *Harpy* you will find it harder to escape me. You will have nowhere to hide. Nowhere."

Lalia said nothing, shutting out his jeers. Let him talk. She had saved Jeremy, and nothing else mattered anymore. Whatever he did to her, her freedom was already lost by the simple fact of his continued existence. He was still her husband. Her cottage a mere memory. A lost dream.

And Morgan?

Another lost dream.

Chapter Twenty-One

Lalia clutched at the swaying ship's rope ladder, fumbling with her feet for the rungs. Her skirts tangled around her ankles, hampering every attempt.

"Damn you, woman! Hurry." Her captor prodded her bottom with his pistol.

Hurry? For what should she hurry? There was nothing aboard this ship for her but pain, humiliation and ultimately death. At last she made the deck and hard hands pulled her over the rail.

"Hear me, bitch. When you become more trouble than you are worth, in that second I will kill you." Her husband fastened his fist in her hair and shook her. "Do you understand me?" Lalia nodded. "Very good. Now stand where you are." He smiled slyly. "And stand very still."

He snapped his fingers, and the great hound that had attacked her at Merdinn bounded to his side. "Styx! Guard."

Lalia cringed, taking a step back. The dog lunged and snapped. Lalia screamed. Hayne laughed.

"I told you to be very still. I especially like his name, don't you? Styx, the barrier between the living and the dead. I have only to give the word and he will tear your throat out. Now I wish to be away before your lover sights us. I do not want him to find you too soon.'' He strode away, giving orders.

Lalia stood very still indeed, terror clutching at her throat. If she so much as shifted her weight, the dog was in her face, fangs clashing mere inches from her soft flesh. The sun beat hot against her bare head. The wind whipped her hair around her, flicking her face. She would have liked to restrain it, but every time she moved her arms, the dog was on her.

Despair began to creep over her. Was it possible that Morgan would find her? She didn't doubt that he would try, but the ocean was a huge place, the world beyond it even larger. If Hayne succeeded in leaving the area, Morgan would have no idea where to start looking. And if Morgan did eventually find her...

What would be left of her?

After what seemed an eternity, her husband returned to her. He dragged a keg nearer to her and sat, taking his ease while she struggled to stay on her exhausted legs. He smirked. ''Are you enjoying Styx's company? He came with this ship.''

Lalia stared ahead of her, disdaining even to look at him.

He laughed, a short, ugly sound. ''Nice of you to ask. I took the ship from the man whose decaying form so distressed you. Of course, he was not decayed at the time.'' When she still did not respond, he laughed again. ''When we first met, he thought it a great joke that we looked so much alike. You might say he died laughing.''

A shudder ran through Lalia in spite of herself.

''I had not expected to be so lucky when I fled in the *Sea Witch.* I was planning to survive by smuggling. Killigrew and the parson and the others had been working for me for months.'' He sneered. ''But the gullible fool sailed this fine ship right into my hands and made it possible for me to 'die.'''

Without turning her head, she looked at him out of the corner of her eye. With his blond hair and muscular build he might have been a very handsome man. Yet, somehow, the evil in him, the bitter hate, leached through to the surface, leaving its corrosion on his face.

He reached out and fingered the fabric of her gown. ''That's a lovely gown, my adulterous wife. No doubt a payment for your services. I fancy I ruined most of your reward. But never mind, I have ample time to cut that one off your body—to shred it to ribbons.'' He cackled with laughter when she winced. ''I mean the dress, of course.

''You are trembling, dear wife. Is that from fear or simply from fatigue? Perhaps if you walk to me and sit upon my knee with wifely affection, Styx will forget his duty.'' He rose, with a bark of laughter. ''Or...perhaps not.

''Stand very still, Lalia.''

The water was becoming too rough to bring the *Sea Witch* into the cove, so Morgan was obliged to use the ship's boat. As his men rowed him nearer the rocks, the forms of Veshengo and his men, waiting on the strand, became clear. He'd seen them waving a bed sheet and had come ashore to find out the purpose of the signal. Morgan was out of the dinghy while the surf was still knee-deep.

Lalia's uncle hurried to meet him, his arm wrapped in a bloodstained bandage. ''Ah, my Lord Carrick, thank God you saw us. I have grievous news.''

Morgan's heart stumbled. Lalia? Jeremy? "What? Out with it, man!"

"My niece has been taken by the pirates. They would have had young Jeremy, except for her intervention. He is safe, but one of your men was wounded. We could not move on them, because he was threatening the boy's life, until Lalia sprang at him."

"Hold a minute." Morgan held up a hand. "Who is 'he'? Who took her?"

"The man to whom she was married—the one thought dead. He took her to his ship."

Morgan stood in stunned silence. At last, he shook his head. "You mean, Cordell Hayne? He's alive? Are you sure?"

"Yes, my lord. Unless, in fact, his *muló* has taken…"

"*Muló* be damned! How…? Never mind. He must have gulled all of us." Morgan spun around, making for the boat. Then turned back to Veshengo. "Did you see his ship depart? What heading?"

"Southwest. Pulling away from the coast."

"We must find him before he loses himself to us." Morgan leapt into the dinghy and turned to the men at the oars.

"Pull, damn you. Pull!"

The thought of the atrocities he now knew Hayne capable of chilled him to the bone. Morgan could only pray that her husband had not yet killed her.

Her husband! Great God!

No. He would not think of that, either. One way or the other, Cordell Hayne would soon be dead. Morgan fervently hoped that Hayne would die in the coming fight, but if he did not, then he would shortly hang. Morgan did not even consider that he, himself, might be the one to die. He could not die. If he did, Lalia would be left to her husband's nonexistent mercy.

He left her alone for the most part, pausing near her now and then to make some threatening comment on the fate of unfaithful wives. Lalia was beginning to understand that, as bad as his treatment of her had been in the past, it would be infinitely worse in the future.

Cordell Hayne had passed some indefinable border between reason and insanity, between humanity and animal. The hatred in him had eaten through his heart and brain to explode in an orgy of cruelty. No one would be safe from him now. Ultimately he would be hunted down and killed like the brute he was.

But that did not help Lalia now.

Hayne stalked the deck, occasionally peering through his spyglass, but never moving far from her. Suddenly he leaned against the rail, his body stiffening. "Bloody hell, there is someone in our wake." He adjusted the glass. "And in a cloud of sail." He turned to Lalia and sneered. "I believe your betrothed has found us, after all. A pity. I had hoped to prolong his suffering a bit longer." He licked his lips. "By prolonging yours. Well, it doesn't matter. I will soon have you both."

He stepped away from the rail and seized her hair, jerking her nearer. The dog snarled and lunged, but subsided when Hayne placed her a few feet from himself. "Carrick can hardly miss that flag of hair. If he is sure you are aboard, he will not fire on us." His eyes narrowed in thought. "I want that cutter. It is the only craft in these waters that can move with so much speed."

Lalia braced her feet against the motion of the ship. Her legs quivered. How much longer could she stand immobile? The weather was getting rougher. Even though they were far from the shore, she could hear the boom of the breakers as the tide and the storm rolled in. The sound was getting closer as Hayne ordered the sails reefed, slowing to let the *Sea Witch* approach.

Lalia had but one thought now.

How could she best help Morgan?

She could see him now, legs spread, standing strong and steady at the rail of the *Sea Witch*. His black hair rippled in the increasing wind as he shouted orders to his men.

Hayne watched his approach with feral joy. "I have him now. By God, I do!" He yelled an order and one of his men handed him a musket. "Let him but get a little closer and I can put a ball in him." He turned to sneer at Lalia. "But don't worry. I don't intend to kill him…yet."

She spoke for the first time in hours, fury rising in her breast. "He will kill you first."

"Oh, no. He can't fire at me with you so near. In this weather there is no knowing where a shot might go. But I don't care who I hit." He squinted at the cliffs. "But we best board them quickly, or we will all be on the rocks." He jeered again at Lalia. "Watch closely. The entertainment is about to begin."

Leaning over the rail, he lifted the musket to his shoulder and took careful aim at Morgan. Lalia's breath stopped in her throat. Without a thought for the consequences she flung herself at Hayne's back. She didn't even hear the dog's bay. She landed on Hayne, fighting to grasp the musket. With a curse he tried to throw her off. At that moment the huge dog struck her. Its weight and the momentum of its lunge carried her over the side.

Lalia didn't even try to save herself. Instead she closed her hands with desperate strength around Hayne's wrist. Woman, man and hound all plunged into the roiling sea.

The green water closed over her head. Hayne's foot struck her as he kicked away from her. Lalia struggled against the water, arms and legs flailing. Her head broke the surface. The dog swam strongly for the beach. Hayne was shouting for a line.

Lalia went under again.

She kicked desperately, but her skirts, now soaked, wrapped around her legs. Dark water reached up for her like a nightmare. Panic surged through her. She managed another thrust and came up into the air again. Hayne was being swept away by the capricious currents. There was a resounding crash, the vibrations rippling through her. Cannon! The ships were firing at each other.

She began to sink.

Morgan. Oh, Morgan, I love you. She tried to kick, but her exhausted legs moved feebly. Her hair drifted upward like the weeds of the sea as her body slid lower into the hungry depths. Her lungs began to scream for air. *My Morgan, please stay safe.*

The light was fading.

I love you, Morgan. Be happy. Keep safe.

Suddenly she felt a tug on her hair and then a firm clasp on her arm. She was going up. Lalia gritted her teeth, determined not to open her mouth, not to take the breath her lungs demanded. She burst into the light with her fist in a ball. If it was Hayne who had her, she would fight to be free, fight to drown if that was her only other choice.

"Here now!" A strong hand grasped her wrist and turned her about. A strong arm slipped around her waist. "Don't hit *me*."

"Morgan!" A sob of relief rose in Lalia's throat.

"The same. I have you. Don't fight me. I have to get us out of here. Those rocks are getting too damned close."

Lalia looked around her. The *Sea Witch* had opened fire on the *Harpy*. It was listing badly. Men were dropping into the water from its deck. As the swells lifted her, she could see what she took to be Hayne's head moving toward shore. They were drifting that way, too. Morgan stroked powerfully for open water, but she could see that with only one arm, he could not defeat the sea.

"Morgan, let me go. You can't swim for both of us."

"We'll discuss *that* brilliant notion at another time. And don't you dare struggle, or you'll drown us both." His mouth was set in a grim line. He tightened his hold and kept swimming.

Suddenly with a whoosh of spray, the gallant *Sea Witch* came racing between them and the breakers. As she swept by, a line came sailing over the side. With a desperate lunge, Morgan grabbed for it. Another thrust of his muscular legs and he wrapped a turn of it around his arm. They were pulled along as the line tightened. Slowly the distance between them and the ship lessened as busy hands reeled them in.

"Valiant fool," Morgan growled. "She'll go on the rocks with us." Nonetheless, he held fast to the rope. The *Sea Witch* changed her heading and broke for the open sea. She gradually drew away from the threatening shore as Morgan and Lalia were hauled upward onto the deck.

The ship's master hurried to their side. "My lord, are you all right?"

"Well enough, thanks to you, you brave idiot." Morgan clapped the captain on the shoulder, and shook his hand vigorously.

The man grinned. "Can't let a good employer drown."

Lalia's legs failed her and she plunked down hard on the deck. Morgan knelt beside her and put his arms around her. They stared through the rail at the men swimming in the water. They would save those they could, but many were being pulled by the currents toward the jagged boulders lining the shore.

"That's him." Lalia pointed at the first head to reach the surf. She could see Hayne's familiar form as he struggled up onto a boulder. The breakers snatched at him as he fought for purchase, slipping down, regaining the height, and slipping again.

Suddenly a giant wave broke over the rock. They watched spellbound as it lifted him high into the air, then dashed him down with incredible force. As his head struck the stone, a sharp crack carried to them on an errant puff of wind. Hayne's limp body slid off the stone into the water, quickly disappearing under the surface.

"I think...I think he is gone." Lalia covered her eyes with her hands.

"I damn well hope so." Morgan pulled her closer and drew her head against his shoulder. "He will not trouble you again."

Lalia nodded. Too weary and shaken to speak.

Morgan lifted her chin and brushed his lips across hers. "Do you know what frightens me the most at this moment?" She looked up into his face and shook her head.

"It is when I think that I very nearly allowed myself to become as full of hate as he was."

The three of them sat together on the sofa. One of Morgan's arms held Lalia as tightly to him as was humanly possible and the other wrapped securely around Jeremy where the boy sat in his lap. His relief at having them both in his care once more formed a lump in his throat that threatened to choke him.

"Is he really dead, Uncle Morgan?"

Morgan cleared his throat, but spoke hoarsely. "Yes, Jeremy. The man who tried to take you is dead. He cannot hurt you anymore."

"But is he really, really dead?" Jeremy clung to him fiercely.

"Yes. His body was found in the rocks. He is undoubtedly dead." Morgan tightened his hold even more.

"I know how you feel, Jeremy." Lalia snuggled her head into Morgan's shoulder and patted the boy's arm. "I can't quite believe I am safe, either, but I saw him, too. He is dead and his men are either dead or being taken to prison. We are safe with Uncle Morgan now."

"Is he going to be a ghost?"

Lalia squeezed his hand. "No, he was just pretending to be a ghost before. I was foolish to be frightened."

Jeremy pondered that information in silence, then voiced another worried question. "Is Joseph going to die?"

"No, I don't think so. He is badly hurt, but he is young and very strong. I believe he will be well again soon."

"He was very brave, wasn't he? He didn't cry." Jeremy hung his head. "I cried."

Morgan hugged him tighter, a tear leaking from his own eye. "There are times to cry, Jeremy. I was very scared myself."

Jeremy gave him an astonished look. "Not you, Uncle Morgan!"

"Yes, me. It is wise to be afraid when you are in

danger. If you are not afraid, then you are not really being brave, just foolish. You kept your head and ran when Miss Lalia told you to. That is the important thing.''

Jeremy sighed and clasped Lalia's hand. ''You won't go away again, will you, Miss Lalia?''

''Only for a few months. I must go back to my little house for a while, but I will come back one day soon.''

Morgan stiffened. Over his dead body! He was never going to let her go again. ''We will have to talk about that. Now, Jeremy, here is Mr. Grantham to take you to dinner. I will come and tuck you in later and sit with you for a while.''

Jeremy slid reluctantly off his lap. ''Well, if you will sit with me…''

Lalia waited until the tutor had lead his charge away before speaking. ''Will you tell him about his father?''

Morgan shook his head. ''He is too young to understand, and he would just be confused.'' He scowled. ''Now…what is this nonsense about your going back to the cottage?''

''I must go, Morgan.'' She touched his cheek tenderly. ''I must recover from my fear of him in my own way and feel like a whole person again before I can be a wife to you. I can't remain your dependent forever.''

''But I *want* you to be my dependent. I love you, Lalia. Marry me. Immediately. As soon as we can make the arrangements.'' He closed his fingers around her hand and brought it to his lips.

''I will marry you, Morgan. You know I will. I love you so much. The only thing I could think when I went into the water was to pray that you would be all right and to grieve that I would not be with you.''

He pulled her into his arms, the horror of that sight

almost suffocating him. "May I never again have such a moment! I can't bear to let you go anywhere."

"The danger is past now. I'll come back. I will marry you in due time—I promise. There is nothing I want more for the rest of my life." She looked up at him and Morgan felt himself falling into the depths of that aquamarine gaze. "You promised me time, Morgan. I still need that time."

"But you *will* marry me?" Morgan grasped the promise like a lifeline, sighing with relief when Lalia nodded. "Then allow me to announce our engagement. I will send the notice tomorrow. We need not set a date yet."

She smiled up at him. "Very well, if it will make you feel better. I will not keep you waiting long."

"But you will *not* go tonight." Morgan steeled his expression. "Tonight you are staying here. I am not going to let you out of my sight—and don't even try to argue. I will not even hear of allowing…"

Lalia put one hand over his mouth, then cupped his face in both hands and kissed him gently.

"No, Morgan. Not tonight. Tonight I need you. And I will always need you, Morgan because I love you."

Epilogue

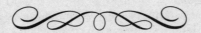

Cornwall, England, 1825

"Well, you leave in the morning. Do you still feel ready for a voyage alone to faraway places?" As he straightened from adding a log to the fire, Morgan smiled at his nephew.

Jeremy answered with a grin. "Of course, I am. It is what I have been wanting all my life. I know that sixteen is too young to become a ship's master, but I intend to learn every job on the craft."

"I expect you to do so. That is why I am sending you, though I expect that will take more than one short trip." With pardonable pride, Morgan looked at the boy he had reared—almost a young man now. "I have every confidence that in a few years you will be captaining your own vessel."

"Thank you, sir, I won't disappoint you. Will Aunt Lalia be in for tea? I want to tell her goodbye."

"Yes, she is tucking the children in."

They watched the fire in silence for a few moments. When Jeremy spoke, it was with a certain hesitation in his voice. "I have been meaning to ask you... I think I should know before I set out... Not that anything will happen, of course."

Morgan's gaze sharpened. "No, I expect a good outcome. You are going with our best captain. What is it?"

"It is about my father. I mean, I know, even though you have never actually said it, that I'm... Well, you know...that my birth is not legitimate. And I don't mind that. I don't want to own a lot of land and have to be a farmer." He wrinkled his nose. "Richmond may inherit Merdinn with my good wishes. But..."

"But?" Morgan cocked a questioning eyebrow.

"Years ago—when that man took Aunt Lalia and tried to take me—he said that I was *his*. Did he mean that he was my father?"

Damnation! Morgan sighed and gathered his thoughts. He had always known this day would come. Perhaps he should have approached it earlier, but... Well, it was damned hard to do. But Jeremy deserved no less than the truth, now that he wanted it. He drew a deep breath. "Yes. That is what he meant. Does the knowledge distress you?"

His nephew appeared lost in his own thoughts for several heartbeats. Finally he looked at Morgan. "I don't like it, but I have suspected it for some time. I want to know for sure now that I'm leaving. Did he hurt my mother? You have told me that she was a lovely person. She wouldn't have..."

Morgan looked into his questioning eyes. More difficult truth. "No. She would never have disgraced herself."

"So he forced her." Jeremy stared into the fire. "And he *would* have killed me, wouldn't he?"

"It had nothing to do with you, Jeremy. He didn't know you at all."

"I hate to think I am the son of a man like that."

"I'm sure you do. But you know that many excellent men are the sons of scoundrels. You are in no way like him."

"Lord, I hope not." Jeremy sat silently for a few more moments. "You are right. I am *not* like that—I *will not* be like him. I will cherish my wife and children as you do yours—as you have me, even though I was not really your son."

Morgan blinked back tears. "To me, you are my son."

"I feel that I am." Jeremy's smile was also a bit damp. "And you didn't have to make me that. You chose to. As I shall choose to be like you."

Morgan could hardly speak. "Thank you, Jeremy."

God grant that he might be worthy of that honor.

*   *   *   *   *

ITCHIN' FOR SOME ROLLICKING ROMANCES SET ON THE AMERICAN FRONTIER? THEN TAKE A GANDER AT THESE TANTALIZING TALES FROM HARLEQUIN HISTORICALS

On sale September 2003

WINTER WOMAN by Jenna Kernan
(Colorado, 1835)
After braving the winter alone in the Rockies, a defiant woman is entrusted to the care of a gruff trapper!

THE MATCHMAKER by Lisa Plumley
(Arizona territory, 1882)
Will a confirmed bachelor be bitten by the love bug when he woos a young woman in order to flush out the mysterious Morrow Creek matchmaker?

On sale October 2003

WYOMING WILDCAT by Elizabeth Lane
(Wyoming, 1866)
A blizzard ignites hot-blooded passions between a white medicine woman and an amnesiac man, but an ominous secret looms on the horizon....

THE OTHER GROOM by Lisa Bingham
(Boston and New York, 1870)
When a penniless woman masquerades as the daughter of a powerful marquis, her intended groom risks it all to protect her from harm!

Visit us at www.eHarlequin.com

HARLEQUIN HISTORICALS®